Michael J. Urban was born in Livermore, California, on October 17, 1967. The youngest of four children, he and his family lived coast to coast growing up, so that is where Michael developed his passion for travel and the history of the land around him. With his wife of seven years, Natalie, they have raised five children between them, living an adventurous life in Kansas.

Thank you to my wife and love of my life, Natalie, who encouraged me the entire time to continue my writing even when I was having a bad day. To my children, my mother and father, and the rest of my family for always supporting me no matter what shenanigans I think of.

To Reed and Melinda Marcum for being the best neighbors and knowing just what we needed to be helped out with when we were in a time of need.

Also, my appreciation to the people of Leavenworth, Kansas, and my friends.

Michael J. Urban

LEAVENWORTH CITY

AUSTIN MACAULEY PUBLISHERS™
LONDON • CAMBRIDGE • NEW YORK • SHARJAH

Copyright © Michael J. Urban (2020)

All rights reserved. No part of this publication may be reproduced, distributed, or transmitted in any form or by any means, including photocopying, recording, or other electronic or mechanical methods, without the prior written permission of the publisher, except in the case of brief quotations embodied in critical reviews and certain other noncommercial uses permitted by copyright law. For permission requests, write to the publisher.

Any person who commits any unauthorized act in relation to this publication may be liable to criminal prosecution and civil claims for damages.

Ordering Information
Quantity sales: Special discounts are available on quantity purchases by corporations, associations, and others. For details, contact the publisher at the address below.

Publisher's Cataloging-in-Publication data
Urban, Michael J.
Leavenworth City

ISBN 9781645751922 (Paperback)
ISBN 9781645751939 (Hardback)
ISBN 9781645751946 (ePub e-book)

Library of Congress Control Number: 2020908344

www.austinmacauley.com/us

First Published (2020)
Austin Macauley Publishers LLC
40 Wall Street, 28th Floor
New York, NY 10005
USA

mail-usa@austinmacauley.com
+1 (646) 5125767

Dedicated to my brother,
but not my twin.
Kenneth Stanley Urban
March 31, 1964 – July 1, 2020.

Thank you to the following:
Michael Coakley, proprietor of The Saint George Hotel who gave me permission to use the historical hotel in my story.
David Hawley, owner/founder of The Steamboat Arabia Museum who gave me permission to use a little bit of the story in my moments of Leavenworth City history. 1856.com

Saint George Hotel
500 Main Street
Weston, Missouri 64098

Steamboat Arabia Museum
400 Grand Blvd.
Kansas City, Missouri 64106

I would also like to thank the Weston Museum on Main Street, in Weston, Missouri, for their contributions of pictures as well. Also I would like to show my appreciation for the citizens of Leavenworth, Atchison, Weston, Saint Joseph, and Kansas City, whose knowledge guided me on the right path for history.

Table of Contents

Synopsis   11

Chapter One   12
Returning to Leavenworth

Chapter Two   20
The Hidden Tunnel

Chapter Three   25
A Journey Back Through Time

Chapter Four   36
Weston, Missouri

Chapter Five   48
Kansas Territory

Chapter Six   55
Popular Sovereignty

Chapter Seven   62
Leavenworth City, Kickapoo City, Atchison, and Delaware City Is Born

Chapter Eight   68
Where the Wild West Begins

Chapter Nine   79
Crossing the Lines: A Territory Divided?

Chapter Ten   87
A Civil War Begins in Kansas Territory

Chapter Eleven 92
A Small City Grows Bigger

Chapter Twelve 102
Battlefield Kansas Territory Popular Sovereignty Is a Double-Edged Sword

Chapter Thirteen 114
The Pendulum Swings in Favor of Free-State Kansas

Chapter Fourteen 122
Laws of the Land

Chapter Fifteen 128
Underground Railroad

Chapter Sixteen 139
Saloons, Breweries, and Brothels

Chapter Seventeen 148
The People of Kansas

Chapter Eighteen 158
Abe Lincoln Visits Leavenworth City

Chapter Nineteen 167
On the Road to Statehood

Chapter Twenty 173
The Battle in Kansas Territory Becomes the Nation's Civil War

Bibliography 181

Special Thank You To 189

Pictures Provided By 191

Synopsis

This is a story of true historical facts chronologically written by a fictitious newspaper reporter. He wrote in his journal this epic adventure surprisingly found in a tunnel that was used in the Underground Railroad in Leavenworth, Kansas. The unbelievable events start from April 1854 in Hannibal, Missouri, a riverboat ride across Missouri on the Missouri River to the city of Weston and the founding of Leavenworth City. The city that grew from an idea that 32 men in Weston Missouri to being a city with over 10,000 people and writes until June 1861.

Murders, lynchings, and hangings were the laws of the land and whoever had the most sympathizers, controlled the land. Kansas Territory is where the Civil War started when the Kansas-Nebraska Act was passed in 1854. Pro-slavery men fighting against the men who believed Kansas should not have slavery.

The childhood home of William Cody was in Salt Creek Valley and his first job was with Russell, Majors, and Waddell, the freighting company started in Leavenworth City. They were the firm who created the Pony Express. Abraham Lincoln visited Leavenworth City in 1858, as well as Horace Greely and many other famous people throughout the history of Leavenworth City.

Chapter One
Returning to Leavenworth

As my wife Natalie and I were watching a professional stock car race on a hot and lazy summer Sunday afternoon at our home in Clemmons, North Carolina, the home telephone rang unexpectedly, making both of us jump. The caller identification revealed that it was my parents' number, as it appeared up on the corner of the television screen. So I answered the phone knowing that it was my mother because my father would never call, at least not actually dialing the phone for himself; he waits until Mom dials, and then picks up on another phone extension after the person on the other end answers the phone.

"Hello, Mother," I remember answering and then adding something like how are you and Dad today? Then I somewhat recall how Mom blurted out how she tried calling both of our cellphones first, but neither of you answered; she then quickly added what I think was, "Your father is not doing well right now! We just came home from the hospital and you two have to come back here to Leavenworth as quick as you can. Your father had another heart attack and we don't know how much longer he is going to be with us." I vaguely remember saying "Yes, of course, we will be on the earliest plane we can catch." I know that I was in shock but at the time I was able to calm Mom down a bit telling her I think was that I would call their five grandchildren that Natalie and I have, and tell them about their grandfather's health situation.

We then changed the subject and I think I asked Mom about what all my other siblings were doing, and when they would be arriving in Leavenworth. My mother had already talked to both of my brothers and my sister, and they were also going to call their children and tell them the news as well also that they are going to get back to Leavenworth as soon as they possibly could make it back there.

As my wife Natalie was making the arrangements for our trip online and calling her aunt, I started calling our children to tell them about their grandfather's condition. Michael and Cera live in Wichita, Kansas, while Laura, Hope, and Christina still live in the Kansas City area.

That night we also had called my childhood friend, Randy, who lived in Winston to see if he would be able to drive Natalie and I to the Winston Salem-Greensboro Airport the following morning. Being a good friend, he obliged me saying that he would be happy to.

After all of our phone calls, we gathered the suitcases and packed our bags with appropriate clothes for church, socializing, and also at least a week's stay in Leavenworth. I have a cousin, Shelly, in the airline business and she was able to get us special fares. Thanks to Shelly, we were able to save money on the last-minute airfare prices they charge. She was also able to secure us a rental car so no one would have to pick us up from the airport. Life is easier when you know the right people in the right places.

After a night of little sleep, we awoke to an early alarm clock and rolled out of bed. We showered, dressed, and then had a quick breakfast allowing us to finish just as Randy arrived at our house at the correct time. Randy and I looked for dragons in the sky during our ride to the airport like we used to as kids growing up in Clemmons after watching all the dragon movies in the early '80s that had influenced our lives. We made it through traffic with ease and he was able to drop us off early so we could go through the security inspection at the airport. Our flight was on time and we were able to board the plane with no problems. It was a very short flight to Atlanta with an hour's layover there, and then we were off to Kansas City. It had been a few years since we were back home in Leavenworth. Mom and Dad liked coming down to visit us and our old neighbors here in Clemmons where we lived here in my youth.

We arrived at M.C.I. (Kansas City's International Airport) at about 2:30 in the afternoon, and retrieved our rental car. It is just a short half-hour drive to Leavenworth from the airport in North Kansas City. As we left the airport, we drove north to Platte City where the memories of the old Sonny Hill car commercials with the big orange water tower made me chuckle a bit when we drove around a bend and saw it in the distance.

Returning to my parents' home started flooding my mind with all those old familiar scenes and forgotten memories that I had lived as a child growing up in the small town of St. Joseph, Missouri. While driving down to Leavenworth in our station wagon, I was of course in the third seat that faced backward—if anyone remembers that seat—as we journeyed to visit all my relatives (No, none of them were in jail. Just thought I would add that in). I had Natalie call my brother, Ken, who should have been already in town. He answered, "Terent," and I replied with the same peculiar word as a greeting also, a goodbye that we learned in Gravois Mills, Missouri, for a few years from the James Gang. We were both on the road, therefore we made the conversation brief while we arranged a place to meet with him when we got to town, so he could inform us on what was going on with Dad and his condition.

As we were driving through Platte City, we stopped and bought us a drink to share at a little convenience store before we went into Leavenworth. When we were walking out, we noticed the visitor information rack inside the store that holds all the brochures about attractions in the area. We saw that there were quite a few antique malls in the area, but the brochure that caught my eye was the one for Weston, Missouri. When you visit Weston for the first time, there is something in the air that just makes you fall in love with the quaint little town. At one time it was a bustling river town, but when the river changed directions after one of the many floods, the river ended up a mile away from the town, and the town almost disappeared. If it wasn't for tobacco and whiskey, I do believe there would not be a town there today. My wife and I used to love going there on Saturday mornings and just walk around and explore the little shops on Main Street, so we grabbed a few pamphlets and we climbed back into our car, continuing on our way to Leavenworth. Natalie called the kids to get updates on their time of arrivals, and all of them said they will be arriving by driving in around noon tomorrow, she was able to find out as we went through the rolling hills on those curvy winding road that took us nearer to Leavenworth. We passed through the little area of Beverly that was built in the late 1880's as a train crossing depot, and today is still basically a crossroad area instead of a town. Before I realized it, we were almost there, and the buildings on Fort Leavenworth appeared on the bluff across the river in the trees. As we drove on the long flat road of Highway 92 leading to the Big Blue Bridge, as I call it but it is actually called 'The Centennial Bridge,' I looked into the open fields and recalled that the first attempt in 1827 to build Fort Leavenworth was on the Missouri side in the flood plain and this made me laugh a bit. I recall wondering aloud about how long the army of Leavenworth stayed camping in the bottom area after they were flooded out. Natalie came back with something as we drove over the Centennial Bridge into Kansas. "Till the First Time!" Even the French fur traders in 1744 built Fort de Cavagnial (who were just north of the fort on the river bank before the river changed course); the fort sat high on the cliff side overlooking the river, as the ruins were seen by and written about by Lewis and Clark and documented in their journal in the year 1804. Lewis and Clark camped at where Leavenworth would be built fifty years later, then continued up river to present day Atchison, Kansas, camping and then passing by the ruins of the old abandoned French fort that was clearly observed by the boats on the river at that time.

As we crossed over the Missouri river and entered Leavenworth, memories kept flooding back, and then I recalled when that bridge used to cost a dime to cross. The old toll booth was on the Kansas side, placed in the middle of the street where the money was collected by booth operators from the travelers. We arranged to meet my brother at the pharmacy at the corner of fifth and Cherokee where he would be to pick up Dad's prescription, so our mom would not have to get out of the house. As we pulled onto Delaware, the scenes of how the old town looked like over one hundred and fifty years ago filled my mind, and the feeling I had when I drove down the streets of Leavenworth gave me a feeling of déjà vu. "I should have brought my cowboy hat," I said as my wife Natalie looked at me and laughed.

Then she said, "Yea right!" and then adds, "But I do get the same feeling when we are in Weston. Like I have lived there before."

We arrived at the pharmacy and then pulled into space close to the soda fountain entrance doors, and we could see my brother sitting in a booth inside through the windows on the building. We got out of the car, and Natalie and I were both looking up and down the street at the impressive architecture of the buildings, which were erected over one hundred years ago or more on Delaware Street.

"Wouldn't it be cool to go back in time and see what this place was like when it first was built," I said to Natalie.

"You're weird," she said and then laughed and shook her head. The pharmacy sign said it had been in that building since 1871, but the place was built in 1854, like Mom and Dad's new old house on the Esplanade that was built in 1854 or 1855. Of course, this was not the original 1854 structure because there were two major downtown fires in the early days of Leavenworth. We walked in the establishment and my brother Ken informed us he was ordering a Green River, so I threw in that he buys me a Sarsaparilla, and to my surprise he actually did.

"These are some great old-time fountain drinks," I said and we all laughed. We gave each other that brotherly hug that said we've missed each other, and then we grabbed a booth and started finding out what was new since we last spoke a week ago.

He started with they had a good flight from Florida and had arrived a few hours earlier. They had already unpacked their bags, and then he said, "Denise and I grabbed the best room too, ha-ha!" He then informed us, "Our other siblings are arriving in town sometime today but they are driving in from their homes. Also tomorrow night our children will be arriving, and Dad went into the hospital Sunday, keeping him in for observation overnight as a precaution." My brother Ken then also informed us, "We had better get to Mom and Dad's house soon or she will be calling soon to see where we are at." We all laughed, and then got up leaving the drugstore, and then headed outside to our cars.

Our parents only lived a few blocks west on the street called The Esplanade, and then a couple blocks north. It was the first road that ran alongside the Missouri River, and the house was up sitting high on a hill overlooking the town, the river running north and south, and they could also see the old town of Farley on the Missouri side. They purchased this beautiful big old house a few years ago after striking it rich with a rare antique they found in the bottom of a box. They had purchased the box at an estate sale for a dollar not even realizing what they had until they unpacked the box at their house and looked it up on the internet.

As I stated before, the house was built in fall of 1855. The porch was built so it totally wrapped around the house, and was very beautiful to sit on in three out of four seasons of the year with ceiling fans mounted in various positions for cooling the guests as they relaxed around the porch. In the front corner of the house, there were round rooms going up to the height of the house to the attic, where there was a crow's nest which had this amazing view over the river and the downtown area of Leavenworth. Above the front door was a beautiful stained-glass window with a Masonic Freemasons symbol placed in the middle of the window.

We had to pull up and park on the street in fount of Mom and Dad's house because my brother slid into the driveway before us with a move he stole from the Dukes of Hazzard. As he was sliding into the driveway, he almost drove into the yard because it was a very narrow entrance originally built for horses and carriages, not for modern-day cars. We laughed at him because that was just the way Ken drove, and that brought back more stories of my youth and how he crashed his vehicles a number of times. Ken almost ran me over once when I was on crutches; in fact, he was the one who broke my leg playing soccer. I remember my friends Randy, Matt, Tate, and I were looking at a full lunar eclipse on the side of my backyard one night, and my brother saw us and hit the wet grass, then he lost control of his Nova and ended up straddling our retainer wall on our driveway. Mom, Dad, and the neighbors enjoyed that late night wake-up crash. There was one other time he was doing donuts in a different Nova. Ken was in a KFC parking lot in Clemmons when he hit a parking block, and then went airborne with the nose of the car going about six feet up the post, hitting the post so hard the bucket was swaying back and forth, almost knocking the Colonel's bucket off the sign post. But I digress, as I mentioned before, the driveway at Mom and Dad's house was for horses and buggies laid in brick still that went up the front yard and then went under the side of the house. The roof extended over the porch and driveway on the north side of the house. From there, the driveway led to the Carriage House that was located behind the house. He had to make an abrupt stop because there were already two other vehicles parked in the drive. It appeared that my sister and other brother had made it in earlier and were parked in the driveway arriving when Ken was meeting us at the corner drug store, so it looked.

"Great," I said aloud, "now we get the worst room in the house, the basement," pulling up to the front walkway on the street.

Natalie laughed and said, "It will be all right, we are here for your dad."

I said, "Yes, it is. All that matters is Dad and Mom, and you're right as always, my love." We got out of the rental car, and then started to unpack the trunk where we stored our traveling cases.

We then entered the yard through the old, black, rod-iron fence gate that had mounted gargoyles on the brick posts; also, the gargoyles were placed on each side of the driveway. The fence was at least six feet tall all around the perimeter of the property, and as we entered the gate, a huge trellis was built and covered in red roses then in full bloom as we passed under them. The trellis curved over the sidewalk making a tunnel of roses. Natalie and I saw my brother, Ric, and my sister, Tammy, and her husband Mark standing out in the gazebo part of front side of the porch and waved to them as we approached the house. The porch encircled the front and sides of the house. I noticed that their baggage was still on the porch, so the first thing I said was, "Dibs on the upstairs room."

Ric laughed and then said, "You are too late, little brother. Tammy, Ken, and I already picked our rooms so you guys get the leftover servants' room on the main floor." We then laughed together, then Ric said, "No, really we did, you're in the room off the kitchen on the main floor."

I said, "That's OK. We're here for Dad, just glad to be in the house."

Ken showed up on the porch, and it was the first time all of us had been together in five years. We all started walking toward each other and began to give each other our family hugs. "Where are Mom and Dad at?" I asked.

Ric said, "Denise and Ann are in with them right now, they are in the parlor room relaxing and watching television."

"Cool beans, and how is he feeling today?" I added.

"He is doing well, but tired and still weak," Tammy replied.

"What did the doctors say was wrong with him?" Natalie asked.

"Mom overworked him at the city yard sale at the Riverfront Community Center," Ken answered.

"They do not need to go to those anymore," I said.

"Oh they are bored, retired, and just like making a little bit of extra money," my sister said and then added, "They still want to find another rare find and strike it richer."

I then said, "They do not need any extra money. Dad's eighty years old and he should be playing with his model railroad downstairs."

We grabbed our bags and all of us headed into the house. Tomorrow was going to be a busy day with all our cousins and some of our old friends coming by to see Dad and Mom. As we entered the house, Mom was walking into the foyer and greeted us with hugs and kisses. Her hair was grayer than the last time I'd seen her a few months ago when they came to visit Natalie and I, and she looked very tired but was very happy to see all of us together.

"I heard laughing outside and I wanted to see who it was," Mom said to us after we finished our hugs. We then walked into the parlor room and saw Dad in his recliner taking it easy. Mom settled back into the chair beside him. Dad started to try to get up out of the chair, but we told him not to get up but he tried to anyway.

Hardheadedness ran in our family. Ric, Ken, and I went over and helped him up from the chair and started giving him hugs, and then everyone else said hi to him and gave their hugs.

We all took seats around the room and started seeing how Dad was and what we could do for him and Mom. "I am fine," Dad said, "I just got a little weak and lost my balance the other day at the riverfront."

"You are not as young as you used to be," Ken added, "and Mom needs to take it easy on you." We all laughed, then we proceeded to get caught up on all of our families' recent events. About an hour later, we all went to our rooms to put our clothes away and refreshed a bit.

Natalie and I went into the servants' quarters as it used to be called, and Mom and Dad still used it as an extra storage area for their yard sale items. It was a bedroom on the main floor built all the way at the back of the house. It was a good-sized room with a beautiful four-post bed, dark oak moldings, hardwood floors with intricate designs that made you wonder how they built like they did back then. It even still had a wallpaper ceiling with flowery designs complete with a rosette around a hanging crystal light fixture that could pass as an old gas light.

There was a bay window in the room with a settee built into the wall so you could sit there and look out into the flower garden. There was even a fireplace in the room with a marble hearth and old stone walls with a huge opening for the fire. This was actually a very cool room even without the view of the river. It was still very comfortable to be in. I said to my wife, "Those guys are idiots for not grabbing this room."

She laughed and then added, "This is a very nice room but I would rather look out across the river and the valley on the other side."

I nodded my head in agreement as we got ready for going back out to the family and see what else was going on. It was about 5:30 in the evening when we were ready to join the family again.

We joined my siblings in the kitchen. Dad had dozed off in his chair, so we continued our conversations where we previously left off, and some of our cousins and remaining aunts dropped by to see how Dad was doing. We had a house full of people by the time evening rolled around. Dad woke up from his nap and greeted everyone that had shown up while he was resting. My brothers and I made a huge meal for all the people that were still there. We ate, drank, and laughed remembering all the crazy antics we all did together growing up together. The broken bones, achievements of greatness, heart breaks, travels, and how silly we were back then. We laughed and talked even when Mom and Dad decided to go to bed. It was about 11:00 now, so we all said goodnight to Mom and Dad, then helped Dad get to his room. We came back and everyone still hung out until about 12:30 in the morning, then everyone agreed to go home to sleep and that we would have breakfast at Homie's Drive-In in the morning for those who didn't sleep in too late. Everyone departed and my brothers, sister, and I decided to retire to our own rooms for a good night's sleep with our spouses, because everyone was coming back tomorrow to do it all over again with us. We always had a good time when our huge family got together.

Natalie and I went to our room and started getting ready for bed. I was sitting on the window settee looking around the room at the exquisite architecture of the moldings and the wallpaper ceiling when I noticed a rock that looked like it didn't belong in the mantel on the fireplace wall. I looked at Natalie and asked her, "Do you see something strange about that rock in the fireplace mantel? It is smoother and darker than the rest of the old rocks that were used."

She looked at it and agreed with me that it was a different rock than the others up there. I got up and walked over to the fireplace, and started feeling around the smooth rock and pushed in on it a bit, then all of a sudden we heard a click, and then the front panel of the settee slid vertically across into the wall. A secret door with a passageway was revealed to us!

Chapter Two
The Hidden Tunnel

I saw Natalie's jaw dropping to the floor as my own mouth opened widely trying to utter any words of bewilderment to escape from my mouth, but nothing but a grunted moan came out of my mouth. We had just witnessed the wooden panel that made up the front of the settee quietly disappear into the wall, thus revealing an opening to a secret passage that went down into a dark tunnel. As we slowly inched closer to the mystery door, we saw the top part of a ladder going down as we gazed into the newly found secret of the old house. We looked at each other in amazement. I could tell she was as freaked out as I was. My heart was racing a mile a minute. I was able to finally say, "Holy crap, what in the world did we find?"

Natalie looked at me with an expression of bewilderment all over her face, and in amazement she said, "Quick, go try to find a flashlight and let's see where it goes?"

Since we were in the room just off the kitchen, I ran to the next room and rummaged through the junk drawer that every kitchen has, finding a flashlight. I then hurried back into the room we were staying in. I turned the flashlight on and we peered down into the tunnel. The walls were made of stone like the rest of the foundation of the house, a round configuration built like an old well. The ladder was made of hedge trees tied together with what looked like hemp rope. Thick branches acted as round rungs extending downwards quite a distance, at what looked like an opening to a tunnel at the bottom of the ladder.

"Wow," I exclaimed as we looked down into the depths of darkness. "How safe do you think this ladder is?"

She looked at me and said, "I do not know, but you are going down first!" I then found my shoes and put them back on, reaching into the open doorway through the dusty spider webs. I grabbed hold of the ladder and tried to see how secure it was before descending down the antique climbing tool. I placed my hands on the ladder, and I noticed that the ladder actually did not move. I looked it over closely, noticing it to be secured by wooden pegs into the frame of the house. Feeling safe, I then turned my body around so I could maneuver easier as I attempted to descend the ladder. As I slipped into the hole, letting my feet take care of the remaining spider webs, I placed my feet gently one at a time onto the ladder applying gentle pressure on the limbs that make up the steps.

Natalie was holding the flashlight as I crawled into this tunnel not knowing where it went, or what it was used for. I slid more into the tunnel, being cautious as I started to move my feet down further, taking extreme precaution as I proceeded down the ladder. I made sure my feet were securely on the ladder. I was now fully entered into the newly found old passageway Natalie handed me the flashlight and I shone it down to the bottom of the pit, looking all around the floor and the walls to see what was there. The bottom lay about fifteen feet down and I spied a large arched opening at the base of the ladder that appeared to lead toward the east, the direction of the river.

Looking at the walls, I believed it was built at the same time the construction of the house began. I successfully got to the bottom of the ladder, and where I was standing on looked like a stone floor with a brick arched doorway about five feet tall and three feet wide. I shone the flashlight down the tunnel and saw wooden beams used as support through a narrow hallway about every ten feet down. Stones were stacked making up the walls. The northside wall of the tunnel looked like the house's foundation in the basement.

I called up to Natalie, "OK, it is safe to come down here and you will not believe your eyes when you get down here!"

I shone the light up so she could get her footing on the ladder, and then she proceeded down and joined me at the bottom of the ladder. When Natalie stepped off the last ladder rung, her foot tripped another switch on the stone floor. The panel of the settee closed above our heads, making it completely dark except for the beam of light coming from our flashlight.

Natalie and I both looked down the tunnel shining the light slowly and over as much as we could, inspecting the walls and floor for anything that did not belong down there, which was anything that caught our eyes. Along the walls we saw torches hung about waist height at all the braces about every ten feet on one side of the tunnel. We spotted what looked like trash, maybe bottles of some sort in a pile against the side of the wall down about twenty feet down the tunnel on the left-hand side, and then noticed that the tunnel went downhill a little past that point. We both couldn't really stand upright as we entered the tunnel, but we could stand side by side, walking into it hunched over just a bit.

Both of us proceeded cautiously down the tunnel stopping at the pile of bottles, shining the light all around the bottles of strange colors and sizes. I picked one up and started to examine it while Natalie was holding the flashlight so we could see our discovery better. The bottle I picked up appeared to be an old medicine bottle with a cork and dropper with some medicine still in the container.

It was a bit dirty so I said, "I cannot really read the bottle's name," so I playfully said, "It says snake oil."

"Really?" Natalie exclaimed.

"No," I said, "it's too dirty, I can't read it that well down here, we need better light."

We placed it back down, then picked up a few others just to acknowledge what was there. We examined the other bottles but not as closely, and then I said, "We will pick them up on our way back so we won't break them."

The tunnel then started going downhill with about a thirty-degree slant. The tunnel was still heading in the eastern direction. We could see about another fifteen to twenty yards and then we spotted what looked like a round or square object or something hanging from the wall on one of the torches hanging on a support post about twenty feet further down the tunnel on the right-hand side.

We shone the light all around and moved down the tunnel as we approached the object. We notice it was a pair of old leather saddle bags. Covered in dust, we looked at them without touching the surprise find. Tapping it with my hand, we did not hear any sounds or any odd movements coming from the bags. The bag swung on the wooden torch, the leather strap still holding the bags, so I reached across and pushed it up by the middle leather strap that held the bags together.

"It is kind of heavy. I think there is something in here," I said to Natalie. As I pulled the bags toward me, there was another noise from down the tunnel where we thought the tunnel was caved in at about fifteen to twenty feet further down. When I took the bags off of the torch, what we thought was the end of the tunnel due to a collapse was another false door. The tunnel appeared to continue going east. Shining the flashlight back at the bags, when the light hit the bottom of the bags, we saw a huge spider jump out of the saddlebag that was on the wall side.

She looked at me and said, "Before we move that anywhere, there better not be any more spiders in there or other critters anywhere down there!"

We looked over the saddlebags with the flashlight seeing the best we could. We spotted a hole in the lower corner of the bag that the spider was in; we unfastened the leather strings that banded it closed for who-knows-how-long, to see what appeared to be documents of some sorts; handwritten letters to and from different people. A few of the bottoms of the papers on that side were chewed upon by the rats or mice over time close to the hole we found in the bottom of the one bag, but you could still barely read the cursive writing of the names of the recipient and the sender of the letters and other documents in the bag. We then started to unwind the other straps on the other bag; we peered inside and only saw what seemed to be three different books, all the same size.

"Let us take it back up to our room and look at it up there."

I nodded my head in agreement and said, "The lighting will be a lot better up there to examine our treasure."

As we got up, I rewrapped the leather string on the side with the books. We looked back down the tunnel with our flashlight and saw that the tunnel was still open about ten to twenty feet further. We figured the tunnel led to the riverbank where runaway slaves used to use it as an escape from Missouri, and gain their freedom over here in Kansas, or continue their journey to Nebraska. My mind filled up with visions of people with hope and panic going through this same tunnel a hundred and more years ago to be free people.

Natalie and I looked at each other and she then said, "Let's go back to the room and see what we have here."

I agreed with her by saying, "Yes, and the light will be much better up there. I do not think this tunnel is going to lead us anywhere."

We headed back to the ladder and after picking back up the bottles and placing them in the saddlebag with the paperwork, we started heading back up the tunnel to the ladder that led us to our room. Natalie went up first and when she placed her foot on the first step, the panel slid open at the top. I held the flashlight so she could climb up the ladder safely. She climbed off of the ladder into the room and then I put the saddlebag over my shoulder and started to ascend. After I climbed out of the settee, Natalie closed the panel by pushing the rock again on the fireplace and closed the hidden panel. We both started heading across the room to the desk.

Our adrenalin was going so fast in our bodies, we looked at each other with excitement and bewilderment. I said to Natalie, "And neither of us are tired now, are we?"

"What are the books in the bag?" Natalie exclaimed.

I shushed her and said, "Keep it down, honey. You don't want to wake anyone up yet!" Then I flipped the bags gently onto the desk from off of my left shoulder so that the bottles we picked up did not break.

Natalie turned on the lamp beside the desk. I then started to untie the leather string that kept the flap down again, and then grabbed the bag and tipped it slightly up so the light of the room could fill the bag contents. "They appear to have some sort of writing on the covers," I said, as I reach inside the saddlebag and removed one of the books, handing it to Natalie. Dust had also found its way in the bag and laid itself down onto the leather covers, but very lightly.

We both blew a little dust off of the books in our hands, and then I reached down and took off one of my shoes and pull off a sock and then started to wipe the covers off.

Natalie looked at me then said, "It's OK this time, but any other time I'd smack you for doing that!"

We both started to laugh, and then nervously we both looked down at the covers in our hands and now could clearly read the title. What I thought was ink was actually burned into the leather on the cover: *The Early Days of Leavenworth City, by James Michael Urbaniak.*

"It appears to be a three-volume set," I said as we searched the outside of the books and saw the numbers on the spines of the books. We both set down at the desk, and turned the lamp shade to see the book's better. We started to inspect the books and found the bookmarked volume one. They were beautiful hardbacks with leather covers. Very nicely written in old style calligraphy was the name of the title with the author's name, and I was right in saying that the title was burned into the leather. A stitched circle surrounded the names in the center of the cover. After a better cleaning, we inspected the edges and found they were gold-edged pages. Very high quality for books made back in those days. As we started to open the first book, we looked on the inside cover and saw written on the page in black ink: 'For my wife, Marisol. For making this adventure come true and would not be possible without her support and understanding.' Signed by James Michael and dated April 1854. It appeared to be a journal of sorts as we flipped the pages without really reading the text. There were also some hand-drawn pictures on some of the pages throughout the journal.

We looked at the clock on the mantel and noticed it was two in the morning. "Should we go to bed or see what is written in these journals?" I asked Natalie. I could tell that both our hearts were still beating a mile a minute.

"My curiosity has me wide awake even though we have almost been up twenty-four hours," Natalie replied.

"I know how you feel, let's read for a bit then get some rest," I said to Natalie, who was nodding her head up and down in total agreement with my last comment.

We got into our pajamas and got into the four-post bed. The lamps on the wall above the bed in between the posts gave us plenty of reading light. We propped our pillows up and got comfy under the sheets, and then proceeded to open the first book with anticipation of what was ahead of us.

Chapter Three
A Journey Back Through Time

"These books are actually in pretty good shape," I said to Natalie. "For being over one hundred and fifty years old, they are not worn or brittle at all." As we gazed at our unbelievable find, the first book we picked up was marked as volume one. We opened it carefully, turning the pages with curiosity of what we would find, and the excitement of the unknown. After the third page, we found an inscription: 'This is for my darling wife Marisol. For whom without the love and devotion she rained upon me to live my life, and our life, with honesty, and integrity. She made it possible to survive the early days of Leavenworth City.' And there was a signature at the bottom: 'With Love. James Michael Urbaniak.'

Natalie and I looked at each other with tears forming in our eyes, and we leaned over and gave each other a soft gentle kiss. Then we snuggled closer, with Natalie putting her head on my shoulder, holding her in my arms. She was holding the book turning the pages; as she turned a few more pages, we found an entry that appeared to look like a journal entry. We snuggled closer and I read the following writing:

    April 4th, 1854   Aboard the steamer ship Polar Star
    Tuesday Night   Missouri River

Greeting and salutations to my family, to my friends, and to anyone else who is fortunate enough to enjoy the personal passages of my adventures westward which began in the town of Hannibal, Missouri, during the springtime in early April 1845. To explain the why's and the where's, and the how I am where I am now, I thought it would be best to begin the story.

I am named James Michael Urbaniak, as my introduction should be noted. I am a correspondent reporter for the *Hannibal Wig Messenger*, formally the *Hannibal Journal*. Approximately one month ago, the new publisher of the newspaper approached me with the idea about a reporter going west and sending back the news on the edge of the frontier. What Mister League called, 'Living on the Edge of American Civilization.' Of that being only two hundred and fifty miles to the west on the other side of the state of Missouri.

William T. League had enjoyed what the last editor of the journal, Mister Orion Clemens, published when his brother Samuel, a close friend with whom I still correspond with in Saint Louis, went east and reported back to Hannibal the newest trends and worthy news from Philadelphia and from New York City. Mister League is sending me to a town called Weston, Missouri, in Platte County. It is a thriving river town that is growing very quickly and Mister League thinks this could be the place to be when the Douglas Kansas-Nebraska Bill passes in Congress.

I honestly must say I did not agree to this assignment at first, because I did not want to be away from my wife or family for any period of time, and with the unknown passing of the Douglas Bill, we did not know when we would see each other again. After lots of discussions with my wife, Marisol, about the advantages and disadvantages of the position, we decided that it would further my writing career and my articles would be sent to other newspapers out east, so I will be writing nationally. So I am off on this adventure and job to set up a new life for my family and me; also to send for them when I have established our new home for us to dwell in. For now, I know nothing about the Indians or the territory I will be living in.

Since all journeys on the Missouri River start in Saint Louis and it is appropriately called 'The Gateway to the West,' on this very morning of April 4th, I boarded on the Saint Louis Iron Mountain Railway running from Hannibal to Saint Louis. From there, I will board the Steamship Polar Star and travel up the Missouri River to Weston, Missouri. The train station was bustling with lots of activity as we approached the station in our carriage. I climbed out then assisted Marisol down, and then assisted the children who also came to see me off on my adventure. Then I went to the back of our carriage and unloaded my steamer trunk. I flagged down the baggage handler and had him take my trunk to the baggage car as Marisol and I said our goodbyes. The children gave me hugs and kisses as tears started to flow from all of our eyes. I gave my wife another hug and kiss then boarded the train as the train conductor called, "All aboard, last call for Saint Louis." I jumped aboard at the last minute as the wheels started turning and the whistle blew. I chuckled at the children as they covered their ears as the whistle sounded. I blew them a kiss and entered my traveling car.

The tears from my eyes were still flowing down my cheeks as I took my seat aboard the train.

I had a window seat and tried to enjoy my view of the Mississippi River and go through some notes about the area I am traveling to. I occasionally looked up from my reading to see all the activity on the river. There were ships and boats of all shapes and sizes traveling up and down the strong current of the water. Steamboats, keelboats, and the famous Mississippi flat bottom boats, snag boats, and log rafts of various sizes floated on the water. The Steamboat Minnesota was headed upriver pulling five keelboats behind her full of merchandise for towns up north.

After a few stops at other towns along the route, about two hours later we finally arrived in Saint Louis, Missouri. The train pulled up to the Seventh Street Station around noon. As I disembarked the train, I retrieved my trunk and then found a porter for the Polar Star, and he took my belonging to the steamer at the levee. I then hailed an omnibus that was headed in the direction I needed to go to purchase some supplies for my expedition.

My first stop was at a paper supply house where my lovely wife Marisol had ordered me five leather-bound journals with my initials embroidered on the covers. She wanted me to keep a daily account of my activities so she can read them at a later date. I also purchased quills, ink, and loose paper so I may send back my stories to the paper. The store was very helpful and had my purchases delivered to my ship so I would not have to carry them to my other stops.

I hailed another omnibus to make one last stop before boarding the ship. As we passed by the courthouse at Fourth and Market, there was a slave auction happening at the time. There was a very large crowd gathered there on the steps outside of the building where four years prior, Dred Scott started his lawsuit against slavery. I am a Missourian but do not condone the practice of slavery. The bus took me a few blocks further to the Hawken Gun Store.

It was about one o'clock when I arrived at the gun store. I was not due to depart till four, so I had some time to pick out my firearms. Samuel and William both assisted me in my purchases, showing a varied and large collection of shotguns and muzzleloaders. I chose one of their finest traditional woodsmen fifty caliber muzzleloader with a hardwood stock. As I also wanted to purchase a pistol for my protection, they recommended I go to the hardware store of Henry Shaw down the street a few doors down. It is there that I purchased a newly-developed pistol sidearm made by Horace Smith and Daniel Wesson. I purchased what they called a volcanic repeating pistol that will fit my needs if I couldn't load my muzzleloader fast enough against the fierce creatures and Indians of the unknown frontier.

I was only a few blocks away from the levee at this time so I decided to walk the rest of the way to the levee. The cobblestone streets were covered with mud even though the streetcleaners with their slop carts try to keep the city sanitized so disease does not spread again through town. I can tell the wood plank sidewalks were a new addition to the existing buildings. There was a great flood ten years ago that made the river stretch its borders into the town about twelve miles wide going all the way up to Second Street. Then in 1849, there was a terrible cholera outbreak in Louisiana that also hurt Saint Louis.

As I walked past the Cathedral, I noticed it was the only remaining building still standing from the fire of 1849.

The story goes that on May 17th of that year, a paddlewheel steamboat by the name of Whitecloud caught fire as it was attached to the levee. The fire spread onto the freight on the levee and then spread to the buildings, burning down fourteen blocks of the city. Over four hundred buildings were destroyed during the blaze. Being a newspaper man, I recall that this was the first time I ever saw in print the death of a firefighter killed during the line of duty. I am sure deaths have happened before but nothing was accounted for in print that I'd ever seen or heard of.

As I walked closer to the river area, the number of saloons and houses of working women become more and more abundant. I had some time to relax before boarding the Polar Star, so I entered a saloon of Polish origins being that my great-grandfather and great-grandmother came across the ocean from Poland seventy years ago. There was a new polka playing in the saloon that I was not aware of with the name of 'Belles of Saint Louis.' It was a catchy tune and a few patrons were twirling around the dancefloor in fine Polish tradition. I sat down at the bar and ordered a whiskey since I had some time before I had to be aboard the Polar Star. As I was leaving the establishment, the mayor of Saint Louis, John How entered while thinking he swung doors and shouted, "Drinks are on me!" The crowd roared with delight with that announcement, but I had to get to the levee and board my steamship.

The Saint Louis levee is six miles long on the eastern border of Saint Louis. At this date, it is considered to be the second largest port in the United States only surpassed by New York City as far as volume of trade. The heavy smoke from factories and steamships become more apparent as I approach the levee landing. The homeless children roam this area picking the pockets of unsuspecting travelers and stealing food from the street vendors. The females at the bordellos flash their bosoms to passers-by of their establishments to earn a few pennies while they are not busy with gentleman callers. The activity at the levee was like nothing I have seen before; pedestrians, horse riders, wagons, buggies, carriages, omnibuses, and hacks fill the streets and sidewalks. I can see why the pickpockets chose here to do their profession because of the constant bumping into people all around you. The chaos here reminds me of bees in a beehive, everyone crawling on top of each other and still being productive. Besides all the people, there are stacks of freight scattered around that are being loaded onto wagons offloaded from the riverboats.

    As I reached the riverbank, I was amazed at all the different types of vessels that travel the river. The larger boats were stacked three deep at some points and smaller ships moved between them and offloaded their product. The street vendors were selling their goods to the travelers shouting what product they sell above the whistles and bells of the steamers that arrive at the levee. The variety of ethnic food filled the air with smells that make your mouth water, and the sound of the tambourine girls, organ grinders, and boot blacks made this area quite entertaining and very loud. The cigar salesmen and cure-all tonic sellers did their pitches to any passerby that looked their direction.

    As I was walking my way to the Polar Star, I gazed upon the magnificent showboats, Goldenrod and the J.S. Deluxe. Many other paddlewheel and side wheel steamships like the Paul Anderson, Sam Cloon, War Eagle, The Delta Queen, the Sadie Fisher, and many more filled the shoreline. Every open inch of shoreline was occupied by some sort of vessel.

    I saw the Polar Star further down as they were still loading the firewood for the engines and assorted freight destined for the cities along the river like Westport, Liberty, Weston, and Saint Joseph Missouri. I notice the New Lucy and Highland Chief flank either side of the Polar Star as I approached the gangplank to board the vessel I will be traveling on.

    The ship's captain was standing on the balcony of the Polar Star watching the loading of the merchandise and passengers. Captain Tom Brierly has earned a reputation of being one of the best Missouri River pilots setting a record for the fastest time from Saint Louis to Weston with the time of two days and twenty hours in the fall of last year during August. Being spring now and the river is high due to the melting snows up north, I do not believe we will set any records on this voyage.

    Before I stepped foot on the gangplank, I shouted an "ahoy," to Captain Tom and in return he gestured back to me that I may climb aboard. When I stepped off the plank, the porter showed me to my room. The paper sent me to the frontier with style that I am sure will be missed when I reach my destination. My steamer trunk was already in my stateroom at the foot of the bed. I placed my new purchases on the bed and prepared myself for a journey of unknown adventure and excitement across the state of Missouri.

    I arrived at the Polar Star about an hour before departure. After putting my supplies away, I changed out of my suit into my new attire including the new holster and sidearm. The weight I am not used to on my hip, never having to carry a weapon before. With this new stationary, Marisol would like me to scribe all accounts of this adventure so while the ship is still docked and loading, I will give a brief description of the area to where I am traveling and the town of Weston, Missouri, of where I will be staying for some time.

Starting with the Saint Louis area, this was once occupied by the group of Indians called Mound Builders. The Cahokia Tribe built huge villages that the Spanish encountered when they first explored this land from the southern region while the French made their way down the Mississippi River from the north. In 1803, Thomas Jefferson bought a large landmass from Napoleon Bonaparte calling it "The Louisiana Purchase," doubling the size of the United States of America. In 1804, Meriwether Louis and William Clark began their adventure to explore this new land and report their findings from a French trading port that was called Saint Louis.

Missouri was added as a territory, and then became a state in 1821 after the controversial Missouri Compromise. Missouri expanded further to the northwest in 1837 with the Platte Purchase that extended Missouri to the Iowa border of which became a state in 1846. The Missouri River, where it heads north, is now being called the dividing line between the Indian lands and white settlers with an invisible line heading south to the Texas Territory that became a state in 1846 also.

At the end of the war against Mexico in 1848, the United States expanded again in the southwest gaining what they call New Mexico and California. The town of Santa Fe became the largest city for trade west of Saint Louis. Four years ago in 1850, California became a part of the United States after a large population of people traveled to the territory and discovered gold. Also in 1850, a large religious sect called the Mormons ventured to the west and created the Utah Territory on their search of religious freedom. I must not forget to mention that there is a state called Wisconsin to the north above Iowa that was admitted to the union in 1848. As I noted previously that the land west of the Missouri River is called Indian Territory and a rumor tells from Washington City that there shall be a bill passed soon that will open up the land from the Missouri River to the mountain range to the west called The Rockies. More and more people want to invoke their Manifest Destiny and reap the spoils of the new land.

The Polar Star's whistle blows off as we prepare for departure. I hear the captain shouting orders as the gangplanks and ropes are removed from the ship, and as the engines are being stoked to engage the waterwheel. I believe I will join my fellow passengers on deck and watch us depart from Saint Louis. I will give more information on Weston as the voyage upriver continues.

| April 4, 1854 | Aboard the Polar Star |
| Tuesday late evening | Missouri River |

    The Missouri River was flowing fast and furious as we avoided debris from upriver all afternoon and evening. Captain Tom believes it is due to all the snow melting from the northern part of the river, where there was a considerable amount of snow last winter, and also from the many other attributes that melt into the Missouri River. Being so dangerous to go upriver at night, we docked in Washington, Missouri. The scenery was magnificent as we went between huge cliffs overlooking the river. The trees and spring foliage are erupting with color, and the sun sat down in the west as we reached the Missouri flatlands giving us a spectacular spectrum of colors from horizon to horizon. We passed by a few small trading posts and towns set up along the river. The fur trading business will greatly increase now that spring is here.

    Besides watching the scenery, I also read on the topics of native animals, trees, and some on prairie cultivation in the Missouri region and some history on the Kansas territory. The trapping industry has already been a major source of income for the western pioneers. Deer, raccoon, opossum, rabbit, turkey, quail, pheasant, goose, black bear, cougar, coyote, and partridge are some of the critters that roam the wild woods of Kansas territory and upper Missouri. Further west there are buffalo, elk, and antelope. In the rivers and streams, you will catch rock or catfish that sometimes can weigh over one hundred pounds. In the lakes and ponds report that there are perch, bass, and bullheads of enormous sizes and shapes.

    The many species of trees that grow in the Platte Valley Region have as much variance as the critters. There are many species of evergreens, along with walnut, oak, hickory, ash, maple, sassafras, sycamore, butternut, mulberry, cherry, and still many more varieties. The land is fertile for fruit as well, apple, plum, cherry, pawpaw, grapes, and strawberries. The land is also used for growing different cash crops like corn, barley, beans, but the most popular crops are the tobacco and hemp that come from this region. Rye, oats, potatoes, and any vegetable succeeds in this climate being very warm in the summer and winters that are mild compared to the northeast. The candle is about extinguished so I will retire for the evening, dreaming about the adventure that is ahead of me.

| April 5, 1854 | Polar Star |
| Wednesday late evening | Going west on Missouri River |

The first full day of travel is complete and tonight we have docked in the town of Rocheport, a short distance downriver from the town of Sandy Hook. As myths go, it is my understanding that the town of Sandy Hook was actually started by the wood saved from a sunken steamer by the name of Plowboy; with that material, they began construction of their shelters and shops.

The capital of Missouri is Jefferson City, and it is raised high above the riverbank as we anchored by their levee this afternoon. It was a very busy port but we were in and out within an hour to drop off mail, passengers, and some freight.

My research today consisted of the Platte Purchase of 1837. This acquisition from the Indians took Missouri to the Iowa border. Many towns sprung up rapidly in northwest Missouri after that land opening. From Westport Landing to Council Bluffs and the small Indian Trading Post in the Black Snake Hills started by Joseph Rubidoux became the town of Saint Joseph, Missouri in 1840. The towns of Parkville, Platte City, Weston and a few others in the crossroads grew up immediately. Weston is located on the Missouri River just north of Fort Leavenworth. Weston is the busiest port on the Missouri River, also being a major trade exchange for the army at Fort Leavenworth. A military road was built from the arsenal in Liberty Missouri to Fort Leavenworth with ferry crossings, bridges, all maintained by the army. The road crosses the Platte River in Platte City and continues over Bee Creek to Rialto.

The means of travel in this part of the country consists of walking, horse or mule, wagon or stagecoach, and different means by river travel. Train travel at this point goes as far as Saint Louis but will be moving west within the next few years. The roads are well worn by wagon tracks and it is safer to travel in groups. There is another military road that goes south from Fort Leavenworth to Fort Scott with that trail crossing over the Kansas River at Grinter's Trading Post. The California and Oregon Trail also has a trail from Fort Leavenworth heading west, and a trail that leads north to Fort Kearney and Calhoun. There is also a trail offshoot from Fort Leavenworth that connects to the Sana Fe Trail. I must add that the city of Santa Fe was established in 1610 by the Spanish, making it the second oldest colonization in United States Territory. Saint Augustine Florida is the oldest colony again established by the Spanish in 1565. Trade routes opened to Santa Fe after the Spanish War with Mexico, when Mexico won their independence from the Spanish in 1820. William Becknell was the first trailblazer to establish a route from Saint Louis to Westport to Santa Fe.

April 6, 1854   Aboard the Polar Star
Thursday Evening   Missouri River near Indian Territory

Today we traveled from Rocheport to the town of Westport Missouri and the city of Kansas that is building up around Westport a short distance away from Indian Territory. The Polar Star was paddling up the river with all its steam, but Captain Tom is still at slow speed due to the fast current of the Missouri River. We passed by the Steamers Excel, E.A. Ogden, and The Orion on the river today going down river. The Excel was stuck on what they call the Baltimore Sandbar about ten miles downstream from Lexington, Missouri. The Excel was being assisted by keelboats trying to offload the freight to lighten the load on the steamer so it may disengage from the sandbar.

The Westport Landing was a natural rock levee. High bluffs are on the south side and trails or roads were cut into the side of the hills so wagons and travelers can ascend or descend the hills with ease. Westport is about four miles from the landing so pioneers have started building closer to the river for easier access to trade on the river. Many great adventurers have stood where I am standing now. The greatest frontiersman, Daniel Boone, loved to hunt in this area after leaving Tennessee to explore the great unknown of the American West. Zebulon Pike, Jedediah Smith, Kit Carson, and John C. Fremont have also traveled on the trails that I am now traveling.

While the Polar Star was unloading some of her freight, the dinner bell rang out at the Troost House located on the south side of the bluffs overlooking the Missouri River. The sixty-room inn was very busy, and the dinner was delectable, but anything would be after having to eat river fish the last two days.

As I sit here, I ponder my location about only being a few miles from Indian Country. There are about four missions established just west of Westport, Missouri, that were established after the Indian Intercourse Act of 1834, when over eleven thousand native Americans were relocated to. I had my first Indian sighting today as I walked past some of the shops in the town of Kansas. They were very pleasant and dressed in very colorful garments. The largest is the Methodist Shawnee Mission run by the Reverend Isaac McCoy a few miles from Westport. The Intercourse Act also prohibited any settling on Indian land by white settlers. Only missions, trading posts, and military farming were allowed. The trails were safe to travel as long as you stay on the trails, and trappers could not hunt the land without the local tribes' consent to the trappers. Almost every religion has set up missions, as they say, to help civilize the natives.

Tomorrow, the Polar Star will be arriving at Weston and I am very nervous about this task I am taking on in a strange town on the frontier. I will finish this scribe in my journal and then read more about this land I am settling in. I will not be burning the midnight oil tonight knowing I have a full day tomorrow.

    April 7, 1854   Saint George Hotel Weston, Missouri
    Friday Night   Room 302

We were able to depart Westport Landing around eight o'clock this morning. The excursion up the river today was very relaxing as I stood on the deck of the Polar Star. The scenery around here is breathtaking as we rounded what was called Kaw Point, and then around the bluffs of Parkville, Missouri. The steamer Orion passed us heading downriver and a short spell later, Captain Brierly pointed out a group of Delaware Indians on the west bank of the river casting nets near a creek flowing into the river. A group of men grabbed their sidearms being ignorant of the fact that the Delaware Indians were very friendly if not provoked. A few climbed to the promenade deck and others went to the pilothouse where Captain Tom told them to stand down, they were no threat to us. The men grumbled and disarmed themselves, but the tension was much higher on board now.

Almost three quarters of an hour later, we could see the landing at Fort Leavenworth. We dropped anchor and set the planks down so a few new recruits could disembark and join the army. The steamships Twilight and The Sacramento drift by us heading south, blowing their whistles as we prepare to depart the fort's landing. As we departed, a man approached me and we began a conversation about the river ride and Weston. He was a pleasant man who introduced himself as Benjamin Stringfellow, a lawyer in Platte County. He has been in this area for a while and is excited about the Douglas Bill that if passes will change the face of our nation, and he swore from tooth to toenail that popular sovereignty will prevail for the good of our country. I must also note that he said that I will be in for an adventure of a lifetime.

In a short amount of time, the boat whistle blew and in the distance church bells rang out as we approached the Weston Levee. We said our goodbyes and hoped our paths would cross again; I went to my quarters and prepared my steamer trunk and other belongings for departure off this vessel. When the Polar Star set its planks down, it was almost one o'clock in the afternoon. I shook the captain's hand as I departed and thanked him for a safe journey. I then found a porter on the levee from the hotel my paper had acquired for me to stay for six months to see if this assignment will pan out with the different views of the people about slavery and expansion west. This is the biggest city on the Missouri river with the exception of Saint Louis. It is my understanding that the population in this town is close to five thousand people.

As I wander up the hill on Main Street in Weston, I see tobacco and hemp warehouses, and buildings of every business you can think of in a four-block area on one street. I walk into The Saint George Hotel and check into my room. The porter has already dropped off my trunk in room 302, the top corner room overlooking the whole Main Street scene. The street is as busy as bees in a hive. Swarms of people, wagons, horses, and oxen fill the streets below me trading their goods and buying them for their trek across the Great Plains of the Frontier. This shall prove to be an exciting adventure.

Polar Star Newspaper Ad

Chapter Four
Weston, Missouri

Natalie and I read the journal until we noticed the sunlight now coming through the windows making the room brighter. Even without sleep, we were still energized about our incredible find and as we were still in bed, we heard movement outside our door in the kitchen. Very quietly we grabbed the saddlebags and placed them in the armoire. Getting up, making more noise, Mom's voice from the kitchen called out, "Rise and shine, we are burning daylight." We were able to get into the shower before everyone else and that revitalized each of us. We readied ourselves and met up with some cousins at "Homies," a restaurant actually called Homer's on 4th Street.

After breakfast, we drove around looking at the old beautiful houses on Broadway Street, and then headed home to Mom and Dad's. We gathered everyone who was in the house in the kitchen and then escorted them to the room Natalie and I were staying in. Getting everyone's attention, I pushed on the rock, and the panel opened up under the window like before. A few curse words were exclaimed as they slowly eased their way over to the new opening in the wall. As they were looking at the ladder, I opened the armoire and pulled out the saddlebags and showed them the books.

With amazement, they looked upon the finds and I explained what we did and saw last night. I had grabbed more flashlights before we came back and played show and tell, so I gave them to my brothers and brother-in-law. I went into the hole first, then one by one each of them came down into the tunnel. I managed for no one to step on the trigger to shut the door from on the floor until everyone was off the ladder and then we proceeded down the narrow passage.

It was actually quite humorous seeing everyone squatted over to walk except me because I was the shortest of the group. When they approached the pile of trash, we could read the bottles a little better with the extra lighting and were able to tell that one was marked with Kansas Territory writing on the bottle. We explored further down the tunnel, and they enjoyed the discovery as much as Natalie and myself.

When we reached the collapse, we were able to notice that there was still an opening on the other side of the boulders and dirt. We decided at a later time we would come back and excavate the tunnel to see where else we may go. As we headed back to the ladder, we each picked up what we wanted to look at when we reached daylight again. We returned to the room and looked at our new treasures. The interest went back to the journals and we agreed that we would read them together in the family room later that evening when the entire family is present.

The children and grandchildren arrived in the afternoon, and we all caught up on everyone's lives as we chatted and snacked throughout the day until after dinner. That is when we all put on our comfy clothes and gathered in the family room around the fireplace waiting for the story to continue.

    April 8, 1854   Weston, Missouri
    Saturday Evening   Saint George Hotel, Room 302

On this beautiful spring morning in my new home for a spell, I enjoyed a wonderful breakfast served at the Saint George. They served a nice ham and egg platter with sausage and grits. The coffee was almost as good as Marisol brews up, and the confectionaries were simply delicious. I will most likely gain weight during my duration here. My companions during the meal were Benjamin Stringfellow and Doctor George W. Bayless who were discussing the soon-to-be new territory and the prospect of them starting a town when the bill passes in Washington. With the bill leaning to popular sovereignty, they could possibly influence others to join their cause of making the new territory a slave region. I listened to them very intently, trying not to show my disbelief of owning someone for any purpose. As I finished eating, I asked the gentlemen where I could procure a horse and accessories to explore this area, and learn about the people and ideals. They informed me of a few places to purchase my needs.

I bid them a good day and continued my morning going to the Weston Reporter, the town newspaper, and inform them of my assignment, also if they wanted me to sell my articles to them as well as my own paper in Hannibal. They were very honest and informed me that they would look at my scribes and decide then if they can use the stories.

This week's main story in their paper was the arrest of a woman, the wife of a Jacob Forth, along with her brother and sister for poisoning his jug of alcohol. Another gentleman whose name was James Morgan, both had taken drinks from the tainted jug, killing Mister Forth and making Mister Morgan violently ill. Mister Morgan is not expected to live from the poisoning. The Deputy Marshall H. D. Herdon had the three suspects in the Weston City Jail until their trial.

The family went to trial last week in front of Judge George W. Gist who did not find enough factual evidence to suggest that they were the culprits who poisoned the jug. After two days of court, the family was set free seeing how there was no witness proving the accusations against wife and other family members.

As I exited the reporter's office and began my way to the stables, the streets of Weston were filled with wagons, horses, oxen, and men and women all of different nationalities speaking their native tongue. This is a different world than I was accustomed to back in Hannibal, Missouri.

I strolled by the hemp houses. The sounds of the hard workers filled the air, pulling and pressing the fibers to make different products that they ship downriver to Saint Louis and New Orleans. The slaves are stripping down the hemp and making bales of different sizes. Another prospering business for this town is the whiskey and beer trade. The breweries here store their product in caves they dug deep into the hills keeping the temperature extremely cold. The whiskey is some of the smoothest I have ever encountered in my travels.

The bells of the Presbyterian Church ring out to inform the town that another riverboat is approaching the docks to be unloaded. Meandering down to the levee, I pass the hardware store I was told I should buy my leather goods from for my horse. Some slaves were busy working on unloading wagons at Elijah Cody's Store, while he was busy working inside the store. I waved to him as I passed by with him acknowledging me with the same gesture.

As I looked up and down the busy Main Street of Weston, Missouri, a badged gentleman was approaching up the wooden sidewalk. As he came closer, I waved and asked for a moment of his time. We introduced ourselves and the man with the badge was Marshall Perry Wallingford of Platte County. He appeared a little dismayed when I explained my purpose in town and would like to know of any troubles or shenanigans.

He told me with disgust, "I reckon that there were a lot of new faces in town that were not welcome because of what they are saying the laws would be about the new possible territory of Kansas and Nebraska. Popular sovereignty shall cause shouting matches to gunfights. Mark my words, just you wait and see." He also mentioned that Missouri is a slave state and the new territory will be also; he and other fellows would stand up to the Uncle Tom cabin ideas and not protect the abolitionist's welfare. I wished him a good day and did not mention to the southern gentleman that I personally had a copy of that writing in my room at the Saint George.

Plat of Weston, Missouri

The offices of Diefendorf and Moore, attorneys-at-law, was just a few buildings down from where I was standing, so I made that my next stop for the day. I overheard their names as fair gentleman a few times while eating breakfast. I entered into a large front office with desks on both sides of the space behind a fence of newel posts and railing. Behind each of the desks sat two very distinguished gentlemen in very nice suits. I introduced myself to the men and explained them of my assignment and asked if they may keep me informed about any news of the new territory. They introduced themselves as Judge Diefendorf and H. Miles Moore, attorneys-at-law. I then asked their opinion about purchasing land now or wait for the new territory. They obliged me and suggested I wait for the new territory to open. Prices would be a lot cheaper than buying land in Platte County. The latest news from Washington and Senator Atchison is that the Douglas Bill will pass in Congress soon. The gentlemen also mentioned to me also that there were in the discussing stage of creating a new town across the river and when the time permits itself for the endeavor, it shall be the greatest town in Kansas Territory.

It was close to midafternoon when I arrived at the levee at Major Ogden's supply tent. He was very knowledgeable of all the Indian Missions and all of the different tribes that were still in the territory. He was called away to a ship that was just arriving, so he asked me if I could possibly meet him next week at his office and he would let me look at maps of trails and where the tribes were located. I agreed and we departed.

The stables and blacksmiths shop were close to the levee just a block back up the hill. I entered the stables and then I had asked the proprietor if he was selling any good trail horses. I was going to explore the area, so I needed a good riding horse. He nodded his head and came back with a beautiful Pinto maybe three years old and about thirteen hands high. He said he was keeping it for himself, but he will part with it for one hundred dollars. I knew that was a lot of money for the horse, but the paper gave me expense money, so I did not haggle and paid the man what he was asking for. I also threw in a stipulation that I can board him here at half price because of my duration of stay in town.

I walked away with my new horse that I immediately started to call Wildfire. We walked up the hill a bit further to Elijah Cody's store so I could purchase the proper leather goods for my adventure in Western Missouri. Mister Cody was assisting George Keller and his son-in-law A.T. Kyle. They were two farmers from Fancy Bottoms, a little valley just north of Weston. So I moseyed around a bit and met Elijah's nephew, Bill, sitting on a stack of flour watching all the excitement of the town and listening to the pioneers' stories of their trek to Weston.

After a short wait, Mister Cody was able to assist me and all my needs to journey across this area. I was able to purchase everything I needed for two gold slugs that was still part of my expense money from the paper. I rode Wildfire around town for about an hour, getting an outlay of the town. This is a busy town that thrives on the river travel and trade. I rode back to the stables and put my new horse away in his stall and brushed him down, then made sure he was taken care of for the night. I then headed back to the hotel for some dinner. It was a very long day and tomorrow will be longer.

Sunday April 9, 1854   Palm Sunday
Saint George Hotel   Room 302, Weston, Missouri

I awoke this morning putting on my Sunday best and heading to the Holy Trinity Catholic Church built up on the hill from the hotel overlooking the town of Weston. It is a beautiful stone church that can hold almost one hundred patrons. Father Francis Rutowski offered a beautiful mass that was set in the most glorious setting I have ever attended. It reminded me of my old parish in Poland as a child.

After mass, I was able to speak with the Father about all the beautiful decorations hanging in the chapel, and he was able to tell me that they were all donated by his friends at his old congregation in the region of the Upper Silesia of Olesno. Of course in the small world that we live in, that was the same area that I grew up in as a child before coming to America.

As I walked back to the hotel, I decided that it would be a nice day to ride Wildfire around the countryside around Weston. After a big lunch at The Saint George, I made my way down to the stables and saddled Wildfire. I headed north along the river, following a nicely formed road toward a small town they call Iatan. Newly planted fields of tobacco, hemp, barley, and corn line the roadside as I came nearer the town. Apple trees surrounded me, before crossing over a small wooden bridge that are starting to show signs of apple blossoms starting to flower. After crossing over the bridge onto Main Street, I noticed the hemp house of A. J. Alexander, whose slaves were busy working on combing out the hemp and stringing it to make rope. In this part of the country, I guess Palm Sunday is just an ordinary day here in the west. Some of the steamboats and other river boats were docked for the day, but there were a few steamboats moving up and down the river. I noticed a few Indian dugouts on the bank of the river full of furs and I believe to be from the Kickapoo Tribe that lives across the river.

The general store in Iatan is owned by a man of the name A.G. Smith and it looked like the place everyone congregated in town. This was also the post office, stagecoach stop, liquor store, motel, and restaurant, all under one big roof. I tied Wildfire up to the hitching post and went through the swinging café doors. I heard a big, "Howdy, what can I do for you stranger?" Mister Smith bellowed out from behind his counter. He was a very pleasant man who he listened as I told my story of my purpose of my being in the area, and then after I explained my mission, I asked him for a story or two about this area and some history.

He had time, so he agreed and came out from behind the counter. We took some seats at a table and then asked me what in particular I wanted to know. I replied with, "Tell me about the town and the surrounding area, please." He smiled and started with how the town received its name, and from what I recollect from this morning, it went something like this: The town was named after a local Otoe Indian Chief who saved the lives of white settlers in the year 1824 when this was still Indian land. He sacrificed his own life to save the pioneers. He then started a tale about the island in the river and why the landing is here. Many years ago, French trappers stopped on the island to check their supplies and stretch their weary bones. They started to gather firewood to cook their meal when they heard the mooing of a cow that wandered out of nowhere on this island. It was the only notable living animal on the island, so the Frenchmen named the island, 'Isle au Vaches,' or 'Cow Island.'

He continued with another more mythical of a story of how the island was named and being bizarre, I have to pass this story on also. Someone had constructed a house on the island believing it was a safe spot to stay. All the farming creatures were there, cows, chickens, pigs. One day, a cow was born with two heads on the island, and it became an attraction for all around to come gander at being the oddity of nature it was. A third more reasonable name for the island is that Indian boys of an unknown tribe stole the cow from a traveling group of pioneers heading west. They moved the cow as far as they could before they gave up trying to get the animal across the river and just left it on the island. He finished with the cow probably fell of a boat, got swept away by current upriver, or fell of a boat and ended up on the island.

I order a Sarsaparilla as Mister Smith continued his tales about Iatan. He mentioned the founder of the town, John Doughtery, and how he started the boat landing here. He threw in a few more names that I do not know but wrote them down for later reference. As follows, the names are Andrew Henson, James Palmer, and an Abraham Risk.

After an hour of conversation with Mister A.G. Smith, I purchased some jerky from him and grabbed a few apples for Wildfire. As I was leaving, he recalled a tale about an old French fort and trading post across the river, built when the French started exploring this land. There was also an outpost called Cantonment Martin either on the island itself or in this area. No signs exist of the cantonment anywhere.

I rode Wildfire down to the levee and spoke to a man by the name of Nimrod Farley, Nimrod was the of brother Joseph who founded the town of Farley north of Weston near where the Platte River flows into the Missouri River. I wanted to make it back to Weston before the sun sat down in the west. So I began my ride south going back on the same trail we traversed before. We entered Weston at dusk as the sun was setting, so I made it to the stable and took care of Wildfire, then I meandered up to the hotel where I fed and watered myself before coming up here to my room and enter this journal. It has been a long day and will be a longer tomorrow. Goodnight.

April 10, 1854   Weston, Missouri
Monday   Saint George Hotel, Room 302.

After a semi-quiet night of slumber, I decided to give myself a change of scenery for breakfast, so I walked across the street to the international hotel to meet other travelers headed west traveling through Weston. I arrived at the eatery and took a seat by the front window, so I could watch people and listen to various conversations occurring around the room. I acknowledged the people around me with morning pleasantries and they were returned by all. I introduced myself to the gentleman sitting across from me, and he in return introduced himself as Charles Dunn. He also stated that he worked for Elijah Cody at his store and farm. Another gentleman entered the establishment and everyone greeted him as Reverend, as he greeted them in passing by, who eventually took a table by myself and Mister Dunn. He introduced himself to me as the Reverend Frederick Starr, the minister of the Presbyterian Church and the new school in Weston. He asked what denomination I was and when I told him Roman Catholic, he shook his head and said he will say prayers to save my soul. He then smiled and laughed, extending his hand out to shake mine.

Entrance to Trinity Catholic Church

We had a very casual conversation as we all ate our breakfast not talking local politics or beliefs on matters, but mostly our families and the possibility of the expansion of the west into Indian Territory. I finished my meal and said my good days to the gentlemen and thanked them for the morning conversation and fine entertainment. I then proceeded back to my room at the Saint George and packed my saddle bag for what I figured to be about a week's journey around Platte County, Missouri.

For the very first time in my life, I strapped a revolver to my hip. The feelings I was having were that this was a part of my life now and in this turbulent time may save my life out in the frontier. My intent is to visit the towns around the area to get the popular feelings of the majority of the people living in this area and how they treat passers-by. After I finish this entry in my journal, I will begin my adventure. I grabbed my saddlebag, rifle, and headed down to the stables where Wildfire was awaiting me.

April 13, 1854   Parkville, Missouri.
Thursday   Thanksgiving Day

Platte City is located about eight and a half miles east of Weston on the Platte River. The slow ride on horseback was through some of the most beautiful land I have ever seen. Rolling hills filled with forests of apple and peach trees along with fields of hemp, corn, barley, sugar, and grape vineyards. My trail out of Weston took me south to Bee Creek that empties into the Missouri River below Rialto, and from there I headed east along the creek till I reached Martins Ferry Crossing. Along the way to Platte City, a caravan of army wagons passed me on the way to Fort Leavenworth from Barry, Missouri, where the army holds an arsenal of weapons for defense against the Indians who try to up rise. Behind the army was a small group of pioneers who were traveling to California via Fort Leavenworth.

Mister Zodor Martin was the owner and operator of the ferry across the Platte River. There were two other gentlemen waiting with me to cross, both riding a buggy together with a horse tied to the back. Sherriff Shepard and Doctor Hollingsworth traveled from Weston to attend a matter at the county courthouse, being that Platte City was the county seat.

It took about ten minutes to cross over the river, only being around 60 feet across at the point of the river we were at. Platte City was also built on the bluffs above the river, so they did not have to worry about the town flooding. It is a bustling town but more established then Weston and reminded me of my town of Hannibal. I arrived at the storefront of L. Rees that I read of the shingle hanging from the building and tied Wildfire up to the hitching post.

This was a very big store that seemed very busy and Mister Louis Rees was behind the counter helping his patrons as I approached. When he finished with them, I was next and he asked me if I found everything I was looking for. I was able to find some apples for my horse and some buffalo jerky for myself. I had also asked him about the town and what I should see while in town before my departure to Parkville where I intended to spend the evening. This town was not like the beehive of Weston, but slower and more of the peaceful feeling in the streets of Platte City. I was passed on the trial by a wagon train of pioneers traveling from Independence, Missouri, to the distant San Francisco, California. They were headed toward Martins Ferry to cross the Platte River. There were at least 40 wagons, and some folk were pulling carts behind the wagons. Following the wagons also was a very large herd of cattle and oxen. The view from this hillside is very beautiful. You can look over the valley and see the hills on the other side. This time of year, all the trees have their leaves retuning and green is seen for miles now instead of the whiteness of winter snow. The center of Platte City has the largest courthouse that I have seen since leaving Saint Louis. The two-story brick structure with each side being about fifty feet wide. In the open space of the square it made all the other surrounding buildings look small in comparison.

It was midafternoon when Wildfire and I departed Platte City. The trail took us due south about sixteen miles to Parkville. The trail was well rutted from all the wagons that have traveled this road over the years. On this route, I passed some travelers headed to California to seek their fortune in gold.

I had reached Parkville just before five in the evening and got Wildfire into the stables before I found a place myself. As I was caring for Wildfire, a gentleman entered and began a conversation with the blacksmith who he called the new visitor, Mister Park. I exited out of my stall when I finished care of my horse, and introduced myself to Mister George S. Park. I also explained my purpose in town and he obliged to speak with me and invited me to Thanksgiving dinner at his house in about an hour just down the street.

I meandered around town for a spell, and then purchased some wine at a saloon located down by the riverfront. The levee in Parkville was busy but not even close to the activity I have witnessed in Weston. The town of Parkville is the next port on the Missouri River after Leaving Westport, the town was named after Mister George Park himself, who also is owner and publisher of The Industrial Luminary, which by the way is an anti-slavery publication in Missouri. Before settling this town, Colonel Park was a war hero in our fight against Mexico.

I arrived at his home and his wife had prepared a huge meal fit for a king. He had invited many guests for the holiday and everyone was merry and thankful. After dinner, we talked for a good while in his home office about his views about the new frontier and its expansion. I wrote a very good article for my paper back in Hannibal and was able to use his back bedroom to sleep for the night. So I am ending this entry in the home of the Parkville Industrial Luminary owner, Mister George S. Park. Good night and Happy Thanksgiving.

    April 14, 1854   Fort Leavenworth
    Friday   Indian Territory

I was awoken on this Good Friday to the sound of steamboat whistles and bells coming to and fro from the riverfront. It is a beautiful morning with still a chill in the air. As I look down at the levee, I can see the Steamships Arabia and Sam Cloon loading and unloading their cargo and travelers watching the activity from the decks of the vessels. Some of these ships travel all the way up to what is called the Montana Territory, where the pioneers west have a shorter distance to travel across the land.

I had washed up and then tidied the room of what mess I had made, if any. Mister Park was not yet at the office, so I left him a note of gratitude and retrieved Wildfire, then headed to Farley, Missouri, located northwest of Parkville about twelve miles away.

I chose the trail to Farley that went along the Missouri River. It again was a very beautiful tour, looking at the sandstone bluffs and all the different foliage colors, and even all the different wildlife that still exists in the woods in this part of Missouri. I was told there were still mountain lions and bears in this part of the woods and hills. This area was an Indian hunting ground until 1820. As I made a bend in the trail northward after about a two-hour ride along the river, I came across where the Platte River empties into the Missouri and I could see the little town of Farley on the hillside out of the floodplain of the Platte River. Platte City is about ten miles down the Platte River from Farley.

Farley had a few businesses and churches, and I stopped at the establishment of Mister Stiles. It was occupied by a few patrons. We exchanged pleasantries and I learned I was fortunate enough to meet another town founder. Joseph Farley was picking up supplies for his brother, Nimrod. I said I had the pleasure of meeting Nimrod at his ferry crossing up by Iatan. I asked their opinions of the near possible expansion of our nation. These were the first gentlemen to not really give me a pro or free answer to the changing frontier, but Farley was very excited at the notion of looking forward to all the money he and his brother will be making from the river crossings. Farley was a newly plotted town, but there was mention of crossing over if there was that necessity.

I thanked all the gentlemen for their time and information, and for giving me more viewpoints. I will send in another article for my paper on the attitudes of popular vote. I feed my horse some apples and ate some jerky myself. Buffalo was actually very good, looking forward to it in a steak very soon.

I took the path to Rialto from Farley, of which is only about six miles away. I passed by Suttons Mill being the first horse-drawn grain mill that I believe I have ever encountered. It was a very big operation with six horses tied to the apparatus that spins and crushes the grains into dust. I do not know why but this area of land was referred to as the Winston Area.

It was about an hour's ride on horseback to Rialto riding through the newly planted crops of tobacco, barley, corn, and hemp. When I reached Rialto, I headed straight for Penseno's Landing, where I was on my way into Indian Territory.

Chapter Five
Kansas Territory

Rialto, Missouri, a town that is mostly comprised of saloons and brothels across from Fort Leavenworth, whose men mostly keep this town alive. One of the first ferry crossings on this part of the Missouri river used to cross into Fort Leavenworth, Indian Territory, also the closest place for drinking and ladies for the soldiers on leave.

It was midafternoon by the time I was entering, passing by the above-mentioned locations and went straight to the ticket office for the ferry boat. The river was very active with river boats. The George Washington tooted its horn as they passed by going north. The Sacramento was a paddleboat enjoying going with the current when it passed by. I hopped off Wildfire and tied him up to a hitching post by a waterhole, so he could quench his thirst. The name Captain John B. Wells was on the shingle above the door as owner operator of this enterprise. I purchased fares for my horse and myself, paying thirty-seven and a half cents for a one-way passage across the river. A total of three bits two for the horse and one bit for me. The ferry was about halfway back from his last crossing of the river.

As Captain Wells landed and tied up his vessel, then laying the planks in place with his deckhands, another steamship, The Twilight, pushed upriver to Weston and who knows where else she will go. As I watched The Twilight go upstream, I saw The Emile, a paddleboat, coming downstream, with both vessels sounding each other distinctive whistles as they approached each other. Captain Wells and his crew unloaded the cargo and passengers that just crossed over. Soldiers, merchants, Indians, and a few fur traders with a good haul of different furs on their mules

Also crossing the river was a family making a journey back to their home in California. The family went by the last name Girard, who said he was a partner in a confectionary business in San Francisco. He offered me a small sample and it was quite a delightful piece of chocolate. In the meantime, Captain Wells had ordered the crew to stoke the fire for the steam engine and we had begun our way to Indian land. We made our way across the current in about ten minutes as I enjoyed the company of my fellow travelers and the beauty that lay before my eyes. I saw flowers that were of every size and color, and trees of many species all in one forest. There were even trees that looked like they had flowers on them. A bald eagle flew over our heads and pulled a fish out of the river about fifty feet from the ferry. The wingspan had to be about five feet across and talons the size of my own hands. A magnificent bird, one of the largest I have ever seen that from what I hear, is very good meat and is hunted like the bear and cougar in this area.

As we approached the landing to Fort Leavenworth, another steamboat was coming down river. The landing has a few buildings built for army supplies to stay out of the weather before being loaded onto the vessels. There are also two small office structures that the ferry uses and the other for the army. The fort was built on the bluff out of flooding area and had a bluff that overlooked the Platte Valley for miles. The wagon trail was well rooted from all the years of use going up and down the slow incline up the side of the bluff. About a quarter mile from the river was the summit of the trail. We entered a beautiful park like feeling. The parade grounds were in front of us. To the north of us, the officer quarters were built and to the south were the enlisted barracks, mess hall, and staff offices. The Oregon Trail and way to Fort Riley continue on past the parade grounds where the stables are and also the blacksmith shops. There is also a cemetery along the western border of the fort of the soldiers who have perished while serving their country at this location.

Very large clusters of trees appear, providing shade in the still unused parts of the military fort. The supply wagons and those of the travelers west also dot the landscape of the majority of the main roads. I was in search of Major Ogden's office as I approached the quartermaster's office, where a group of men were on the porch speaking some form of tribal tongue I am not familiar with, appearing as if they were saying their goodbyes. I learned from Major Ogden after an introduction that the two Indians on that porch were Henry Tiblow, an interpreter and ferry operator across the Kansas River due south about thirty miles from the fort, and Commissioner Manypenny, who is the government-appointed agent for the Indian negotiations on the lands for this new bill being voted on in Washington.

When I did finally arrive at Major Ogden's office, I dismounted Wildfire and by the time I turned and reached the porch, the Major was there to greet me. We shook hands and did our pleasantries, and that is when my two new friends arrived to say goodnight to Major Ogden; they had a very long day negotiating today and wanted to settle in before the storm was upon us. The sound of thunder filled the air and they departed quickly. We entered the office and he immediately went to his maps and started informing me about the operations that have to be taken to sustain a military establishment like this one. Farms are established and taken care of by some Indians and some contracted farmers. Cattle and horses must be raised along with the chickens and cows to feed an army that is in one place. Coal mining in the Kickapoo Hills is being done to heat the buildings on the fort. Most of the land in what he called the Kickapoo Valley is just to the northwest of the fort, this is also where Salt Creek Valley and the Kickapoo Mission are located. The Delaware Indians are the tribe that is currently living to the south of the fort directly.

The weather outside had become violently windy and rain had started to fall from the clouds harder. The Major said he could get me a place in The Rookery close to his home. I was not aware of this storm, so I was unprepared. I graciously accepted and we headed to my room for the night. As the lightning filled the night sky with its intense flashes, the rolling of the thunder was so deep it vibrated the floor. Hail started hitting the rooftop, sounding like we were being bombed in a war. The crackling of limbs could be heard as the winds picked up some more, causing the hail to crack one of the windows in my room. Major Ogden stayed with me awhile, so I asked him to tell me some amusing stories of adventure that he has seen or heard at his time here.

He smiled then laughed and told me of a tale that had just occurred one month previous to my arrival here. In early spring 1854, the Eighth Baronet of Manor Gore, somewhere near Sligo, in Northern Ireland, Sir Saint George organized a hunting expedition that started out at the Chauteau Trading Post but are taking the northern route on the Oregon Trail and passed through Fort Leavenworth. Jim Bridger was the guide and Earl William Thomas Spencer Wentworth-Fitzwilliam, regarded as the richest man in the British Commonwealth, was accompanied by thirty dogs for hunting, also wagons full of seventy-plus rifles and over a dozen different shotguns. Cases and cases of pistols and ammunition filled more wagons along with many kegs of gunpowder. There were two wagons filled with different types of fishing equipment. Rods and reels of every size a person might ever need, even a specialist to make new fly lures out in the expedition.

The expedition would not be without the comforts of home either. The Baron slept under a huge green and white tent at night in his brass bed that was accompanied by his steel bathtub, several camping stoves, and wagons filled with wardrobe for every season. I enjoyed the story even more when Major Ogden informed me that there was a fur-lined commode that traveled behind his wagon.

The windstorm and hail seemed to pass by as fast as it appeared. The rain was still falling but not as bad. Major Ogden departed to his home after we both said our goodnights. As I enter this into my journal from the candlelight of my bed. The lighting I have from my candles and the fireplace still fills the room, so with that noted as I sit at this desk, I believe I glimpse out of the corner of my eye, an apparition of a lady in a white dress walking by my fireplace and bedroom door. My visitor seems to be glancing at me with a disappointing look on her face. I am going to sleep at this point, saying my prayers and laying my pocket rosary on the nightstand beside the bed. Sunrise cannot come too early in the morning.

    April 16, 1854   Weston, Missouri
    Easter Sunday Evening   The Saint George Hotel Room 302

I did not sleep well last night and woke up very early after a night of hearing footsteps where no one can be seen, and laughing children all night when there were no children on the premises. The wind and rain had stopped during the early hours of the night but upon leaving my residence porch, I saw some of the devastation of the storm that had passed. Branches a few inches thick lay across the grass and roads being broken off from the wind. Debris lies all over the fort.

As I started my day off by heading back to Major Ogden's office, I heard a few soldiers speak of what they called a tornado that went through tearing off a few roofs in Salt Creek Valley and many trees down here in the camp. Major Ogden provided Wildfire with room and board last night also and had him waiting for me as I approached his office. When I entered, he was already in a discussion with who he introduced me to as Alexander Majors, a freight transporter who was bidding for the government contract to California and all forts out west. I did not interrupt too long; Major Ogden provided maps for my use and informed me that I may go to the mess hall, there was a meal waiting for me there.

After a fine meal with the last of the infantry unit, I rode out past the parade grounds where the dragoons were doing some drills and training the horses for battle. As I reached the west side of the grounds, the infantry were doing their drills as well. A very impressive sight to behold when they march in unison. I believe I also saw Colonel Thomas Fauntleroy himself, out on the field observing his troops.

The stables, blacksmith shops, wagon makers, and general warehousing occur on the west side of the camp. The Oregon and Fort Riley Trails continue at this point. Many jobs are held by non-military men who live on the Missouri side and cross the river every day. Some are allowed to live on the land they maintain for security purposes on government land. Coal is mined to keep the buildings warm during the winter and cooking in stoves. Crops are grown to feed the soldiers and the livestock of chickens, pigs, cows, oxen, and horses that they raise to use as meat, dairy products, and leather.

As I rode to the top of what they called Government Hill, I saw the splendid beauty of what is called Salt Creek Valley below. Just over a half an hour, I reached Rively's Trading Post. It is a Kickapoo Indian Trading post whose proprietor is a man by the name of M. Pierce Rively, where there is also a bridge that crosses Salt Creek, and then after crosses the trails split directions for the Fort Riley and the Oregon Trails.

My reasoning for visiting the store was to find out more about this land and its inhabitants. The Kickapoo, Delaware, Sac, Fox, and my map showed there was a reservation set aside for half breeds just to the north, about thirty miles or so. I was observing the activity that occurs at the trading post when a pair of familiar faces pulled up on a wagon. Isaac Cody and his young son, William, were heading to the fort to conduct business about a government grant to raise cattle and hay here in Salt Creek Valley. Isaac's brother, Elijah, was mentioned of having a business with the Potawatomie Indians about fifty or so miles to the west.

The men discussed the Douglas Bill that is in Washington right now being debated on by our elected officials. Mister Rively also discussed squatters having tried to settle on the Indian land. A rider approached as they were having their discussion and when he became identifiable by eyesight, Major Rively welcomed the Reverend from the Kickapoo Indian Mission. The Reverend Joel Grover, a Methodist priest. He came to invite all to the Easter service tomorrow morning at the mission at seven, as we Catholics call it a sunrise service.

I spent my Saturday at learning about the area and its resources. There is another bridge at what they called Stranger Creek on the Fort Riley Trail. It was getting late when the Codys left the trading post, and Major Rively asked if I wanted to bunk down there so I could experience an Indian Methodist Mass on Easter Sunday. I accepted and we put Wildfire in his stable. There was a loft in the trading post where some buffalo skins were thrown down as bedding. I placed my saddlebag and rifle down by a thick fur and went back down to where I had dinner with Mister Rively, who stayed in a room at the back of his store.

During dinner, Major Rively told me more stories about the area. He mentioned a settlement, Council Grove, way out west. After dinner, I excused myself and went to bed. They said it was about a half-hour ride on horseback to reach the church mission, so I had to be arisen early to be sure I made the service on time. The morning came too early as I saddled Wildfire in the light of the moon. The sun had not quite risen yet into the valley. I thanked Major Rively for his hospitality, and wished him well as I rode east along Salt Creek to the Kickapoo Indian Mission. The creek runs through the middle of a valley with beautiful hills surrounding it, full of trees and flowers of all colors. The sun was rising when I arrived at the mission. It was about five miles from the trading post. The Mission was a site to behold also in the sunrise. Fog rolling over the land from the Missouri River in between the huts and buildings of the Indians who dwell in them. The blue bright sky rising above the hills, turning into a light blue color, and then the black sky of the night still was above my head behind me. What a truly amazing Easter Sunday Morning. The church was lit up with candles making every window visible, and the congregation were arriving, so as I looked at my pocket watch, I saw that it was a quarter till seven. I tied up wildfire outside on the hitching post and proceeded inside where the mass was spoken in English by Reverend Grover, and the current reverend of the mission, Reverend N. T. Shaler, said the mass in the Kickapoo language after each sentence of mass. The mass in two languages was quite different, when I am used to Latin. Other than that, the service was similar to the service I attend back home.

After mass, the sky was beautiful and the sun was shining fully. Not a cloud in the sky. As I looked around the mission, I spotted in the post a man by the name of Major Dyers, who set up his shop when it was a catholic mission years past. As I am walking toward it with Wildfire, I notice on the bluff to the southwest of my location that there is what looks to be an old fortress overlooking this area. Mister Dryer informed me when I inquired about it that it was an abandoned French fort for about one hundred years, that was named Fort de Cavagnial. He said the Indians used it for a while but now it just sits. I learned that there was another agency station for the Kickapoo at a place called Kennekuk that was ran by a Major C. B. Keith. I may have time later in my stay here but not today. I was making my way to the Iatan Ferry that will get me back to Weston.

We arrived back in town today around midafternoon. I gave my horse a good brushing, rub-down, and a good meal. I treated myself to the Saint George's dinner with a big steak and potato. After this entry into my notes, I am flopping on my mattress for a long night's rest.

Kickapoo Mission

Chapter Six
Popular Sovereignty

April 17, 1854 Weston, Missouri
Monday Evening Room 302 Saint George Hotel

This morning I was awaken by the thunderous sounds erupting from the street below. A major wagon train heading to Salt Lake City had arrived and was looking for supplies to travel west. I opened my window and received the smell of a warm day in the country and surveyed the streets that were full of wagons of all sizes and types. I glanced at the clock in my room and saw it was almost nine o'clock. It was another beautiful day out today, but I understood that as they say, "In this neck of the woods, watch out, the weather could change in an hour." My view from my room also let me look across the city from the levee to the ridge of Main Street on top of the hill, also allowing me to see the main business area of Weston and the beautiful housing area to the north.

   As I was standing there gazing out yonder, another sense became alive in me, and I was smelling something cooking when my stomach growled like a big bear. I washed up using the water provided in the room bowl and pitcher. I then dressed myself for today's adventure, and then I proceeded my way down the stairs to the lobby, where it was full of travelers wanting rooms and departing their stay from here. Porters were carrying bags in and out as fast as they could to and fro. I made my way to the counter, grabbing *The Platte Argus* newspaper, then I attracted the clerk's attention and tossed him a dime showing him the paper. He nodded and waved as he caught the dime and put it in his drawer. It appeared *The Weston Examiner* was already sold out here by the time I arrived in the lobby of The Saint George.

   I made my way across the lobby to the entrance of the dining room and was able to be seated at a table with a window view of the Main Street. It was very busy still out on the sidewalks, and I could hear the voices on the streets speaking different languages. A few I do not believe I have ever encountered before. While I was enjoying my vegetable soup and iced tea, I read an article in the paper about the steamship Excel going up the Kansas River to Fort Riley delivering over one thousand pounds of flour and other necessities to the families at the fort. That will change how some of the transportation will be delivered from Fort Leavenworth being that river transportation is quicker and faster, with the chance of an Indian attack happening on the river very low.

The paper brought me up to the current events I missed in the days I was traveling, also seeing that an *Uncle Tom's Cabin*, an anti-abolitionist portrayal, was playing in Saint Louis this month. I also finished off a plate of steak and eggs this morning before heading out to observe the world, and a piece of mulberry pie to fill my belly. The activity around Weston reminded me of the action that was happening in Saint Louis along the levee and streets by the river. The streets were still muddy from the rainstorm that blew by on Friday, so the people were having a hard time trudging up the hill to the stores. The river's level increased further toward the warehouses but still not in any danger. The church bell of the Presbyterian Church tolled as more steamships arrived at the levee informing the dock workers of their arrival. Each steamship has a distinct whistle on each of the vessels that also helps identify the ship when it is still not in eye-view. There was no sense of tension or panic in the air as I walked the streets of Weston today. The pioneers were looking toward the future of living a dream in the new west. Where gold and silver were being discovered every day. This is the last stop along the trail to pick up any spare parts or other necessities so they must be confident about their supplies and equipment to make the journey across wild America, where you do not know what is around the next corner or hill. Some will make it to their destinations while others end up in places, they have no knowledge about and try make the best of it with what they have with them and around them.

Some of these faces I see before me on the streets of Weston, Missouri, will have their bravery tested every day fighting the natives of the land as well as the animals of the west, and the weather. Most of the stories I hear when I ask why they are traveling west is that they are looking for freedom and riches, in pursuit of gold and happiness in the new frontier. One day maybe I will travel to California, but I admire the pioneers that go out and find land of their own, traveling across hostile and torrent conditions from faraway lands, and now what reports from the pioneers, they have found some of the most beautiful land in the world, but what is in the land makes it also the most deadliest land.

Still taking in the atmosphere of Weston, it is hard not to notice how beautifully laid out the city is on the side of a hill. Everything you will ever need is within a few blocks of the levee. In a four-block area on Main Street and what I can see off the main road, I believe I observe nine dry good stores, two clothing stores, a bowling alley, a drug store, grocery store, two saloons, two livery stables, two blacksmiths, two gunsmiths, a furniture store, saddle and harness shops, a millinery, and a dentist. My list continues with shops on upper levels. Shingles of all shapes and sizes fill the rafters of the porches along the storefronts. Lawyers' offices, Banking houses, a large confectionary, telegraph office, hotels and homes are even down on Main Street. Just off to the south of the levee are the houses where the ladies entertain our troops when they are on leave from Fort Leavenworth. The houses of the upper class are along the hillside to the north of town. On the very top of a few buildings downtown, there are masonic symbols for some of the masons who are in the city. The Weston Court House is very small in comparison to all the other towns in Platte County; a small structure, a block up from the Saint George Hotel, also across from where Elijah Cody resides.

I notice the name Holladay on a few of the buildings and upon some shingles, and the name Holladay was also overheard while eating breakfast on multiple occasions. I inquired at the telegraph office when I was sending a short message to my wife, Marisol, about the Holladay name and what the entire name is involved in. I was not aware but I passed his property on the way to Platte City. Ben Holladay owns twelve thousand acres just east of Weston where he built a spacious sixteen-room brick mansion with stone window corners. The mansion was built upon a sloping a short distance from where I rode last week. Mister Holladay owns a large mill at the southwest of Weston on the road to Rialto. From Independence, Missouri, he runs a very successful overland stage that goes to Salt Lake City, Utah Territory, and he also has an overland freight transportation company like the gentleman I met at Fort Leavenworth, Mister Russell.

In Weston, the name Holladay appears on a saloon, a hotel, and a general store. The general store is managed by his brother, Jesse E. Holladay, and the mill outside of town is managed by Ben's other brother, David. A story I encountered about Mister Ben Holladay was that he had bought a saloon and was able to get barrels of whiskey for a quarter a barrel. So in his saloon he charged a quarter a shot of whiskey and that is where he made his money to venture into the other fields of his pursuit. All that said and done, Ben Holladay accomplished amazing knowledge before he was twenty-one years of age as he owned a hotel and saloon.

As I stood on the corner of Thomas Street and Main, the beehive of activity was still buzzing around me. I walked down the hill to the levee and then back up to the Saint George where I asked where I may find a seamstress in town. I was given an address and then went up to my room to retrieve the garments that I needed mended. Misses Harst lives on the on the corner of Cherry and

Walnut Streets, on the other side of the hill in a large two-story white house. She has the reputation of good honest work, done very quickly.

I finished my walk around the parts of Weston I had not ventured to yet. I returned to the telegraph office to retrieve my messages from Hannibal. The paper loves my stories and is sending them to Saint Louis and Chicago for publication. The family is doing fine but anxious to move to the west. I shall now retire for the evening. Until then.

May 19, 1854	Weston, Missouri
Friday Evening	Saint George Hotel Room 302

There is a great commotion amongst the citizens of Weston about the Douglas Bill being discussed by our leaders in Washington on the floor of the Congress. I understand now why Commissioner George Washington Maneypenny has been working so diligently and traveling the region meeting with the leaders of the local Indian Nations at Fort Leavenworth. I understand from my sources in Washington that the efforts of Commissioner Maneypenny paid off on May 6, 1854, when the tribes of the Delaware, Moravian, and Munsee ceded their land over to the United States. This meant that the Indian land across the river now belonged to the Government and will be up for occupancy very soon. I also learned from my friends in Fort Leavenworth that Alexander Majors acquired a contract to haul supplies to all the forts in the west.

On May 9th, I crossed the river with the help of Nimrod Farley, who was also assisting a large group of Missourians that were headed to Rively's Station in Salt Creek Valley for what they are calling a 'Squatters Meeting.' The meeting was announced by the distribution of pamphlets that were handed out from Saint Joseph to Westport. On my crossing, there were at least thirty men on board the vessel and our horses; a few buggies had to wait for the next passage across. Some of the faces I did recognize and acknowledged them with a tip of my hat or a nod and wave.

It was about a fifteen-minute horse ride on Wildfire, when for some reason, *Camptown Races* entered my head and I began singing that silly song. I had previously passed the Old Mission, and was riding through the fields of corn and hay maintained for the Fort. Civilians would come over from Missouri and work the fields that the government owns. There is also in the hills I pass a coal mining operation that is used by the fort to burn in their fires for winter warmth.

In a conversation I had with Major Ogden about maintaining a post in the middle of nowhere, he told me that a few years back Fort Leavenworth had over one thousand one hundred acres of land under cultivation with over thirty civilian hired hands to work the land. They yielded over twenty-five thousand bushels of corn, oats, and wheat. Also growing hay, straw, raising cattle, oxen, sheep, chickens, and hogs.

As I approached the station, I saw that there were already at least over one hundred men already present. Horses and buggies were tied up all around the front of the station, the buggies making a higher seating area for the men further back. When this first meeting started, there was at least two hundred men present. Some rules and regulations were established by the group, but the main decision was to have another meeting in about a month's time at the same location. I was too far away to fully hear the meeting, but I will get notes from other attendees.

On the next day, the 10th of May, news came that Commissioner Moneypenny had met with the Shawnee Indians, the next tribe south of Delaware, and they had also signed a treaty, ceding over their land to the United States government. As of yesterday, the 18th of May, the Kickapoo Tribe released their land to the government with the aide of Commissioner G. W. Moneypenny. Rumblings from the east have brought to my attention that the emigrant aid companies in Boston and other northern companies are attempting to persuade Congress to bring in the new territories as free, while the southern states believe they should be slave after the last state being a free state. Opinions are being voiced in the streets of Weston as well. The personalities of who I thought were upstanding citizens now voice their opinion on the rights of southern values and morals of gentlemen. The streets at night are filled with debates with activists standing on their soap boxes or buggies, telling me how I should think. I keep to myself for now, protecting my cover and still being able to get close to my sources and view both opinions.

The hotels and boarding houses seem to be remaining full while we wait for news from Washington about the Douglas Bill under debate. Tent cities are starting to appear outside of most major towns along the Missouri River as reported in the newspapers with pioneers who want to start in Kansas Territory over six hundred miles to the Rocky Mountains. No skirmishes have occurred at this time, but temperatures are rising in the streets every day.

June 2, 1854   Weston, Missouri
Friday Evening   Saint George Hotel, Room 302

All the eyes and ears in the west were on Washington for the past few weeks. News spread as fast as the telegraph lines could send the message that the passage of the Kansas-Nebraska Act was voted for and passed through both houses and signed by President Franklin Pierce on May 30th, 1854. The land shall be governed by popular sovereignty. Senator David Atchison had sent word to his friends in Platte County to head across the river and claim the land as quick as you can. Kansas Territory now stretched from the Missouri Border on the East to the Utah Territory border west of the Rocky Mountains and the northern border of Oklahoma, still Indian Territory, to the southern border of Nebraska.

    June 20, 1854　　　　　　　　Weston, Missouri
    Tuesday Evening　　　　　　　Saint George Hotel, Room 302

    The last three weeks have been a tornado of activity here on the border. In less than seven days after the passage of the Kansas-Nebraska Act, every piece of land that became available has already been claimed by squatters in and around the area of Fort Leavenworth. My friend Isaac Cody finished his house and moved his family over to Salt Creek Valley. I ran into Mister Cody when I attended the second squatters meeting at Rively's Station on June 10th. This meeting, I managed to be close and take notes for my newspaper and personal entries. At this meeting, the announcement of the Leavenworth Town Company that had formed secretly in Weston and that land was already set aside for a town south of Fort Leavenworth.

    D. A. Grover was appointed Register of Claims and Malcolm Clarke was elected as the First Marshall in Kansas Territory. Lewis Burnes of Weston was Chairman of the Meeting and J. H. R. Cundiff of Saint Joseph was appointed Secretary. Declarations were made in the Squatters' Constitution that stated that slavery would be allowed in the territory and that there would be no protection given to any abolitionist who desires to settle in Kansas Territory.

    Other men attending the meeting were Jesse Connell, George O. Sharp, Merrill Smith, David Hurley, J. B. Crane, Hugh Miles Moore, H. B. Gale, and a gentleman by the name of William Henry Harrison Goble. There were over two hundred at this meeting as well. There was speculation that the fort would be abandoned and that the buildings would be used to start a new town. Major Ogden later confirmed that the fort had no intention of moving or shutting down anytime soon.

    On the 10th of June, John C. Gist and Samuel Farandis claimed the land south of Fort Leavenworth, in the name of the Leavenworth Town Company. The men moved across river and are squatting on their lands to protect their claims for the company. On the evening of June 13th, 1854, there was a special meeting held here in one of the rooms at the Saint George. The Leavenworth Town Company consisting of thirty-two distinguished men of Platte County of both northern and southern beliefs to create a future town in Kansas Territory. The officers of the new town company are General George W. Gist as President, H. Miles Moore as Secretary, Joseph B. Evans as Treasurer, Amos Rees, L.D. Bird, and Major E. A. Ogden as trustees. The first issue debated on was the name of the town. The Judges Bird and Diefendorf wanted to name the town Douglas in honor of the senator who created the bill but was opposed by H. Miles Moore, who wanted to name the town Leavenworth City with the use of a military installation's name as added protection entering the Wild West. A name that had a sense of security and prominence. The company voted and the name Leavenworth City won out by a narrow margin.

Other members in attendance were Reverend Frederick Starr, L.W. Caples, William S. Murphy, Malcolm Clarke, G.H. Keller, A Thomas Kyle, and Samuel F. Few. More names will be discussed when I obtain them. The town secured 320 acres of Delaware Trust Land that will extend from the southern border of Fort Leavenworth along the Missouri River to Threemile Creek, whose name originated from being three miles away from the American flag post in the center of Fort Leavenworth.

A few days after the founding of The Leavenworth Town Company, on the 15th of June, Uncle George Keller hired a group of eighty men and started the process of clearing the site for Leavenworth City. Also on that very evening, another organization was formed in Weston to protect the values and heritage of Missouri from the abolitionists emigrating into their Kansas Territory or into Platte County, Missouri. I was not present at this meeting so I do not know any of the subjects.

        June 26, 1854   Weston, Missouri
        Monday Evening   Saint George Hotel, Room 302

Even as civilized as I believe the conditions I live in are safe, I am sad to enter this into my notes. My first friends I encountered her in Weston have departed our lives on June 24th, 1854, and are on a journey to heaven. Elijah Crutchfield and his sweet wife were destroyed by cholera on their farm six miles east of Weston.

Chapter Seven
Leavenworth City, Kickapoo City, Atchison, and Delaware City Is Born

July 13, 1854   Weston, Missouri
Thursday Evening   Saint George Hotel Room 302

With Kansas being a new territory for over a month now, a governor of the new land was selected by Senate on June 30th, 1854, with the announcement of Andrew H. Reader, the first man for the appointment of that office. Also announced was Daniel Woodson as Secretary, and Israel B. Donaldson as United States Marshal. They should be arriving from Washington in the next few months.

I was able to enjoy an American Independence Day celebration on the fourth of July over in the Salt Creek Valley, at Rively's Station. Isaac Cody, Reverend Grover from the former Kickapoo Mission, and Major Rively put on a celebration that my eyes have never seen before, and who knows if they will again.

It was a day that consisted of games, eating, drinking, and fireworks that turned night into day again. The games consisted of shooting, knife throwing, roping, horse racing, and buggy racing. The children played running games, and a few Indian games with the bow and arrow, wrestling, and bareback riding. There were two beeves in the pits for the white squatters, and the other for the Indians and coloreds that were at the festivities. Young Bill Cody kept up with the other Indian children in all the games he participated in. Beer and whiskey were carted over from Weston. The tables were set with all the fixings of a family reunion. The men folk talked politics of the territory, keeping all civilized with the women and children around. The celebration went far into the night with the displaying of fireworks that lit up the sky like a battle in war to end the day's events.

I was over in the area where the Delaware Trust Land used to be to witness a meeting of the Leavenworth Town Company, during the day of July 7, 1854.

On the land that had been acquired by G. B. Pauton, also a member of the association. G. W. Gist, presiding president over the association, honored Malcolm Clark and Mister Pauton. Each man was granted eighty acres of land and that a map be started of the squatter lands and a map of the town site platted out. Three trustees were nominated for that: Major E. A. Ogden, Major S. Maclin, and L. D. Bird Esq.

Many members of the Leavenworth Town Association were present, so a request was made for another installment of fees for the town association. Twenty dollars was collected from each member present. The Kickapoo Association at this time has already sent a delegate to Washington, to help with a representative of Kansas Territory. Kickapoo City Association has a city planned for the northern border of Fort Leavenworth where the Salt Creek runs into the Missouri River. The town's mayor was already announced as being Josiah Elliot, a name I have never heard.

    July 30, 1854   Weston, Missouri
    Sunday Evening   Saint George Hotel, Room 302

News from the east is that the pioneers and squatters along the border in Kansas Territory have formed a stock company and have immigrated to here from the New England area of the United States. Many companies formed by people like Eli Thayer, Amos Lawrence, and J. M. F. Williams. They are forming a town further up the Kansas River.

In somewhat of an opposing fashion to all of the free state men on the Leavenworth City Association, Senator David Atchison on the 27th day of July, 1854, along with Dr. Stringfellow and a small group of men about fifteen to twenty miles upriver from Weston to the trading post of George Milton, used his ferryboat to cross over the Missouri River and stake their claim for the Atchison Town Association. Peter Abel was appointed President, and Doctor Stringfellow as Secretary of the Atchison Town Association.

Besides the popular sovereignty issue with Senator Atchison, the citizens and some of the more rebellious citizens of Platte County Missouri , or should I restate that as more pressing of their beliefs than what the law will or should allow, have entitled themselves to be called the Platte County Self-Defense Association. This group of marauders that is led by George Galloway and B. F. Stringfellow attack the free-state pioneers, robbing them of their possessions and forcing them home while letting their southern brothers pass through with no avail. Stores of any merchants that are free-state supporters are vandalized and burglarized. The pro-slavery merchants like Elijah Cody have turned away the abolitionist settlers.

The Reverend Frederick Star was attacked by a lynch mob himself here in Weston. He was accused of riding in a buggy with his negro slave girl in the seat beside him. He is also accused of teaching his slaves how to read and write. One last accusation on the Reverend Star was that he had bought the freedom for a slave by the name of Henry. When the Reverend was able to explain his side of the story and disprove all the allegations against him with his profound manner of speech, he won over his accusers and was able to leave the building in peace.

The Defense Association has been very busy on the trails around Weston heading to any passage across the Missouri River. They turn back wagons and steamships that are organized by the abolitionist pioneers and or dealing with them in any way they have at their disposal.

    August 15, 1854   Weston, Missouri
    Tuesday Evening   Saint George Hotel, Room 302

With the harassment of travelers increasing in Platte County, the pioneers have taken to different directions for furthering their adventures west. They go up north through Nebraska Territory and then travel south into Kansas. Other methods are going up the Kansas River to as far as Fort Riley. Establishing new towns along the river deeper into the new territory as the pioneers face all the difficulties they are trying to escape from whence they came. One of those towns has established themselves are being called Lawrence, being started by Charles Robinson and the New England Emigrant's Association along with Charles W. Branscomb and Samuel C. Pomeroy. Another town going by the name of Topeka is being founded by Cyrus Holliday, both towns of course are for the free-state movement.

Some of the Atchison Town Company have taken it upon themselves to inform Commissioner Manypenny, that the town plot for the city of Leavenworth is still considered to be on the Delaware Trust Lands, and that the proper payment has not been occurred by the proper hands. A delegation was sent to Washington after the Leavenworth Town Association heard of the allegations and speak on the town's behalf to the proper authorities. After a few weeks of jumping through legal bureaucracy, the delegation returned to Leavenworth and the plans for the city were still intact.

    September 8, 1854   Weston, Missouri
    Friday Evening   Saint George Hotel, Room 302

There was a count or what is also called a census of the area of Leavenworth City in the town limits, or in its city proper on the first of September a few days ago. There is already a recording of over one hundred residents of Leavenworth Village. All recorded were males, except for Aunt Beck, a former slave of the Ordinance Sargent Flemmino. She lives in a tent at Threemile Creek where they have plotted for Third Street to end. She made her living there doing the laundry for the workers who are clearing the land and building the new structures for Leavenworth City.

It is said that the City of Lawrence is already over the population of two hundred men in its city limits. Building will be started soon, but a fortress was needed to be established on Mount Oread, to protect the free-staters from the southern sympathizers who attack their camps.

There is also news of a grasshopper swarm arriving from Southern Kansas Territory fairly soon to our area. In a lighter note, the first time in print *New York Tribune* mentioned the towns of Leavenworth and Kansas City in its August 26th edition.

September 22, 1854   Weston, Missouri
Thursday Evening   Saint George Hotel, Room 302

I am writing tonight with an extremely heavy heart. Four days past on the 18th of this month, my friend Isaac Cody was stabbed at the trading post of Major Rively in Salt Creek Valley. I happened to be a witness in the large group of settlers who came to say their piece about the laws of the land. The voices were getting more boisterous when Mister Cody approached the ruckus on his horse. Noticing the arrival of the free-state supporter, the crowd hollered for him to speak of his opinion on the matter of how the Kansas Territory should be governed by its people. Mister Cody was honored by the attention but did not want to speak in front of the large crowd, but the constant persuasion prompted him to dismount and head to the wagon where the speakers were debating.

He climbed onto the buckboard and gave a speech on how he believed that Negros should not be allowed into the state free or slave. Missourians and other southern supporters started yelling at Isaac Cody, calling him an abolitionist and at one-point Mister Cody was pulled off of the wagon by two pro-slavery supporters. Just as he was disembarking the wagon with the help of his non supporters, I noticed that his son and daughter rode up on their horses. Isaac was able to secure his footing and stand, but a friend and worker of Isaacs's brother, a Mister Charles Dunn, rushed up to Isaac Cody and thrust a Bowie knife into his chest with force.

William and Helen watched as their father was stabbed, and fell to the ground. Young Bill jumped off his horse and ran to his father's side. Doctor Hathaway was present at the event and proceeded to address the issue with Mister Cody. A few men were asked to carry Isaac into the station where the wound could be sterilized with alcohol as the doctor dressed the wound. He was then boarded onto a wagon for travel to Weston, where he could recoup closer to the doctor's care and under the roof of his brother. This was the first act of violence against another person I have seen or heard of in Leavenworth County or in Kansas Territory over popular sovereignty. Charles Dunn was dismissed from employment at the Cody Farm and store upon his return to Weston.

Not that there is a brighter side to that story, but Uncle George Keller has completed clearing all the underbrush and land for the building of Leavenworth City. Major Ogden had soldiers help some of the landowners start the construction of their buildings. Tents are scattered all over the city proper, and on the 15th of September 1854, the first newspaper printed in Kansas was under an old elm tree at the corner of what will be Cherokee Street and the levee. A pro-slavery newspaper with the name of the *Kansas Herald* with the proprietor being H. Rives Pollard.

On the north side of Threemile Creek where the creek enters the Missouri River, a sawmill under the shingle of Scruggs and Martin was built and is in business for cutting lumber for the new buildings being erected in Leavenworth City. Construction has already begun on a hotel along the river by the landing.

Last Tuesday, the 20th, there was a Squatters' Trial held in Kansas Territory at Rively's Station. It appeared that there was a claim staked out by J. W. Martin and the claim was jumped whilst Mister Martin was pertaining to business in Liberty, Missouri. Mister Martin hired H. Miles Moore as his attorney to represent him in this travesty.

Each party was represented and gave the court each story of who owns the claim, and at the end of the trial, Captain J. W. Martin was victorious and won his claim back. The Squatters' Court Marshall Malcolm Clark was then asked to remove the claim jumpers from the property and let Mister Martin back on his claim. Being the lateness of day, the order was to be executed the following morning. I showed up the following morning myself at the station and rode out with the posse, and by mid-morning, we arrived at the Martin claim. The man fled during the night, leaving his wife and children to fend for themselves. The Marshall was very much a gentleman and offered her time to get her belongings out onto a wagon with her children. He even offered to help carry the furniture and heavier items if that would assist her in any way, but to no avail; she would not leave the cabin. She barricaded her and the children in the cabin, but after hours of persuading and threats of violence, the cabin was retaken by Marshall Clark and returned to Captain Martin.

The belongings of the woman and children were placed into a wagon and they were escorted away with the woman still screaming that it was their property and she would be back that night to burn the cabin down. As a precaution for the time being, the Marshall placed a guard at the home until Captain Martin was fully living in the cabin again.

Isaac Cody was still on bed rest in his brother's house up the hill from the Saint George. It has come to my attention that most of his hay was burned by the ruffians of Missouri, and that most of his cattle had been run off as well. Young William and his sister took some of the cattle over to where Mister Cody procured more land in what is called Grasshopper Falls about thirty miles west of Salt Creek Valley.

There was then the sale of town lots in Atchison on the 21st day of September that I was unable to attend. The New Lucy left Weston, carrying a large group of people who were interested in buying land in the town. The free-state supporters were warned not to attend the sale today. This is the first sale of town lots that I am aware of in Kansas Territory, even though on paper, Leavenworth City is the first town recorded.

Chapter Eight
Where the Wild West Begins

October 5, 1854   Leavenworth Hotel
Thursday Evening   Leavenworth City, Kansas Territory

It is actually who you know and being at the right time at the right place in order to get or gain in this world. My paper asked me to keep working and sending them news from the frontier and I accepted. With my six month stay ended at the Saint George, I was about ready to check into a boarding house in Weston, but my luck I ran into Uncle George Keller and he is giving me room and board at his new hotel in Leavenworth City called The Leavenworth House. The hotel is to be officially opened on Saturday. The hotel is located on the northwest corner of Main and Delaware Streets. Main Street is also known as the Levee, or Esplanade depending on the location you are at on the street.

    After, Uncle George and a group of eighty plus men spent the summer clearing the land of underbrush and making a clearing for the town proper improvements of their properties started immediately.

    The streets of Leavenworth City are laid out and marked with the names suggested by Major Ogden and H. Miles Moore. The streets running to and from the river, or east and west, are named after the Indian tribes that have lived in this land before us so that they will be remembered as being once a part of this land. The streets moving north and south parallel to the river are numerical numbered streets starting at Main advancing up till Seventh Street.

    The boat landing or the Levee has been cleared, and some steamboats are dropping supplies to the people who are improving their claims. The sawmill of Captains W.S. Murphy and Simion Scruggs is in production of planked wood furnished from the wood cut down by Mister Keller. Doctor Charles Lieb has pitched a tent and started his practice a block from the hotel, and the provisional warehouse of Lewis Rees is in development on the corners of Delaware and Main Streets. The Engleman Brothers built the second store in

Leavenworth City on Main Street between Delaware and Cherokee Streets. Mister Rees's store was all-purpose, while the Engleman Brothers sold only liquor, some groceries, and a few provisions. I now spend my days riding Wildfire around Leavenworth City, Fort Leavenworth, Salt Creek Valley, and to Weston to keep informed about the atmosphere around this new frontier. The tension between the free-staters and pro-slavery ideals is becoming more and more outspoken in the streets of Weston. The voices of the people fill the streets with how the new territory should be governed and who should be the ones to lead their beliefs.

On the 1st of October, I was visiting Major Ogden at his office in Fort Leavenworth when a ruckus started outside his door. It appeared that the new governor of Kansas Territory arrived unannounced on the Polar Star that day. The governor received word about a plot by the Blue Lodges to kidnap the governor when he arrived in Westport. The newly elected Governor Andrew Reeder of Kansas Territory entered into Major Ogden's Office. Following behind the governor was Colonel Thomas Fauntleroy of the First Dragoons and Captain Franklin Eyre Hunt of the Fourth Artillery. Introductions were made by all present and then non-essential personal like me was asked to leave for security matters. The newly appointed Attorney General A. J. Isacks was on the Polar Star from Saint Louis with the governor but continued his travel to Weston.

There are other towns being established along the Missouri River on the Kansas Territory side. Atchison is about twenty miles to the north of the fort whose town was platted to be the same size as Leavenworth City, then there is a smaller town Oak Mills about 10 miles away from the fort, and then there is Kickapoo City a mile away from the fort. All these cities were built at ferry crossings that were established years before to trade with the Indians. They were also built on the military trail that went to Fort Atkinson. I have heard of a free-state town being established up north inland to Senator Atchison's dismay by a man named Caleb May. I believe I heard the name was Pardee. Mount Pleasant Township is another town built along the trail west outside of Atchison settled by a man named Thomas Fortune.

About a mile south of Leavenworth City, the town of Delaware City is being platted across from where the Platte River enters the Missouri River. The Delaware Town Association designed their town with numbered streets like Leavenworth City but chose to name the perpendicular streets of the river after the trees in the territory: Maple, Mulberry, Oak, Ash, and so on.

I just obtained this information from a traveler at Fort Leavenworth who just spent a spell along the Kansas River. Mister E. D. Ladd informed me of the shenanigans occurring at the establishment he called Boston, but after hearing its location realizing it was the new town of Lawrence. It seems the aggressions of the pro-slavery supporters have made the development of the city very difficult. While the men are working on the buildings, ruffians had come into their camp and burned their tents, supplies, and destroyed the squatters' encampment. At this time, no one has claimed responsibility for the damage.

    October 10, 1854   Leavenworth Hotel
    Tuesday   Leavenworth City, Kansas Territory

The past few days have been a whirlwind of activity in Leavenworth City. On Saturday, the 7th day of October, Governor Andrew Reeder officially took office at Fort Leavenworth, making the fort the first territorial capital. Governor Reeder called all the representatives of the towns being formed to the fort to learn about the progress and beliefs of how the territory should be governed. I, by chance, had been present when the town of Weston demanded their say in the matters.

The delegation was led by Doctor Charles Lieb at the headquarters of Captain Hunt on the grounds of Fort Leavenworth. It was a very informal meeting and started with Doctor Lieb addressing the governor with the concerns about slavery in the territory. The governor was able to speak after hearing the delegation and being a politician with a well-worded speech, had relieved the tension in the room. After the governor spoke, the meeting ended with the celebration of success and then I was invited to attend a sermon given by the Reverend W. C. Caples. Even though I am not Methodist, I went to the service. It took place north of the hotel along the riverbank almost at the northern border of Leavenworth City. The Reverend Caples said a fine service standing atop of a buckboard with about seventy people in attendance. His sermon was an inspiration to all present about the new city beginning and the possibilities of dreams coming true in the new frontier.

On the brisk full morning of October 9th, 1854, travelers from all over Eastern United States arrived by wagon, steamboat, and anyway necessary to be present at the auction of land for Leavenworth City. Boats of all sizes were docking at the Levee. The public land auction was telegraphed all over the land a few weeks prior to the event. After a warm meal at Uncle George's Hotel, I attended to Wildfire at his stable. I moseyed on down to the auction being held between Amos Rees Warehouse and the hotel. A well was dug for fresh water at the intersection of Cherokee and the Levee during the clearing of the land, so a water source was nearby for drinking. The auction was set to begin at eleven o'clock in the morning.

The sound and smells of the sawmill filled the air that morning before the land auction took place. Before the auction, there was a description of the land that was to be auctioned off that day and the streets that they were on. Delaware Street was designated the main business street and was grated at seventy feet wide while the other streets are only sixty feet in width. The lots are twenty-four feet across in width and have a depth of one hundred and twenty-five feet. The city block was designed with thirty-two lots per block, sixteen on each side of an alleyway that was designed to be fourteen feet in width across for wagons to access the backsides of the establishments. The lots were staked out and numbered with temporary street signs placed on each corner, so bidders can find their possible new home or business. General George Washington McLane of Weston, Missouri, and W. S. Palmer of Platte City were asked to be the auctioneers and did a splendid job over the two-day event.

I myself was caught in the excitement and purchased a lot on the Esplanade between Seneca and Miami Streets. Bidding for the lots varied from of course on location. Delaware Street lots sold for the highest, around three hundred dollars each, while the side streets were less for around fifty dollars. I paid one hundred dollars but only having to put sixty dollars down and the rest when the title deeds return to the treasurer H. Miles Moore from printing company in Saint Louis.

Marisol and the children will love the view across the river with all the activity and a view of the city as well. All the new landowners were very pleased with how the town was transformed into what it was these days. During the auction, I stayed by the table where the payment was made for the lots. To learn the names and faces of those who have the dream to start in a brand-new land that was only months earlier Delaware Indian Hunting ground. Besides the town company members, I knew a few men who purchased lots on Delaware Street. Elijah Cody and Alexander Majors both are setting up their new stores in Leavenworth City, both because of the closeness to the fort where they conduct most of their business. Mister Major is putting his office a few blocks away from my house on the northeast corner of Seneca Street and Fourth.

This morning the auction continued in the same manner as yesterday but before the action began, the steamship F. X. Aubrey carried to Leavenworth City the new territorial judges. The Honorable Saunders W. Johnson of Cincinnati, Ohio, and the Honorable Rush Elmore of Montgomery, Alabama, walked the plank of the steamship around 10 a.m. Governor Andrew Reeder was present on both days of the auction sitting at the payment table for the event with H. Miles Moore was called back to Fort Leavenworth where he had to issue an arrest warrant for a double murder in Salt Creek Valley. The deceased's names were Davison and Thompson and the warrant was for a man by the name of Samuel Burgess. Before the governor left on his mission, he received five shares from the town company by General Gist for the sum of one thousand dollars as part of the land exchange with the agreement the governor would make Leavenworth City the territorial capital.

I have heard some figures of money made by the town company in the sale of lots; fifty-four lots were sold on Monday and close to the same today, bringing in over ten thousand dollars for town improvements.

        October 17, 1854   Leavenworth Hotel
        Tuesday Evening   Leavenworth City, Kansas Territory

This week I have been as busy as a bee with all the activity happening in Leavenworth City.

Lumber and dry goods are being unloaded at the levee by ships of any size that can maneuver the currents of the Missouri River, mostly large flatboats from Westport or Weston and steamboats from Saint Louis.

Construction on the new lots began immediately after purchases. My plans are to build as soon as possible as well, but I am waiting for the best carpenter in Leavenworth City to become available. The men are working sunrise to sunset building the town, and at night they gather down by the well and drink their beer or whisky by the campfire made for light and warmth while talking work and politics. Tents are set up all over the city in the lots that are not yet being improved and that is where most of the workers sleep, and the landowners also camp out to protect their claim.

I venture back and forth to Weston to send my stories to my paper, *The Hannibal Messenger*, and Mister William T. League. I also transfer money that is sent to me for expenditures from the paper and send my messages back home to Marisol as well. I do this every morning enjoying a hot breakfast in a building that has warmth and comfort. The Leavenworth Hotel is improving daily, but the beauty of the Saint George compares to nothing in Leavenworth City at this point.

There is no ferry boat in Leavenworth City at this time, so I still ride up to the Fort at crossover into Rialto. On my return trip, I stop by the offices of Captain Hunt and Major Ogden to inquire about any other news and information I can obtain from out west, north, or south. The governor will be departing the fort for a two-week tour of Kansas Territory later this month with a huge protection detail to protect him from anyone who believes he will steer this territory in the wrong direction. The Platte County Self-Defense Association and the Blue Lodge Society were aware of his travel plans, but the governor still insisted on this tour. Popular sovereignty is the popular ideal of the southerners, and the northerners are more for the free-state abolitionist, although there are some in both parties who fell opposite. As the governor proceeds to each town, more men will be provided for his protection as the tour goes on.

The city of Leavenworth continues to grow more each day. Stores of all that is needed are being constructed quite quickly as the product is milled by Murphy and Scruggs and being brought upriver from different companies. There is still no catholic church here in town yet, so I still go to services at Holy Trinity in Weston with Father Rutowski. I hope when winter arrives, there will be a catholic mass in town.

November 1, 1854   Leavenworth Hotel
Wednesday Evening   Leavenworth City, Kansas Territory

The weather has been cold but no snow as of yet. The town is continuously growing as more new buildings are being built. The river is close to freezing over, so the river traffic will be no longer, but on a good note I can cross over the ice and do not have to pay the ferryman passage across for a few months. Building has crossed over Threemile Creek with the streets being named after trees of the region. The first house dwelling being built in the new city limits goes to Jerry Clarke. The *Kansas Weekly Herald*, printed by W. H. Adams, has printed his second edition of the newspaper from a small cottonwood one-story house at Delaware and the Levee, and also the Engleman Brothers' Store is almost nonstop full of people.

The latest news I received from the town of Lawrence was that a child was born in Kansas Territory. The first on record to be born in the territory was a boy on October 26, 1854, with the name of Lawrence Carter. They also say he was deeded a lot of the city as a birthday present.

November 16, 1854   Leavenworth Hotel
Thursday Evening   Leavenworth City, Kansas Territory

View looking West from Weston Bend Bluff

The governor returned from his territory tour and issued a proclamation. There was to be represented voting for all towns that currently are in Kansas Territory for sending delegates to Washington. The voting will take place on November 28, 1854. Sources indicate that the Platte County Self-Defense Association and other groups of pro-slavery supporters are in the process of gathering up men and going over and voting for their cause, and to persuade others to vote their way as well. David Atchison was making loud noise in Liberty, Missouri, with a gentleman by the name of Grover for him to start an organization of a voting party for slavery to cross into Kansas and spread their beliefs. At this point, only Lawrence and Leavenworth City were considered free cities while all the other towns are pro slavery.

The weather here is continuously getting colder, but snow has yet to arrive. Mister Adams of the *Kansas Herald* has a new partner in the press. General L. J Eastin took over the editor's position, and a further note about the recuperation of Isaac Cody is of good report. He is mending well still in Weston and should be out of bed sometime soon.

November 30, 1854　　　　　Leavenworth Hotel
Thursday Evening　　　　　　Leavenworth City, Kansas Territory

Before I note the events of the election, I need to scribe the events that lay "heavy on my heart" and mind. General George Gist, a man whom I shall call a friend here in my new residence, and who was the president of the Leavenworth Town Company, departed us from this world on November 21, 1854, in his home he built in the High Prairie area two miles southwest of

Leavenworth City. His remains were found by his wife about one in the afternoon that day.

The funeral was actually held the next day in Weston and it is said to be one of the largest funerals ever recorded in Platte County. Being a Mason of the Royal Arch Chapter as well as being members to other organizations, he was buried with the upmost honors a man of his prestige deserved. He was 59 years of age at his departure and was buried in the Weston city cemetery, Laurel Hill.

Now I will try to recollect the events that transpired from a few days before, the first election in Leavenworth City, until tonight's entry into this journal. The good citizens of Missouri who belonged to the Platte County Defense Association and other non-membered men who desired the Kansas Territory to be a slave state no matter what opposition they encountered.

The association has been terrorizing travels more frequently and their voices are being heard louder in the cities of Missouri along the border of Kansas Territory. Alcohol was fueling anticipation of the ruffians, so on the eve of the election a large group of men set up a camp near the mouth of Threemile Creek so they could be there in the morning to help persuade the voters to agree with their beliefs. The majority of the Missourians arrived the morning of the elections filling up at the Levee on any boat that could carry them to Leavenworth City, others arrived by marching into town crossing over at the ferries.

The voting took place at Leavenworth House with B. H. Twombly, C. M. Burgess, and Mister Smith being nominated to be stand-in judges until the actual county judges arrive in town. As the day progressed, the ballots were placed in an orderly fashion. I find it quite peculiar that the polls took in more votes than over twice the population of the county. By nightfall, the drinking started, and then fights occurred, but there was no harm done by either side. The fights began because others like me noticed the heavier side of the scale was a little more tilted to slavery by over-voting and was not a fair election.

The results of the election, of course, favored General John W. Whitfield with over four hundred votes, while his opponent, Flenniken, only managed to gather ninety votes. Pro-slavery has won in Leavenworth City but shall be fought by the abolitionists.

  December 14, 1854 Leavenworth Hotel
  Thursday Evening Leavenworth City, Kansas Territory

Winter has finally graced us with its presence. It has been bitterly cold and ice has now formed on the Missouri River and the steamboat travel has ended.

I have both happy and sad news in this entry. The joy I am noting is being the announcement of the first child born in Leavenworth City. Cora Leavenworth Kyle, the daughter of A.T. Kyle, son-in-law of Uncle George Keller, was born on December 6, 1854, at the Leavenworth House.

The sad news is that along with birth comes death, and with that said, I have to mention the Missouri River again, because that was the killer of Steven Noble and Joseph O'Neil. The men perished by her swift currents when their boat overturned with the freight they were hauling from Weston to Leavenworth City, where they were new residents. Volunteers from Weston, soldiers from Fort Leavenworth, and people from Leavenworth City searched for the two men after seeing their capsized boat floating down the river, but to no avail; their bodies were never retrieved from the swift currents of the river. May God rest their souls.

In other local news, on the 12th of December, the public land auction occurred in Kickapoo City. The former village of the Kickapoo Indians was the new land for the city north of the fort at the mouth of Salt Creek entering the Missouri river. Being somewhat like Atchison, Kickapoo City did not want free-state settlers in their city, so the town was bought by mostly pro-slavery men. Out of the four towns being built on the river, Leavenworth City is the only city giving opposition to the pro-slavery movement.

I feel safer to be in the United States of America because Pope Pius the Ninth has been declared a patron saint for this country. The Doctrine of Mary's Immaculate Conception, a dogma, also issued that the Virgin Mary be the guide for the United States of America.

I had just heard earlier in the day a message that was being delivered to the newspaper office when I was doing my journey around Leavenworth City. The elections that took place in the city of Lawrence on the 29th day of November ended with the shooting death of Henry Davis, a pro-slavery man, who was traveling back to his home, near a place named Hickory Point, when a man by the name of Kibbee shot and killed Mister Davis because of who he voted for in the election and his beliefs for slavery in Kansas Territory.

December 28, 1854   Leavenworth Hotel
Thursday Evening   Leavenworth City, Kansas Territory

The river has been frozen solid for the past few weeks, so wagons or any creature can cross the river at any point. There is always a supply of fresh meat and furs from all the wildlife still in the area. A bear or mountain lion may be on the same path with you out in the hills and woods. The weather has been bitterly cold so building progress is slow on my house, and of course

Leavenworth City is slowly growing still in winter. Marisol and the children arrived on the steamboat Polar Star last week to spend Christmas with me here in Leavenworth City. Uncle George put extra beds in my room now for the children and said he wouldn't charge me any extra for my family staying. Not many people celebrate this holiday in Leavenworth City with a population of around two hundred people. Some folks gathered down by the well and sang carols on Christmas Eve. I took the family to Christmas mass in Weston and showed them the town. Renting a wagon for the day to carry the family, I showed them all around this new frontier as best as I could with weather permitting. The family traveled back home a few days ago, but hopefully I will see them soon when our house is complete.

> January 10, 1855   Leavenworth Hotel
> Wednesday Evening   Leavenworth City, Kansas Territory

There is not much to mention in this entry, but I thought I would mention that it is now 1855 and what will this year bring to this western town. The nights are filled with gunshots and loud men drunken in the streets still celebrating the new year. The freemasons established themselves with a meeting in Leavenworth City on December 30, 1854, claiming to be the first freemason group to be established in Kansas Territory. I was at the hotel with Uncle George when he asked me to go somewhere with him. Being a friend I obliged, and we went in the shadow of darkness to Rees's warehouse where a group of men, about thirty to fifty men were there in the room but, I could not tell for sure because it was very dark.

The Honorable S. D. Lecompte arrived and started his duties as Territorial Chief Justice. When he arrived at the levee, he boarded a carriage and went to Fort Leavenworth where he set up a temporary office.

> February 6, 1855   Leavenworth Hotel
> Tuesday Evening   Leavenworth City, Kansas Territory

The lodge, as before mentioned, is now called #2 A.F.+A.M. Masonic Order, which is now organized with over one hundred members meeting at Lewis Rees's General Store; the last meeting was on the 18th of this month. On another new item, a new business has been bestowed upon our fair city. After four months of not shaving, keeping my facial area warm, I had the honor of being able to receive a shave and a haircut for a bit from Julius Trummel, who set up his shop on Delaware Street.

The first snowfall blanketed the streets and buildings of Leavenworth City making it look very picturesque. The snow started falling on the thirtieth and continued falling into the next day. I believe we have accumulated around a foot of snow in the last week.

Chapter Nine
Crossing the Lines:
A Territory Divided?

March 10, 1855   Leavenworth Hotel
Saturday Evening   Leavenworth City, Kansas Territory

Spring has arrived in Kansas Territory and along with the blossoming flowers and trees, many towns have come out of hibernation and have emerged full of energy and mischief. I must relate the story that occurred a few days ago. I have not entered this yet because of tiredness at night from assisting the fire damage that swept through the town of Weston on the morning of the 8th of March 1855.

    Before the sun had risen on the Thursday past, I was awakened from my slumber – by the rukus – in the hallways of the hotel. I put on my britches and went outside to see the sky was a bright orange to the north where Weston is located. A group of men including myself ran to our horses and rode to Rialto Ferry and crossed over there.

    By the time we arrived in Weston, the townspeople had started a few lines of a bucket brigade to help the fire from spreading any further across town. My associates and I immediately jumped into anywhere we could to assist to put this fire under our control and extinguish it. Witnesses have said as word spread down the bucket lines that the fire was started in the back of Murphy's Ten Penny Alley. The carpenters' shop and Perry's Livery Stable were also involved on the other side of the bowling alley. Then the fire spread to the U.S. Hotel and then to the north on Main Street. The wooden structures made the battle very intense, but the fire did not reach the Saint George Hotel. The line I was in defended its walls from a fiery demise. All of the buildings I ventured into on Main Street were now in smoking ruin. The Masonic lodges, the telegraph office, saloons, grocery stores, my favorite confectionary shop, and at least forty other businesses in Weston were destroyed that day.

Accusations were made about whom and why the fire was started, and tempers flared up when there were more threats about burning the town down. The yelling turned into an actual fight and arrests were made by the Platte County Marshall of that which also dispersed the crowd. Some of the men who lost their businesses in Weston also had a place of business in Leavenworth City, Kickapoo City, or Atchison, but they still feel a great loss. With the belief of this being an abolitionists' act, guards were hired by the Defense Association to protect the city at night from any more possible acts of violence.

In Leavenworth City news, Thomas Shoemaker, Jared Todd, and Samuel Pitcher were granted a twenty-year contract from the town company for a ferry company that will be at the Levee and Cherokee Streets. They will be docking in a few days to start their business. *The Kansas Herald* is printed only by Lucian J. Eastin, who prints his paper every two weeks. As I ride Wildfire through the streets of Leavenworth City, it is easy to see the growth of all the new buildings going up and all the new shingles hanging on the rafters of the storefront porches. Adam Fisher has a general store opened up, Beyer's and Jennet's Grocery Store, almost beside Elijah Cody's Grocery Store. William Russell has a large dry goods' store and outfitting company. There is another general store ran by Cohn and Abel; George Russell is the proprietor of the stove and tin Store.

There are at least two blacksmiths in town with three different carpenters; a few doctors of dentistry and medicine; a handful of lawyers have their shingles hanging as well. Other hotels are being built to help in the growth of the city. In the area of the boat landing is already mostly developed up Delaware and Cherokee Streets to Third Street. I did not mention we have a shoemaker and a tailor shop. I cannot go to Mrs. Christina Harpist's shop on Cherry Street in Weston anymore, for I will support only my local business. A drugstore is being built in town and should be open soon.

Leavenworth City has a new postmaster with the announcement of Lewis Rees accepting the position for the city on March 6, 1855. Now my reasons to travel to Weston are declining. As fate would have it, my room at the Leavenworth Hotel was placed on the corner very close to where the city well is by the Levee. At night, the talk of politics fills the night air again, with both sides again trying to see who can be the loudest.

I regress and have to enter this event that occurred on Wednesday, February 28, 1855, at Fort Leavenworth with Governor Andrew Reeder. After reviewing the census of Kansas Territory that the governor had taken at the beginning of the year, it was said to claim that over eight thousand people reside in Kansas Territory. The governor has divided the territory up into ten different council districts and decreed that there be an election held on March

30, 1855 for the territorial legislation. He added another proclamation that there would be voting for the thirteen members of the territorial council to represent each district in the house that the governor has created. There will also be an election for twenty-six members to represent each district for representation in local territorial matters.

Earlier in the hours of this evening, the citizens, Governor Andrew Reeder, and more friends of Leavenworth City gathered together at the Rees's Warehouse and held a convention to nominate men for those positions created by the governor. Both sides of popular sovereignty were represented at this convention. The Blue Lodge Members from Platte City were abundantly present while the free-state men were present but not in the numbers like the pro-slavery movement.

Mister A. J. Galoway and B. F. Stringfellow were very vocal over George Bayless, who they wanted in office. They would initiate the crowd to cheer when their candidates said an appealing word, and to make noises when the other candidates are giving their speech. By the end of the evening, both sides are being represented in the upcoming election on March 30th.

March 31, 1855   Leavenworth Hotel
Saturday Evening   Leavenworth City, Kansas Territory

Before I recollect the past events that occurred over the last few days, I first must mention that I have hired the best carpenter in Leavenworth City to build the family home here in town. Samuel Lyons has agreed to build my home and will also find the best stonemason to build my foundation and fireplaces. The river has thawed enough that trade and travel has started again on the river. Leavenworth City is now a scheduled stop on the steamboats' routes up and down the Missouri River. The ferry crossing of Shoemaker, Todd, and Pitcher has been opened and their fares posted in town with a twenty-year contract. Foot passengers are charged ten cents, but cost is two bits when I ride Wildfire across to Missouri. A one-horse carriage is charged a half dollar while a two-horse team is charged six bits.

One of those steamboat stops dropped off the new surveyor general for the Kansas and Nebraska Territories; John Calhoun came to the shore of Leavenworth City and let the citizens expect that he was going to establish his office here in Leavenworth City, so with that expectation, the town company elected to gift Mister Calhoun a share of the town properties that was located on Delaware Street between Second and Third Streets.

So with the arrival of a new person in town, I must now mention the departure of a founding member of the town company who is being reassigned to The Presidio in San Francisco, California. Major E. A. Ogden announced his resignation at the last town company and cleared up his affairs before leaving on his new adventure. The territorial election on March 30, 1855, was to be held at the Leavenworth Hotel, but with concerns expressed by Uncle George Keller about the shenanigans of the voters that the polling should happen at another establishment other than Uncle George's Hotel. After consideration, the event was moved to Benjamin Wood's Saddle Shop at the corner of Cherokee and Third Streets. Ropes were placed to keep the polling lines in order and men were placed outside the establishment provided by the Salt Creek Valley residents, who called themselves the Kickapoo Rangers, to prevent any ruckus from happening. There was an unofficial uniform for the riders of the rangers consisting of mostly hunters and farmers; they had unshaven and untrimmed faces, and wore long leather boots. Bowie knifes are stuffed down the legs of the boots, and revolvers hang on both hips of the horse riders. A rifle is strapped to their backs and a feather of bird hangs from the hat they wear on their heads. It appears to be a turkey feather hangs from the hats and a star is placed either on the brim of the hat or somewhere on the person that it can be easily noticed.

The night before, the election tents were raised at the Threemile Creek with people arriving early for the voting. The boarding houses were at full capacity and the hotels had no empty beds. The New Lucy arrived early in the morning, bringing voters from Weston. Even the ferries that cross the Missouri were at capacity for the voting day at all hours. Mister Ellis of the Kickapoo Weston Ferry almost had his vessel destroyed by the Kickapoo Rangers who believed he was a free-state conspirator who brought over abolitionists to vote. Mister Ellis then posted a notice on his vessel and both docks that he was as sound as a goose, which is a hidden message by the Platte County Defense Association that he is a member and should be left alone.

With no surprise, the population of Leavenworth City had more than doubled on the day of the voting the free-state voters that evening a spokesman was hired by the name of William Phillips, who is a young up-and-coming lawyer, to send a formal protest to Governor Reeder about the unlawful voting in Leavenworth County. William Mathias, H. D. McKeenin, and Archy Payne were the undisputed winners in the election all having the same vote count for each candidate.

In other events, the Reverend Starr was ran out of Weston for being a supporter of the Abolitionist Movement. He was able to leave the town peacefully and was said he will go north until the tides have turned and is safe to return to this land. Because of these events, I do not announce my beliefs in anti-slavery at this time.

      April 14, 1855   Leavenworth hotel
      Saturday Night   Leavenworth City, Kansas Territory

    It was brought to my attention that on the day of the election, the steamer New Lucy was used by the citizens of Weston as a bribe for the citizens of Platte County to vote in the Kansas Territorial elections in Leavenworth City. They were given free transportation to and from Leavenworth City, and on the voyage home was given a buffet dinner on board the New Lucy.

    William Phillips was not the only free-state voter to be prompted to write Governor Reeder. There were reports of illegal voting all over the territory. Accounts from all the border counties have more voter turnout than actual residents. Lawrence and Manhattan also report voting inconsistencies. The influence of the pro-slavery men was felt all over the territory. Lawrence reports cannons were used to scare off abolitionists on the way to the polls to vote. With the results of the election, being over by thousands of votes than lawfully allowed by the census, Governor Reeder has announced that there will be another election on the 22nd of May 1855.

    The pro-slavery advocates in Atchison showed their feeling to a fellow resident of Atchison by tying Reverend Pardee up with rope, putting tar and feathers all over his body, and then placing the honorable Reverend Pardee on a small sailing ship with a flag tied to the mast, and a warning saying that free-state men are not to assist in the transport of slaves in the underground railroad. This was the first warning of this nature I have seen in the new territory.

    Easter was celebrated on April 8th, and I went to the services at Holy Trinity in Weston. It was the longest service I have ever attended on Easter Sunday. It was very beautiful with the smell spring in the air and the foliage blooming all around. Yesterday, Thanksgiving was celebrated in high fashion in Leavenworth City. A huge feast was prepared at the hotel and the gathering room filled up to capacity with the citizens of Leavenworth City celebrating the lives we have and the company in our presence.

      April 19, 1855   Leavenworth Hotel
      Thursday Evening   Leavenworth City, Kansas Territory

    The Leavenworth County Court System held its first session of Territorial Court today, with the Honorable Samuel D. Lecompte residing. The courthouse was established on the second floor of J. L. Roundy's Furniture Store located on Delaware Street between Second and Third Streets. We also have our first bank in town, also on Delaware Street but in between the Levee

Street and Second. The proprietor Mister Bailey opened his doors earlier this week.

   April 25, 1855   Leavenworth Hotel
   Wednesday Evening Leavenworth City, Kansas Territory

More and more buildings are being erected in Leavenworth City every day, and even my own abode is almost to a point where I can live in it while construction is still being done. The town has again doubled in size from its original plot, not only moving southward but further westward as well. I must mention another person that has fallen to the pressures of the pro-slavery men in Platte County. This tragedy belongs to an acquaintance in Parkville. The founder of the city and editor of the Parkville Luminary, George S. Park, and his associate, Mister Patterson, were assaulted and warned to leave town or more harm would come to their families. The newspaper press was destroyed and taken to the river with all its type and thrown into the water at the deepest point. Both men left the town of Parkville in the dark of the night the next evening after securing their homes, departing the city they loved, and forced to leave.

   May 7, 1855   Urbaniak House
   Monday Evening   North Esplanade, Leavenworth City, K.T.

It is with sorrow in my heart that I must now scribe the events that lead to the killing of Malcolm Clarke. It has taken me days to find the words and emotions to describe the events that occurred, to present the story in full detail as I recall on the day of April 30, 1855.

  The Squatters' Association conducted a meeting at the corner of the Levee and Cherokee Streets near or under the Old Elm Tree. The oldest and biggest tree left in the city proper by Uncle George while deforesting the land. The base of the tree being so large, three men cannot touch their hands around the base, also with a height so grand it can be seen almost two miles down the river. It also sits on top of the Levee Hill that also is the home of the city well. But I regress, the newly appointed R.R. Rees and Artie Payne were also part of the Squatters' Association as judges, and Malcolm Clark was there as Marshal for the Court. Salt Creek Valley and all Leavenworth County were represented at this congregation. Tempers started to flare up when accusations were made about the association for holding onto claims that had no improvements on the property yet. The squatters claimed that with no improvements on the properties, it was theirs to claim and claim for their own property.

A man named Cole McCrea is a resident of Salt Creek Valley but whose house and property lay on the outside of the northern boundary for the association. Mister McCrea was being very vocal and becoming unruly, when Marshal Clark approached Mister McCrea and then he asked the gentleman to refrain himself from such outbursts. Not being a member of the association, Cole McCrea truly had no say in the matters of the topic at large. Mister McCrea agreed to calm down, but still expressed his opinion in a very unruly manner so Marshal Clark had to intercede again on behalf of the association. The voting on new resolutions continued until Mister McCrea called this meeting a fraud after a decision was made that he was clearly against.

Marshal Clark again stepped up and called Cole McCrea a liar for not keeping his word to remain calm. The Marshal then reached down to pick up a board that was laying on the ground. The Marshal then took a swing at McCrea, who dodged the blow and then turned to run away from the Marshal. Marshal Clark then proceeded to chase Cole McCrea when Mister McCrea turned around drawing a revolver out of his holster and then pointing and shooting the weapon at the Marshal. Hitting the marshal in the chest, the life of Marshal Malcolm Clark was taken that night under the Old Elm Tree.

A fight broke out as Cole McCrea turned to run away from the shooting. He ran down the hill to the Levee and tried to reach the river where he could escape to Missouri. A lynch mob was quickly formed to find the runaway shooter. Before the mob could get organized and track down the fugitive, Samuel D. Pitcher, who is part owner of the ferryboat in Leavenworth City, and a few other heavily armed men found the shooter and told Mister McCrea to come with them or his life would end from a noose above the body of the Marshal who he just shot. Cole McCrea boarded the army ambulance that Mister Pitcher acquired and with great speed whipped that team of horses to Fort Leavenworth, where Mister McCrea was put into a guardhouse until his trail could commence.

After the commotion and the drama ended, the body of Marshal Malcolm Clark was removed from the streets and taken to Weston for a proper burial. The meeting ended with the appointment of a pro-slavery vigilante committee of thirty men who determined that Mister McCrea had an accomplice to the crime. Someone in the crowd had handed the revolver to the shooter. The committee all agreed that William Phillips was his co-conspirator in this vicious attack. Mister Phillips applauded the efforts of Samuel Pitcher and his associates at the procurement of Mister McCrea. The committee asked William

Phillips to leave the territory by midafternoon on May 3rd or there will be justice served by the committee.

The funeral for Malcolm Clark occurred on May 1, 1855, in Weston, Missouri. He was well-received by all who knew him, both pro-slavery and abolitionist men attended his memory. Respected by all who knew him, his procession through the streets of Weston to Laurel Hill Cemetery was longer than General Gist's. The death of a fellow citizen and the still smoldering remains of the devastating fire set a somber mood in Weston that day. The loss of the Marshal will be felt by all in the region.

On the morning of May 3rd, the Vigilante Committee was having a meeting under the Old Elm Tree when they noticed William Phillips approaching with his brother on Delaware Street. The men were seized by the committee, but William Phillips begged the committee to have leniency toward him as he was leaving town but had some business to conclude and would be gone in two weeks. The committee granted his wishes and let the two men go to finish conducting their business in town and continued their meeting under the Old Elm Tree.

Stephan Naeher's

Chapter Ten
A Civil War Begins in Kansas Territory

May 24, 1855   James Michael Urbaniak
Thursday Night   North Esplanade Leavenworth City

Over one hundred buildings have now been constructed in Leavenworth City with the population growing larger each day. My other news is that there is a new addition to the Cody home in Salt Creek Valley. The arrival of Charles Whitney Cody made the household of Isaac and Mary Ann Cody a warm and delightful place to be, with Isaac still recuperating from his injury of the year past. The mother, father, and baby are doing well, while the other children tend the fields and cattle, both in the Valley and in Grasshopper Falls, a new community north of the town of Topeka.

    I failed to mention this in my previous writings but the army post in the southeast portion of Kansas Territory, Fort Scott, was abandoned last year and its soldiers moved to Fort Riley to protect the new settlers in the plains of Kansas Territory from Indian attacks. The army deemed the fort unnecessary and auctioned off the buildings to the general public last week around the sixteenth. It is my understanding that the town will be named Fort Scott and the buildings will be used to develop the town with hotels and brothels. I mention the other army posts because I have also received notice that my friend Major Ogden's orders were changed and he is now being stationed at Fort Riley.

    I must now rehash an event that happened in my last entry about the Vigilante Committee and William Phillips. On the 17th of May, exactly two weeks to the day that Mister Phillips promised to be out of town, and still under the belief that justice was on his side and he would outcome as the victor, was kidnapped in midmorning by a dozen or so men from Weston.

    These fully armed men took William Phillips under no resistance, bounding his arms and legs, throwing him into the back of a wagon and kidnapped Mister Phillips. They took him across the river into securing him onto the ferry that landed at Rialto. Upon landing on the Missouri side of the river, they placed a hood over William's head and delivered him to a warehouse on the road to Weston. This is where the committee shaved off half of Mister Phillips's hair, and then stripped him of his upper garments to begin the tar and feathering of his upper body. The group, calling themselves the Leavenworth City Proslavery Committee, started to parade William through the streets of Weston and ended the parade at the auction house. Since the fire, the auction house is now across from the Saint George Hotel, where they mounted William Phillips to an auction block and had a mock slave auction.

The committee brought out a black man, the auctioneer named 'Ole Joe,' who started the auction with a one cent bid to humiliate Mister Phillips even more; no one bid any higher so the mock auction ended with a one cent bid. The mob of vigilantes then again started to parade their prisoner around the town of Weston, bringing more shame and humiliation to William Phillips.

Now other distinguished citizens of Weston had had enough of the mob's shenanigans and told the committee so. The mob consisted of lawyers, doctors, editors, store owners, and United States court representatives. Eventually around sundown, the committee released William Phillips and he returned to Leavenworth City to receive medical attention from the tar burns on his upper body.

I must add that on the night of May 16th, the moon totally disappeared from the sky that night in what was called a full lunar eclipse. The animals went a little crazy and it scared a few people that were not aware of this event.

June 10, 1855   Home of James Michael Urbaniak
Sunday Evening   North Esplanade, Leavenworth City

Leavenworth City is still growing at an unbelievable rate due the enterprises of Russell Majors and Waddell. The overland shipping company has brought in more businesses to make sure their wagons and animals are in fine shape for the journeys across America and being able to fulfill the contracts they have with Fort Leavenworth. General Harvey of Fort Leavenworth has just granted the firm of Russell Majors and Waddell that they can by any means protect the wagon trains from Sioux Indian attacks in the prairie. There have been attacks on shipments and many supplies have been lost to the renegades.

The transportation company has brought in more carpenters, blacksmiths, wagon makers, leather tanners, and farmers to maintain their oxen, cattle, horses, and farmers to produce food for the men working on the trails across the plains. The oxen they need to use are herded in the high prairie just southwest of Leavenworth City. The amount of animals needed to run this venture is over a thousand head, which is almost the population of the city. Pilot Knob Hill located to the southeast of city proper is the source of fresh water for our community and is also a sacred burial ground for the Delaware Indians.

As all the nationalities of the world transcend onto Leavenworth City, areas of ethnic groups are being established. Many dialects are spoken in the streets, but in the stores, everyone tries to speak proper English. Northwest in the town at the fort boundary is an area we call 'Goose Town,' because the people living in that area have a large amount of geese at their homes.

There are Polish, German, English, Scottish, French, and Irish settlers establishing their own religious beliefs in their neighborhoods, and bringing the delicacies and cuisine from their native countries. It is almost like the boroughs in New York City, where there are mini cities within the big city. People that have been in the United States for a generation or two are moving into the areas that their ancestors came from and fill in the gaps in between the neighborhoods.

Another sawmill was built in north town to accommodate the construction need for sawn lumber in Leavenworth City. It is running lumber every day and is located almost at the site of our first church service, but who is the proprietor I do not recall at this time of the evening.

An anti-slavery newspaper has started printing here in Leavenworth City by the man named Mark W. Delahay. Mark Delahay was a former resident of Illinois who is printing his beliefs about how this territory should be governed, and being a territory without slavery. General Eastin has not appreciated Mister Delahay arriving in town as of yet.

The latest news from Lawrence is that they had held a state convention of their own accord for the Free-State Movement. Charles Robinson was nominated by the people at that function to run for governor for a free territory.

The house is still being worked on, or should I say my small castle, for my Marisol. I have added a few specialties that I cannot write at this point for my safety.

  June 24, 1855   The Urbaniak Family home
  Sunday Evening North Esplanade, Leavenworth City

The population of Leavenworth City continues to multiply. At this time, many businesses of any needs line the streets of downtown, making the landscape of downtown most entertaining. The other towns around Leavenworth City are coming along but not as fast as this town.

Alexandrea Township is a pro-slavery site in the corner of northwest Leavenworth County. Delaware City is getting larger as well. The town of Easton that was named after the editor of the pro-slavery paper here as I have mentioned before, they have built a beautiful covered bridge that crosses Stranger Creek about where Andre Dawson had his crossing. Eastin is due east from the Hurley House that was built eight miles from the post's flagpole.

Other towns forming in the Northeast section of Kansas Territory are Manhattan, Pawnee, Topeka, Grasshopper Falls, Saint Mary's, Lecompton (formally Bald Eagle from all the Eagle's Nests), Tiblow – Chief Tonganoxie has a trading post wagon stop called Chief Tonganoxie Lodge; Grinter's Trading Post has a small village there now – Shawnee Mission, Atchison, Oak Mills, Mount Pleasant, Port William, Millwood, Fairmount, and Lawrence. The most interesting one though is a place called Mormon Grove just east of Atchison. The Mormons established it for their voyage to the Utah Territory where they are establishing their community.

Today I was invited to the first Catholic Mass that I believe to be held in Leavenworth City. It was at the home of Andy Quinn on Shawnee Street just past Fifth Street. Father Fish preformed the mass with a dresser being turned around and used as the altar for the small congregation that was aware of the service.

There are many churches being built in the neighborhoods. There is a Methodist Church being erected on Third Street, and a Campbellite Church with the direction of Elderman W. S. Yohe is going up on Shawnee Street between Second and Third Streets.

    July 6, 1855   Urbaniak home
    Friday Evening   North Esplanade, Leavenworth City K.T.

If I have failed to mention in my scribbling's past events and bring them up as if aware of the situation, I humbly apologize. I say that because the events that happened with our territorial capital must be written. To recap, Governor Andrew Reeder moved the Office of the Governor from Fort Leavenworth to Pawnee, a venture that Governor Reeder had bought stock in previously from moving the capital there. Pawnee is located on the southern boundary of Fort Riley.

At the time our legislative session for the territory was to begin, the buildings in Pawnee were not fit for occupation, so there was a vote to temporarily move the capital to the Shawnee Mission Indian Trade School. The governor was furious over the moving of the capital to Shawnee Mission.

The rain has been falling almost constantly every day this summer but the work continues on the house. It is almost finished on the inside now, so I will be traveling back to Hannibal and bring Marisol and our children to Leavenworth City.

| August 20, 1855 | Marisol's Castle |
| Monday Evening | North Esplanade, Leavenworth City, K.T. |

I have returned to Leavenworth City with Marisol and the children. They are in awe of the wildness of Leavenworth City citizens, but they love how quaint the town is and its beautiful landscape. Upon my return, I received news that my old friend Major E. A. Ogden has died of cholera at his post in Fort Riley. The disease took half the men at the fort, and word was sent back that Major Ogden stayed mounted on his horse till his life left him. The sickness did not stop him from his duties. He shall be missed. God rest his soul.

Governor Andrew Horatio Reeder, the First Territorial Governor of Kansas Territory, was removed from office on August 15, 1855, claiming that he abused his power as governor and manipulated the last elections with his office making the election unconstitutional as claimed by the free-state representatives. The replacing governor will be Wilson Shannon.

As I was updating my information from Fort Leavenworth since my arrival back from my adventure, while on the post I was told of retaliation to Indians from the Gratten incident a year past. In Ash Hollow, Nebraska Territory, General William Harvey took approximately seven hundred men to a small Indian village of a population of around three hundred. They were sent to have the Indian Chief Little Thunder surrender him and his people to General Harvey.

Chief Little Thunder did not surrender to the general, so the order by General Harvey was to kill all in the village. About one third of the village's population was killed by the army that day.

Children, women, men, and beast were injured or killed and the village destroyed. When the general reported back to Fort Laramie, he confirmed that there would be no more Indian conflict.

Chapter Eleven
A Small City Grows Bigger

September 10, 1855   Urbaniak Home Esplanade
Monday Evening   Leavenworth City, Kansas Territory

One week ago, Leavenworth City held its first city elections. The election was issued by the territorial legislature to help, organize, and establish the laws for the new cities. The elected judges to watch over the elections were J. H. Day, W. H. Adams, and Lewis N. Rees.

This election has given Leavenworth City its first mayor. Thomas F. Slocum was voted in with eight members of his council. The council members are as follows: John H. Day President, Fred Emory, Thomas Doyle, George Russell, M. Truesdell, Adam Fisher, Doctor D. J. Park, and William Marvin.

The new council then appointed city officials to help govern the city. Scott J. Anthony was appointed City Clerk, William McDowell is now the City Marshal, John I. Moore is the City Attorney, and E. I. Berthoud as the City Engineer. The men put into those positions were both pro-slavery and free-state voters.

River steamboats are now stopping at every town that has been established, starting from Westport Landing, to Wyandotte City, to Weidmar City, and to Delaware City, and continues on up to Atchison and further. Also, ferries were put in at those landings along the river so there are many more places to cross the Missouri river. James Skinner was the first steamboat agent to set up in Leavenworth City.

On September 5th, a convention was held in the free-state town of Big Springs, a small town just south of Lecompton, formerly called Bald Eagle. This was a meeting held by the free-state men only of Kansas Territory. Representatives traveled from every established town in the territory that wanted Kansas not to have slavery. The ex-Governor Andrew Reeder, Charles Robinson, and General James A. Lane were among many speakers that stated their views that day. This new organization is to be called the Kansas Free-

State Party. Its members also include H. Miles Moore, Isaac Cody, Mark W. Delahay, and I, as I am in agreement with the morals of this organization. In all, I would say that there was over one hundred people in Big Springs.

With that news, I now have found out that our new Territorial Governor is a southern supporter by the name of William Shannon. This is the second governor Kansas Territory appointed by President Franklin Pierce September 7th, 1855.

September 24th, 1858	Home of James M. Urbaniak on the Esplanade
Monday Night	Leavenworth City, Kansas Territory

On Tuesday, September 11th, 1855, Leavenworth City held its first town council meeting on the second floor of J. L. Roundey's Furniture Store located on the southern side of Delaware Street, in the building between Second and Third Streets. The first city ordinance took effect on September 17th, the ordinance was pertaining to games of skills of chance. In other words, gambling in the proper places. Also that same day, the Leavenworth City Fire Department was established with Miles Shannon as our city's first Fire Chief.

October 2, 1855	Home of J. M. Urbaniak
Wednesday Night	Leavenworth City, Kansas Territory

There are more and more buildings being built in downtown. Most are of wood construction but some are being made out of stone and mortar like our new public hall building across the street from J. L. Roundey's Furniture Store on Delaware between Second and Third Streets. The first factory began its operation on the northwest corner of Fourth and Cherokee as Patrick Fogarty started his furniture factory.

A beer garden has been established in Leavenworth City as well. On the southwest corner of Cheyenne and Second Streets, Stahl's Beer Garden is the first stop for anyone especially the soldiers from Fort Leavenworth or any traveler who want to have a good time after trail riding for months in the west. It is also the last stop for those heading west before their long journey, and again the Fort Leavenworth men before they go on their next excursion. The beer and whiskey are shipped up the river from Weston on a daily basis to keep the customers satisfied with fluids.

October 17th, 1855   Esplanade
Wednesday Night   Leavenworth City, Kansas Territory

Fall has finally arrived after a long hot Kansas summer. The assortment of trees here reminds me of the falls in the Appalachian Mountains. The colors are vibrant and vary in many colors.

The leaves are falling from the trees and blowing all over the city. Marisol and I spend our free time sitting on our porch, enjoying our view of the steamboats and other water vessels on the river, and the levee is just in our sights as well. The bluffs we see in the short distance across the valley on the Missouri side from our porch is a very beautiful sight in the fall.

Leavenworth City has a few furniture manufacturers but the one that caught my attention was Davis, who specializes in caskets as well as any household item. His shop is located on the north side of Delaware Street just off Fourth and Fifth Streets. More specialized manufactures are arriving in this growing city every day. The downtown area has been built up enough that now the city is expanding to the west and south to accommodate housing.

There is an upcoming convention to be held in the city of Topeka and then in the month of November there will be voting for the Leavenworth County Seat. Delaware City, Kickapoo City, and Leavenworth City have their hats thrown in to win the honor.

October 31st, 1855   Esplanade
Wednesday Night   Leavenworth City, Kansas Territory

Today was the Eve of All Saints and in today's changing world, it is now also called Halloween by the Scott and Irish immigrants. Fireworks were set off by some people around town as the night parties continue as I write this. I watched and participated in the bobbing of apples, or dooking as the Scottish refer to the game as.

I must retell a tale that Marisol and I heard earlier this evening. There is an old tale that if on this very night if a young woman sits in a darkened room and stares into a mirror, the face of her future husband will appear or the face of death, which means that the woman will not be alive before she weds. That was the weirdest of the night; we did hear many more ghost stories and sang festive songs throughout the evening.

A week past on October 23rd, there was a free-state delegation from Leavenworth City that traveled to Topeka. At Constitution Hall, a new face in Leavenworth, Mark W. Delahay spoke his mind about Missouri Bushwhackers and slavery. That day he became an acquaintance of mine that I hope will last.

Doctor Charles Robinson was also a forceful speaker from the Lawrence area. I heard a story about Mister Robinson; when he landed in Lawrence, he walked the area until he found his promise land. He named his land Mount Oread in respect to his old home area in New England, and he built a huge house on top of a hill overlooking Lawrence.

The president of this gathering was a gentleman by the name of James Lane who delegated the time each speaker consumed. Samuel Collins, William Moore, John Wakefield, Caleb May, Samuel Wood, John Butler Chapman, and George W. Partridge are names to watch in the growing Kansas Territory political party. With any luck, this gathering may help bring a constitution to the territory.

November 17th, 1855   Esplanade
Saturday Night   Leavenworth City, Kansas Territory

With the free-staters claiming that the latest legislature in Topeka was bogus, the pro-slavery men agreed to have another convention in Leavenworth City that was held three days ago on November 14th. This gathering in Leavenworth City was referred to as a Law and Order Party for those who are opposed the free-state movement. Our newest Territorial Governor, William Shannon, made his first appearance in our city and gave a lengthy speech at the convention.

And so to bring up the local elections, Delaware City is now the county seat of Leavenworth County. At the end of the day of the election, Kickapoo City had more votes, but Delaware City had opened its polls the next day and took in additional votes to make Delaware City the majority winner of the county seat. Construction for the new county jail and courthouse will begin in the next month weather permitting.

November 28, 1855   Esplanade
Wednesday Night   Leavenworth City, Kansas Territory

Rumors have spread down from Kickapoo City that some of its so-called distinguished citizens and the Platte County Self-Defense Association procured a number of arms from the United States Army Arsenal, in Liberty, Missouri. It was reported that over sixty men overtook the arsenal and stole rifles ammunition, cannons, and other items through my source at Fort Leavenworth.

December 14, 1855　　　Esplanade
Friday Night　　　　　　Leavenworth City, Kansas Territory

There have been some recent violent actions by the pro-slavery men in the name of popular sovereignty in the territory at a place called Hickory Point just south of the city of Lawrence.

Charles Dow, a free-statesman, was mortally wounded by a pro-slavery man by the name of Franklin N. Coleman. Eyewitness reports claim that it was a land dispute between the two gentlemen over the woods that was between their land. This did occur in the latter part of November.

Mister Dow and two of his associates approached Mister Coleman's house and with constant antagonizing by Mister Dow and his associates, Mister Coleman placed a bullet into Mister Dow, ending the argument. Thinking his actions were justified, Mister Coleman turned himself into the proper authorities. While on the way to the jail with the Marshall, a mob of free-state men drove Misses Coleman and over a dozen more pro-slavery families out of their homes and burned them until there was only a pile of ash remaining.

A Deputy Marshall by the name of Sam Jones arrested Jacob Branson, a friend of Charles Dow, in connection to the shooting, who they claim started the mob that night. On the way to the territorial jail in Lecompton, Sheriff Jones and his posse were stopped at the Wakarusa Bridge. A large group of free-state men wanted to liberate Mister Branson from the sheriff and his posse. After a long standoff between the two groups of men, Jacob Branson was released to the men who came to free him, the free-statesmen. Not a shot was fired at this altercation and the free-state men retreated to Lawrence as victors. Sam Jones, after that confrontation, sent out fliers and notices in the papers that a militia had to be formed to help defend the laws of the territory.

By the beginning of December, at Lawrence a free-state militia had formed and had built protective forts around the town. Jim Lane has taken control of the forces and is ready to fight the proslavery forces camped on the outskirts of Lawrence. A few days ago, the governor settled the matter in Lawrence that almost escalated to a mini war and the city of Lawrence being destroyed.

With that happening, it is sad to mention the killing of another free-state man on December 6th. Thomas Barber and his brother were riding home from a trip to Lawrence when they were bushwhacked and the life of Thomas Barber was ended by Missouri Ruffians on what is referred to as the Highway of Hell.

5th and Shawnee looking north

December 31, 1855   Esplanade
Monday Night   Leavenworth City, Kansas Territory

Mikolajki, or Christmas season, was very festive this year at our new house in this city in the west. It was a very happy holiday and the new year will be starting in a few hours from my scribblings at this time. The children were surprised by what 'Sweity Mikolaj' (Saint Nicolas) had left under our evergreen tree that we placed in our living room with decorations of popcorn and candles. For the last week, they have been constantly playing with their new toys.

From all around town, I can hear the shouts of celebration and gunfire into the sky from the festive townsfolk. Fireworks are also being fired off around Leavenworth City for the midnight jubilation. The sound of singing and music also is carried into the house on this bitterly cold winter night. Many people are out and about tonight at the saloons and beer gardens, enjoying the last hours of 1855.

In other news, before I retire for the evening, the criminal Cole McCrea at some point in the month of December escaped from the confinement of Fort

Leavenworth and was reported to be in the Lawrence area. He was still awaiting trial for the murder at the Leavenworth City levee.

  January 20, 1856   Esplanade
  Monday Night   Leavenworth City, Kansas Territory

  It was a very cold and bitter winter this year. The river has been frozen over for over a month so supplies are brought over by wagon across the ice in the safest places. Travelers heading west have settled in town or have made shelters outside of town and are waiting till spring to continue their journey. The fires of hatred and popular sovereignty are still burning hot even in the frozen Kansas Territory with the gentle persuasion toward a few of our newly elected city officials, a few men have decided to step down from their positions for health reasons. Their lives were threatened to end by the Missouri Ruffians if they did not leave their position in the city. Mayor Thomas Slocum and George Russell, a city councilman, stepped down and was already replaced. Our new mayor is William Murphy, a pro-slavery man to the fullest extent.
  Speaking of the pro-slavery movement, the Kickapoo Rangers added more to the number of murdered free-state men in Leavenworth County. After a day of voting in the town of Easton at Thomas Minard's Farmhouse, a free-state man named Stephen Sparks and his kinfolk were headed home at a late hour on the 17th of January. A bitterly cold night, a night said to be the coldest in Kansas that has been remembered, Stephen Sparks was detained by a band of drunken Kickapoo Rangers. Witnesses of the detainment told of the situation to the free-state men in Easton.
  Reese E. P. Brown, a newly elected representative for Leavenworth County, and a small group of men mounted some horses and wagons and headed out to the area where the Kickapoo Rangers were detaining the Sparks Family. When the free-state men arrived at the scene, weapons started to fire from both sides. A Kickapoo ranger, John Cook, was injured at this shooting and the son of Stephen Sparks was also injured in this encounter.
  The rangers retreated to Dawson's Crossing, and his men made their way back to Easton to recuperate. The next morning, reinforcements from Kickapoo City arrived at Dawson's Crossing, starting a posse to look for Sparks and other free-state men who were part of the events of the prior evening. Not knowing a larger group of Kickapoo Rangers awaited Reese on the trail back to Leavenworth City left Easton with his small group believing the events were over.
  The Kickapoo Rangers overtook the smaller free-state party with guns drawn but no guns were fired. The Rangers took the weapons of the Reese

party and escorted them back to Easton at Dawson's Store, where there was a debate about what to do with the prisoners. It was decided that they were to be let go when a ranger named Robert Gibson recognized Reese Brown as one of the abolitionists who shot John Cook, who passed away from his wounds the previous night.

Everyone but Reese Brown was released by the Rangers, who was taken back into the store to be interrogated on the location of Stephen Sparks. After some debate, tension was rising with no retaliation for the murder of John Cook. With Reese Brown one of the men in the sights of Robert Gibson, Mister Gibson took a hatchet from his belt and lunged at Reese Brown, swinging the hatchet into the temple of Reese Brown's skull. Throwing the limp bleeding body of Brown into a wagon, the Rangers rode for a while not knowing where to take the body. After a few hours and as noted being the coldest night in Kansas history, Brown was still alive. So the Rangers left Dawson's Crossing and headed to the McCrea Farm, where Brown and his family was staying.

Riding in like a windstorm, the Rangers pulled the wagon as close to the door as they could and kicked the door of the home open, pulling the body by the boots and dropping the body into the middle of the doorway to the house. After terrorizing the women of the house and plundering Robert Gibson in his last bit of meanness when he was leaving the home spit a huge block of tobacco onto the wound of Reese Brown and kicked him in the head as they left the house. A neighbor heard the screams of the distressed women and rode to the McCrea homestead. The neighbor pulled the still-breathing body into the house since it was too heavy for the ladies to move. The best care was provided for Mister Brown but the wound took his life that day. The coldness kept him alive enough to say goodbye to his wife when he came back to life for a moment. His body was placed at Pilot Knob Mountain southwest of Leavenworth City.

February 20, 1856   Esplanade
Wednesday Night   Leavenworth City, Kansas Territory

The winter has brought this town to a standstill. Some wagons make it into town but their loads are light and mostly lumber and furs from frontiersmen. I attended another funeral for another friend of Leavenworth Thomas C. Shoemaker. Mister Shoemaker was a partner at the riverboat at the levee along with Jared Todd and Samuel Pitcher. Mister Shoemaker along with mister Pitcher apprehended the criminal Cole McCrea and took him to the Fort Leavenworth Jail.

Apparently, Thomas Shoemaker spoke his mind about the new mayor William Murphy, and although Thomas spoke the truth about the new mayor, it was very abusive and some of the drunken Missourians in the crowd did not appreciate the words of Mister Shoemaker. Taking matters into their own hands and defending the mayor, the Missourians ganged up on Thomas Shoemaker and beat the man to death. Mister Davis has started making caskets in his furniture business on Delaware Street. He was laid to rest on top of Mount Oread.

Pilot Knob Hill was renamed to Mount Oread. The Indian burial grounds will be left intact beside our new burial ground. No charges were ever filed against the ruffians who murdered Thomas Shoemaker.

In other noteworthy news, the county seat of Leavenworth County is officially Delaware City and construction of the new county jail, courthouse, and other buildings are under way.

>
> March 17, 1856   Esplanade
> Monday Night   Leavenworth City, Kansas Territory

The river has started to thaw, the trees are greening, and the flowers are budding with bright beautiful colors, unearthing themselves after the long hard winter. Two new establishments have also emerged from the winter coldness. The Brewery of Fritzlen and Mundee on the Esplanade south of the downtown area was dug into the hillside to keep the beer and other spirits cold in all seasons. They built a two-story stone structure with the sales floor upstairs.

The other business worth noting is the Abernathy Furniture Company that I am able to see from my house. They have built a huge factory on the corner of Second and Northwest Corner of Seneca Streets almost taking up the whole block.

View looking south from Rialto Landing

Chapter Twelve
Battlefield Kansas Territory
Popular Sovereignty Is a
Double-Edged Sword

April 10, 1856　　　　　Esplanade
Thursday Night　　　　Leavenworth City, Kansas Territory

Since I have been in Kansas Territory, I have heard and witnessed some unbelievable events that have been accomplished, but the story I am about to scribe is one of the most unbelievable stories that have come across my ears. The other night I had the honor to dine with Major Ogden and Alexander Majors who both witnessed the event of what I am about to tell. Both swore on a Bible after they told me of this tale, I must add.

A few years back before Leavenworth City was even a thought, Major Ogden and Mister Majors did not know each other at this point but both had business to conduct in Westport, Missouri, at this particular time. This is a story of Thomas and his Windwagon. There was a man named Thomas who created a Conestoga wagon that had a mast and sail on it, like a boat, and he had the idea that he could sail across the plains like a boat across the water. The high gusty winds of the west should make him go faster than a multiple horse team wagon. Thomas had claimed that he just crossed the plains from sixty miles away in one day.

The story continues that he was laughed out of town and as he was crossing the plains at full sail, heading to Council Grove across Indian Territory, he came across a wagon train that was under attack by the Indians of that area. The Indian attackers noticed the white sail wagon with no horses moving quickly toward them. Almost mesmerized by the spectacle, the wagon train men were able to shoot some of the attackers and being scared and now under fire, the Indians rode off not retuning. Thomas and his wagon saved the pioneers and they, including Thomas, made it safely across the country to California.

They shared another story of a group of people down around the Fort Scott area that has established a village of vegetarians. About twenty miles west of Fort Scott, a community was formed called Octagon City. Their idea was to live off the vegetation of the land and there was to be no eating of any meat. Henry S. Clubb settled the one hundred and eight souls to farmland in southern Kansas Territory. We all wished them luck on that venture and I will try to keep my ears open on any further news from that community.

Locally, the news has been rather slow. The river thawed out enough last month that the ferries began operation again, and so I took the family to Holy Trinity in Weston for Easter Services. It is a beautiful little church. It was a beautiful day that day and we spent the day in the carriage riding around the area and had a picnic.

May 10, 1856　　　　　Esplanade
Saturday Night　　　　Leavenworth City, Kansas Territory

The tension is rising between the abolitionists and pro-slavery men, and is happening because of the Popular Sovereignty Act of Kansas Territory. Both the free-state newspapers and pro-slavery ones are throwing insults into each other's faces and the gloves are to come out and slap someone's face. The city of Lawrence is also being very vocal on what they are calling the bogus legislature of the territorial government at Shawnee promoting the legislation that occurred in Topeka with the free-states choice of leadership. Both sides are saying that each side have equal rights and powers.

May 30, 1856　　　　　Esplanade
Friday Night　　　　　Leavenworth City, Kansas Territory

The war of ideals and way of life has erupted here in Kansas Territory. Should this new territory be a state of slavery or a state where all men are free? The pro-slavery voted in government of Kansas Territory decided that the people in charge of the Topeka Constitution should be arrested for treason against the territorial government. Warrants of arrest were issued with seven names posted on May 14, 1856. George Washington Brown, John Brown Jr., Henry H. Williams, Judge G. Smith, Gaius Jenkins, George Dietzler, and Charles Robinson of Lawrence.

Charles Robinson was arrested on May 10th, 1856, in Lexington, Missouri, and then transported here to Leavenworth City on May 24th. The Kickapoo Rangers were very persistent about terrorizing the free-state men of

Leavenworth County, in particular the men who have changed their morals about the issue and are no longer slave owners.

My friend and acquaintance H. Miles Moore was also wanted for treason for the same reasons of being part of the Topeka Constitution. H. Miles was partnered with John Sherman and Messrs. Howard. Mark Perrot and John's younger brother, William, has helped on occasion. On May 27th, the Kickapoo Rangers stormed into the streets of Leavenworth City and went straight to the offices of the lawyers armed with muskets. Warning the men about their actions against the territorial legislature will have consequences and left as quickly as they entered town.

The next day, the Rangers appeared back in town at the same office and arrested H. Miles Moore, Mark Perrot, and John Sherman. They were escorted east down Delaware Street to the corner of Second and Delaware, where a warehouse built by Russell, Majors, and Waddell was being temporarily used by the Platte County Defense Association for the trial and hanging of H. Miles Moore. A small group of men left heavily armed and returned a short time later with a man named Robert Riddle, who was a resident at the Leavenworth Hotel. Some other men were arrested as well that day but were taken to different locations in the city.

The four men were held overnight in the warehouse and in the morning Marc Perrot and John Sherman were released only if they promised to leave the territory and never return. Mister H. Miles Moore, a founding father of Leavenworth City and a member of a masonic lodge of whom he is of great importance, was grabbed by the pro-slavery men and placed on a stool with a noose around his neck that was hanging over the rafters.

The stool was about to be kicked out from H. Miles's feet when a shot was fired from Colonel Clarkson's pistol, and with extreme accuracy the Colonel sliced the rope in half just above the head of H. Miles. A few friends of H. Miles grabbed him off the stool and led him out the back door that was just a few feet away. In the alleyway outside the back door, there was a horse saddled and waiting for Mister Moore to jump on and ride away under a hailstorm of bullets from the angry pro-slavery mob.

As I mentioned earlier, the pro-slavery men of the territory are on a manhunt for all the people that were involved in the Topeka Free-State Legislature. Lecompton was another city that prisoners were being taken to, to be held for trial. Rumors got to Sheriff Sam Jones about many of the treasonous men were back in the town of Lawrence. The Sheriff was there previously in April on the 23rd looking for the men in question, but while still arresting six men in Lawrence, Jones was shot in the back by an unknown abolitionist.

With revenge in the heart of Sherriff Samuel Jones, he returned to Lawrence with a full army of Missouri Ruffians and artillery. They circled the city on May 20th, 1856, ensuring there could not be any escapes, and at the highest point in the city where Charles Robinson built his house, Mount Oread was taken over by the ruffians. The Sacramento and Kickapoo Cannons that were stolen from the Liberty Arsenal were pointed to the center of Lawrence from the top of Mount Oread.

The army of Sam Jones took over the city that day, pillaging and plundering the city and arresting almost a dozen men. Not satisfied getting the men they wanted, the Sherriff returned the next day with orders to destroy the town. Destroying the home of Charles Robinson, Sherriff Jones along with twenty men and two cannons headed into downtown Lawrence.

The cannons were placed in front of the Free-State Hotel and after a series of attacks against the structure, it still stood. It was a very well-built stone structure as it turns out. Now with more anger the building did not collapse, Sam Jones filled the Free-State Hotel with gunpowder and fired his cannons on the structure again, this time with a huge explosion; the Free-State Hotel was destroyed. Now he was paying his attention to the newspapers' offices and any other abolitionist-ran establishment. The newspaper printing presses and stamps were tossed into the river, and the papers and offices were all destroyed. The men ravaged the city again, setting it on fire as they went building to building again downtown. Every house and building were burned down in the town of Lawrence and destroyed by the Pro-Slavery Army of Sherriff Sam Jones. It appears that only two souls were lost in the Attack of Lawrence coming from both sides of the altercation.

On May 23rd, 1856, Captain John Brown of the Kansas Volunteers, who was late in the arrival to defend the city of Lawrence, set up a camp on Pottawatomie Creek with his five sons and three other men for the night. The sons of John Brown were Frederick, Oliver, Owen, Salmon, and Watson Brown; the son-in-law of John Brown Henry Thompson accompanied the family. Two other abolitionists were along for the cause and their names were Theodore Wiener and James Townsley, who owned the wagon the group was traveling in.

The Brown Party heard that there were participants in the Lawrence Raid along the Potawatomie Creek, and came upon the home of James Doyle and family. A small series of questions was asked by John Brown to Mister Doyle and not liking the responses of James Doyle, John Brown shot Mister Doyle in the head. The Brown boys jumped off the wagon and hacked and sliced the sons of James Doyle with scythes and swords. Leaving all three Doyle men dead, the Brown Party headed further downstream to the home of Allen

Wilkerson near a ford crossing. Wilkerson was surrounded at his place by the Brown Party and escorted off the property so his wife would not witness his killing. The Browns again hacked the body of this pro-slavery man until he lay lifeless at their feet then tossed him off into the bushes. They then continued their mission and headed toward the house of James Harris when they came across a man named William Sherman, who heard the screams of Mrs. Wilkerson. Again not liking the answers of Mister Sherman, they took Mister Sherman down to the creek and beat him to death, leaving his body in the current of the Potawatomie Creek.

This news of Brown's revenge started an uprising of debates on both sides of popular sovereignty. From the Kickapoo Rangers and the Leavenworth Volunteers having their antics being played in our region, to the nation's capital where Senator Preston Brooks attacked Senator Charles Sumner, and with a cane on the Senate floor, hit Senator Sumner so many times the Senator was almost beaten to death.

    June 10, 1856   Esplanade
    Tuesday Night   Leavenworth City, Kansas Territory

There was a small war raging in Kansas Territory this week led again by John Brown and his militia of Kansas Volunteers, instigated by Henry Clay Pate and his pro-slavery posse. After the incidents at Potawatomie Creek and Wakarusa, pro-slavery supporter Henry Pate formed a posse to capture John Brown and his party.

The posse went to the home of John Brown and did not find any of the men from the raids in the home but took into custody John Brown Junior and a younger son named Jason. As the posse was taking the prisoners to Lecompton, they were met by a larger group of abolitionists who believed what the posse was doing was wrong. So the abolitionists liberated the Brown boys from their hands and then sent Henry Clay Pate and his posse on their way back to Lecompton with no shots fired.

Now unfortunately, Mister Henry Clay Pate did not take his humiliation lightly, so a few days after his embarrassment, Henry Pate formed a larger posse and sacked the town of Palmyra, seizing horses and weapons for their cause on the Sunday morning of June 1st while the citizens of Palmyra were in church. Arresting four men that were abolitionists while still looking for John Brown, the posse then headed to the town of Prairie City in hopes of John Brown's capture. John Brown's camp was just outside of Palmyra that the posse rode by earlier before sacking the town. He had sent messages to other volunteer men on his side and raised another nineteen men for his army that day and then set out to find this Henry Clay Pate and end his posse. The two sides found each other in an area called Blackjack Ravine, and after a long fire fight between the two armies, Pate and his posse of twenty-three men thinking they were surrounded surrendered to Brown and his Volunteers.

Colonel Sumner of Fort Leavenworth arrived after the battle and surrender of the posse, who on his arrival released the men to the dismay of John Brown and his men. There was a warrant to arrest John Brown, but it could not be produced at the scene to be enforced so the three armies departed Blackjack Ravine in three different directions, calling the day a draw.

On June 4th and 5th, a group of abolitionists from Lawrence heard of the location of the cannon Sacramento was close by in a town named Franklin, a pro-slavery town that was prepared for the attack and defending the cannon. It was reported that only one person was mortally wounded, but many others were wounded. The cannon remained in the hands of the pro-slavery town.

On June 7th, 1856, the town of Osawatomie was attacked by the pro-slavery forces in retaliation for the attack on Franklin. Many other skirmishes occurred between the abolitionists and pro-slavery men, keeping the patrols of Fort Leavenworth always on the trails trying to stop this expression of freedom. The Popular Sovereignty Movement is causing there to be a war over slavery in the Kansas Territory.

July 6, 1856   Esplanade
Sunday Night   Leavenworth City, Kansas Territory

With all the ruckus and shenanigans in the territory and in the area in general, the city council of Leavenworth City issued their first warning flyer to the citizens of Leavenworth City about discharging of firearms in the city limits is prohibited and that you can be arrested for disturbing the peace of the city.

A few weeks ago, the Leavenworth County sent delegates to what is the first Republican convention in Philadelphia, Pennsylvania, with the hopes of John C. Freemont as their choice for President of the United States. My friend Isaac Cody was one of the men sent to the convention. The main issues of the convention were to make Kansas a free state, the polygamy by the Mormons, and the issue of slavery in the nation.

While we were celebrating Independence Day in Leavenworth City, another free-state legislature formed in Topeka. Governor Daniel Woodson heard of this new gathering in Topeka and ordered Colonel E. V. Sumner with five companies of dragoons, mounted with cannons and artillery, to march to Topeka and order the men to end their antics and go home. The men gathering in Topeka were having an illegal gathering not recognized by the Territory of Kansas and that they can be removed by force if they do not leave peacefully. The representatives dispersed the building with no violence by either side.

       August 28, 1856   Esplanade
       Thursday Night   Leavenworth City, Kansas Territory

An unarmed free-state representative was brutally murdered on his way home from a resolution meeting between Captain Saunders and his Ruffians meeting. Major David Starr Hoyt was found by his friends, who went out after Major Hoyt when he was not home at his expected time. His body was found in a ravine shot multiple times, his weapons and belongings missing. It is believed that it was an unsuccessful meeting for Captain Saunders and he ordered the bushwhacking of Major Hoyt on his way back to his home in Lawrence.

It is whispered that James Lane and John Brown have a trail from southeastern Kansas Territory to the Nebraska Border, and then into Iowa, trying to avoid the pro-slavery forces while they take liberated slaves from Missouri to freedom in the north. On August 12th, 1856, Jim Lane and his forces stormed the town of Franklin, this time capturing the cannon Sacramento. Other weapons and ammunition were seized that the town had stored for pro-slavery forces. Jim Lane had a successful campaign.

A few days later, Governor Shannon began a desperate plea to the citizens of Kansas Territory to stop their mercenary war and compromise on their issues. Of course, neither side budged in any direction, and Governor Shannon, seeing no answers, resigned his post on August 18th, 1856. Our newest man to attempt to govern this territory is John Geary.

On August 16th, a little skirmish took place outside of Lecompton close to the Kansas River at the home of Colonel Henry Titus. It was rumored that Colonel Titus was the man who ordered the destruction of the *Herald Freedom* news presses of Lawrence. A man by the name of Samuel Walker wanted revenge for the sacking of his town of Lawrence and retake the materials stolen from Lawrence and return them to the rightful owners, taken from Sherriff Samuel Jones and his men back in April.

About fifty men from Lawrence led by Samuel Walker went up to Lecompton and faced about three dozen pro-slavery men at the house of Colonel Titus. A short battle occurred and the house, or what they called Fort Titus, fell to the hands of Samuel Walker and his men. Five pro-slavery men were laid to rest that day along with one of the men from Lawrence. After negotiations were discussed at meet by both parties, the prisoners were released and Samuel Walker and his men returned to Lawrence.

The trail from Leavenworth City to Lawrence has become to be known as the Devil's Highway. It is controlled by the pro-slavery men who live on the road. The main leader of Devil's Highway is said to be Captain A. B. Miller. A man named Hoppe, who was from Germany, dropped his wife off at an acquaintance in Lawrence and was returning to his home in Leavenworth City when he unfortunately ran into a drunken Charles Fuget on Devil's Highway, who earlier that day, unbeknownst to Mister Hoppe, Mister Fugat swore in one of the bars he was frequenting at the time with witnesses around him, that he was going to kill the first abolitionist he saw that day on August 19th, 1856. Somewhere just outside of Leavenworth City, the two men faced each other on the trail. After a few words between the men, Fuget drew his weapon and removed Mister Hoppe from his carriage. The shot sent him flying into the grass edge of the road where Charles Fuget scalped Mister Hoppe for proof of his earlier promise of killing the abolitionist. Feeling remorse for what he had done, Charles Fuget escaped to Missouri with the scalp of Mister Hoppe.

Leavenworth City streets are really controlled by the Kickapoo Rangers and the Four Horsemen. Terror is sometimes in the feelings of most of the citizens at night and when the army is deployed out into the wilderness. Even in groups, it is hard to travel if you are not in a freighting wagon train.

The last skirmish I will mention in this entry occurred in an area that is called Middle Creek, somewhere near Parker Kansas Territory. Approximately one hundred and twenty-five men led by David Atchison were spotted by a free-state militia camped in that area. On August 25th, shots were fired by both armies and thankfully only one casualty was reported by the free-state militia. Lieutenant Cline was mortally wounded that day. The battle lasted fifteen minutes by some witnesses. There were previous encounters on the Fort Scott Fort Leavenworth Military Road in-between David Atchison's Missouri Ruffians and John Brown and his militia.

September 2, 1856   Esplanade
Tuesday Night   Leavenworth City, Kansas Territory

Captain Martin and his Kickapoo Rangers have controlled Leavenworth City and the entire county. Violence and corruption are their form of communication when there is a disagreement upon the morals of the individual and a pro-slavery state when it comes for the time to vote.

The violence seems more extreme to the south of Leavenworth City in Osawatomie. John Brown and his Free-State Militia continue to fight the pro-slavery elements on the border in southeastern Kansas Territory. Pro-slavery General John Reid and his troops received word that Jim Lane and John Brown would be traveling to Topeka to receive orders from the free-state leaders.

On August 30th, 1856, the Reverend Martin White escorted General Reid and his troops into the town of Osawatomie in search of any abolitionists on their wanted posters. Frederick Brown was in Osawatomie that morning and started to approach the army to see what was happening. The Minister of the Baptist Church noticed the young Frederick approaching and drew his revolver, ending the life of Frederick Brown. While General Reid was still in Osawatomie, John Brown and his troops arrived and a small volley of firearms was exchanged between the two armies.

The exchange of gunfire lasted about fifteen minutes and with John Brown's knowledge of his son's demise, he wanted to continue. They took off in the terrain knowing all the surroundings after emptying all their weapons and escaped into the wilderness undetected by the pro-slavery forces of General Reid. Reid was so upset by the escape that he ordered the entire town of Osawatomie to be burned to the ground. Every building was destroyed and half a dozen men were taken prisoner. The women and children were left standing in the streets in the smoke and destruction of their town.

Besides Frederick Brown, six other souls lost their lives that day. David Garrison, George Partridge, Theron Parker Powers, and Charles Kaiser, all free-state supporters who perished for their freedom, and two unidentified pro-slavery men also had their lives taken as well. Reid continued his plundering northward until he almost reached Topeka.

Meanwhile back up here in Leavenworth City, as I mentioned before, Captain Morgan and his Kickapoo Rangers have been terrorizing the citizens of this town with their forcefulness and violence. There was a municipal election yesterday but we knew there was going to be more trouble when on Sunday there was an encampment of approximately two hundred men at Threemile Creek. Captain Fred Emory and his band of ruffians that are known as the Bashi Bazouks, are some of the men at the camp.

Early Monday morning, the Four Horsemen and their band of ruffians terrorized the streets of Leavenworth City. Horses riding and men marching down every street and alleyway looking for anyone they recognized as a free-state supporter. The Kickapoo Rangers escorted over one hundred and fifty persons into the river that day. Some might have been fortunate to be on a boat but most of the men were ran into the river with whatever belongings they carried on their persons. Houses were plundered and destroyed and many men were wounded in this unnecessary act of violence, but the worst event of the day happened at the home of William Phillips. The young lawyer, who was tar and feathered for speaking his mind on the past bogus elections, was still in the eyes of Captain Martin and Captain Emory.

Captain Fred Emory and his band of ruffians were riding west on Shawnee Street, passing Fifth Street about halfway down the block on the north side, when they noticed the young lawyer in his home and Captain Emory called William Phillips out of his house. William Phillips answered the call by making himself seen on his bedroom balcony on the second floor. William Phillips came out to his balcony overlooking one hundred ruffians, fully armed pointing their weapons at him and his home.

Before any words could be exchanged, Captain Emory shouted, "Fire," and just as William Phillips was able to get a shot off from each revolver in his hands, he received at least fifty bullets to his body and collapsed over the railing, falling into Shawnee Street. His brother Jarad was on the first floor and was shot in the arm through the window by a ruffian who saw him on the inside. The wives of the men were spared of any harm that day.

So it is safe to say that Doctor F. W. Few did not win the election for Mayor as a free-state representative and that Mayor William Murphy will retain his chair. Many free-state men avoided the Kickapoo Rangers by hiding in the thickets and traveling by creek. There are only five reported murders that day that we will call Bloody Monday, but hundreds of lives were affected by the violence of the Kickapoo Rangers.

September 17, 1856   Esplanade
Wednesday Night   Leavenworth City, Kansas Territory

More blood has spilled in Kansas Territory over popular sovereignty since my last entry. News has traveled north from Lyon County about one hundred miles to the south of Leavenworth County. The killing of the first woman in Kansas Territory happened when Sarah Carver, a seventeen-year-old new bride, was shot in the home of her and her abolitionist husband, who was defending it from Missouri Ruffians on September 10th.

The actions of the Kickapoo Rangers have attracted the attention of our new Governor Geary, who actually traveled to Leavenworth City to put an end to the mercenary antics in the county. On September 9th, Governor Geary and troops from Fort Leavenworth marched into town and arrested Captain Emory for his actions on Bloody Monday. There have been other skirmishes in the region involving different militias. One event occurred on the 11th of September, three miles north of Oskaloosa in Slough Creek.

A free-state army led by Colonel James Harvey was sent for by the governor to Leavenworth City to help the citizens from being harassed by

Missouri Ruffians. There were no reported killings that day but the free-state army took six prisoners' ammunitions, and a flag from Charleston, South Carolina, the home of the pro-slavery army at Slough Creek.

Grasshopper Falls, a town started by Isaac Cody, was burned down by a pro-slavery group, and General Jim Lane was in Topeka and started to help the people of Grasshopper Falls, but in an area called Hickory Point General Lane encountered a group of pro-slavery supporters from the Carolinas. A small gun battle ensued but the southern sympathizers held onto their stronghold. General Lane sent for reinforcements and when Colonel Harvey arrived, he arrived with the cannon Sacramento which is now in the hands of the free-state forces.

Colonel Harvey took his forces straight down into the camp of the pro-slavery army. There were five men killed in the battle known to be from the free-state army. The only name I received was Charles Nehall, who was killed by a cannonball and five other men were wounded on the abolitionist side.

My last entry for tonight is about another murder in Kansas Territory. Another free-state man by the name of David Buffum was murdered by the Kickapoo Rangers while attending his field outside of Lawrence near the Devil's Highway. He was shot and left for dead but was able to get his story off to no one other than Governor Geary himself, who was riding by after the incident. David Buffum was able to tell the governor who shot him and the reason why before he breathed his last breath. He was shot for not giving up his horse to the Rangers.

I must now share with you the fate of the steamboat Arabia that was sunken by an oak tree submerged underwater on the evening of September 5th. The beautiful two-sided paddlewheel Arabia was three years old when she went down south of Delaware City, taking supplies and travelers up the Missouri River to Nebraska Territory and the other territories up north.

Dinner was being served on the vessel when the ship slowed suddenly according to the one of the hundred and twenty-nine passengers that survived the incident. The only known death was a stubborn mule that would not move off the ship as it was sinking. The Arabia went down quickly with all the freight on board that included supplies for the clothing stores, weapons, shoes, silverware, dishes, and spices with every amenity that one could need to survive comfortably in the west. The next day, all that was visible was the pilot's cabin and the tops of the steam pipes.

October 7, 1856   Esplanade
Tuesday Night   Leavenworth City, Kansas Territory

I am thankful to the God above that I am able to scribe this entry tonight. I was on an assignment to Lawrence a fortnight ago when I made the mistake of traveling alone on Devil's Highway. I had just passed Chief Tonganoxie's Stage stop when I heard the sound of a rifle nearby. Wildfire staggered and then fell onto his side. Looking at his side, he was shot by someone in the unseen woods. I grabbed my saddlebags and rifle, and crawled into the bushes and into the gully on the side of the road. I heard the sound of horses galloping on the road approaching from the north, so I cocked my rifle and prepared for the worst.

I heard a few voices as they stopped and looked at the situation; they were about to get down and search the men when were startled off by the sound of more horses approaching from the south. A stagecoach with an army escort that was at Chief Tonganoxie's heard the shot and came galloping to my rescue. I exited the bushes and told the men who I was and they remembered me from the stop. I received help to put Wildfire into the bushes and retrieve my saddle. I was able to ride the stage to Leavenworth City, where I will have to replace an irreplaceable horse.

Chapter Thirteen
The Pendulum Swings in Favor of Free-State Kansas

December 3, 1856 Esplanade
Saturday Night Leavenworth City, Kansas Territory

As winter becomes harsher in the territory, the aggressiveness of the Kickapoo Rangers has become weaker or at least until spring arrives perhaps. More abolitionists from the northern states are living in Leavenworth City, making it more difficult for the pro-slavery element to enforce their beliefs. The elected officials are pro-slavery in Leavenworth City, but I fell that the feeling of the territory and nation are changing with the times. Leavenworth County now has nine towns in its borders and all of them governed by the pro-slavery element. More small towns are being established all along the trails heading west in all the counties in Kansas Territory.

Alexandria Township is a growing community founded by Joseph McAleer, Samuel Pitcher, and James M. Alexander, the town's namesake. Alexandria was established on the Fort Riley and Fort Leavenworth Military Road that is approximately ten or so miles northwest of Leavenworth City. The main source of income there is a coal mining operation that began in the fall of 1855.

Also investing in the town of Alexandria is William G. Mathias and Lucian Johnson Eastin, editor of the *Kansas Herald*, and who founded the town of Eastin halfway between Leavenworth City and Alexandria at where Andre Dawson had his ford to cross Stranger Creek.

Before Eastin put his money into the area, there was a settlement called Martinsburg about a mile south of where Eastin was platted. With the popularity of a town on the Military Road, the romance of Martinsburg died and so did the community. High Prairie is another community that is in Leavenworth County to the west of Leavenworth City. Up above the hills west of Leavenworth City, the land levels off and becomes rolling plains as far as the eyes can see. In 1854, when the land became available, Caleb Shearer bought a quarter section of that area or one hundred and sixty acres of land, mostly to be used for farming. A large group of people reside up in the High Prairie region.

Kickapoo City is of course just north of Fort Leavenworth on the Missouri River where Salt Creek enters the flow of the Missouri River. A very dominant pro-slavery town that will do anything to become the county seat. North of Kickapoo City, the town of Oak Mills that was the landing on the Kansas side from Nimrod Farley's ferry crossing. Port Williamtown is another town along the Missouri River. Delaware City, south of Leavenworth City of course mentioned in previous writings, is not growing as fast as the town had wanted.

Leavenworth City is growing more each day with the success of the freighting company of Russell, Majors, and Waddell, who have brought thousands of jobs to Leavenworth City and are helping build the interior roads and bridges in Kansas Territory for their freighting needs. The city's population now is about five thousand and grows more every day. As I stated before, as more people arrive new businesses are established as well.

There is a dark side of a growing town near a military installation and that is all the brothels, bars, saloons, beer gardens, and gambling dens. When the army is in town and when there are the wagon riders with the freighting teams in town, the above-mentioned businesses are open twenty-four hours a day, causing all sorts of drunken shenanigans in downtown. The music and the merriment that comes from all of the establishments make the evenings a festival every night.

There is one more town to mention that is being established across from Parkville on the Kansas Territory side called Quindaro. It is in lower Leavenworth County. The name comes from the wife of Abelard Guthrie, who was a Wyandot Indian. Quindaro is the only free town port on the Missouri River that with the help of Charles Robinson made a trail to Lawrence so the Pro-slavery Ruffians would not steal or burn the product for abolitionists in the western towns.

    January 20, 1857   Esplanade
    Tuesday Night   Leavenworth City, Kansas Territory

The Missouri River is completely frozen over with a foot of snow covering the ground above the ice, but even in these frigid conditions the battle in Kansas Territory continues to rage out of control. I am happy to say that the Kansas Free-State Militia has run the Kickapoo Rangers back to Kickapoo City earlier this month on January 4th.

On the 12th of this month in Lecompton, the Proslavery Law and Order Party changed the name of their organization during a conference to the National Democratic Party. Let us hope it will change the morals of its constituents as well. Our beloved Mayor Slocum had enough of the antics of both parties and resigned a few days before the election that was held on the 15th of January.

Word has come to my attention of a tragedy that occurred in northeastern Leavenworth County on voting day last week. The altercation took place at the polling station in Eastin when a group of Rangers tried to overtake the station and steal the votes. The votes were defended by a small group of free-state supporters with Stephen sparks of the Alexandria Township leading the free-state men of Leavenworth came to help at the polls. Captain Reese P. Brown, Henry J. Adams, J. C. Green, and Joseph Byrd held the Rangers back with one man from the Rangers being mortally wounded. A man by the last name of Cook was the person who was shot.

Staying in Eastin after the polls closed, the following morning the Leavenworth men left Eastin heading toward Leavenworth City on the Military Road. Nearing David Hurley's house, the group was met by an army of fifty Kickapoo Rangers led by Captain Martin and Captain Dunn. The Kickapoo Rangers captured the men and their wagons and escorted the men that were headed to Leavenworth City back to the town of Eastin.

In one of the stores in Eastin, the men were tied up and held prisoners by the Rangers where a trial was to be conducted for the murder of one of their men the previous day. Captain Reese P. Brown was put on trial for the shooting by a witness of the Rangers who saw Mister Brown pull the trigger. Mister Byrd was kept as a witness and the other men were allowed to escape while they could.

During the set-up for the trial, some drunken angry Rangers stormed into the store led by Robert Gibson, who in the blink of an eye had pulled out a hatchet and split the top of the skull of Captain Brown. Captain Martin ordered the still-breathing body to be thrown into the back of the wagon and they would dispose of the body. That day was the coldest day in the history of Leavenworth County. So in the back of the wagon, the still-living body of Captain Reese P. Brown was taken to Smith's Saloon in the Salt Creek Valley so the men could warm up. After more torture and tobacco being spit onto Captain Reese, it was there that they decide to drop the body off at the home of Cole McCrea, where they found out that Captain Reese's wife was socializing.

Taking the wagon full speed and spinning in front of the cabin, the Kickapoo Rangers kicked the door open of the McCrea home and dragged the still-breathing body of Captain Brown down off the wagon leaving a small blood trail in the snow across the porch where they dropped the body halfway in-between the opening so the door couldn't close. At the sight of her husband, Mrs. Brown fainted and Mrs. McCrea screamed out in horror at the sight of the bloody man.

After ransacking the house, the Kickapoo Rangers left the women who were still trying to remove the body from the doorway. Hearing the ruckus, a neighbor, David Brown, came to the aide of the women and helped move the body out of the doorway and into the house so they could close the door.

Captain Reese P. Brown passed away a few hours after being dropped off at his wife's location. The coldest day of his life kept him alive to be in the arms of his beloved wife for his final moments on Earth. He was buried at Mount Aurora Cemetery on the top of Pilot Knob Hill the next day.

February 22, 1857   Esplanade
Sunday Night   Leavenworth City, Kansas Territory

Mother Nature has let Jack Frost gone crazy at the end of winter. Temperatures are below zero, so using the privy at night has become quite a task to stay warm. The snow continues to pile up and the river continues to be frozen solid ice. I was able to venture to Lecompton on assignment last week and witnessed an action that keeps popular sovereignty alive in Kansas Territory.

At Constitution Hall, the newly appointed Sheriff William T. Sherrard, who replaced Sam Jones in Douglas County, was attempting to retrieve his commission that was not allowed to him for being a free-state supporter. The new sheriff attempted this same task a few weeks earlier at the governor's office where threats and spitting had occurred in the faces of Sheriff Sherrard and Governor Geary.

Sheriff Sherrard was allowed to address the members of legislation about the corruptness of the Governor and other members of this territorial legislation. A pro-slavery supporter named Sheppard in the crowd, who was against what the Sheriff was speaking, stood and started an argument with Sheriff Sherrard. Not liking the words of his debater, Sheriff Sherrard pulled his revolver out of its holster and fired upon Mister Sheppard, hitting him in the side. Mister Sheppard, drawing his weapon, returned fire, striking the Sheriff with a bullet, injuring him as well. Thus prompted a volley of gunfire from almost all the men on the top floor of Constitution Hall that day but was quickly extinguished by the guards in the room.

When Sheriff Sherrard was pulled away from the group in the hall, the secretary for Governor Geary, John Jones, jumped up in front of the Sherriff who was being held by the guards and shot the sheriff, mortally wounding him there on the floor of our territorial capital building.

    March 26, 1857   Esplanade
    Thursday Night   Leavenworth City, Kansas Territory

A few weeks ago on March 4th, a new President of the United States was sworn into office. Franklin Pierce has stepped aside and James Buchanan is the fifteenth man to fill that office since George Washington. In our local elections, L.F. Hollingsworth was appointed Justice of the Peace for Delaware City and the Constable Wilson Fox, who have already requested money to build the proper structures for the county seat to function in Leavenworth County.

It is with a heavy heart what I am about to scribe onto this note. My dear friend and old acquaintance, Isaac Cody, has passed away due to complications of his stabbing a few years back. Pneumonia was said to be the final cause by the doctor. The funeral of Isaac Cody was the largest procession that anyone there had ever witnessed. From the viewing of his body at his home in Salt Creek Valley, he was taken to Mount Aurora Cemetery, Pilot Knob Hill, where he was laid to rest overlooking the territory he helped develop.

The Free-State Movement took a blow to equality for all when the Supreme Court finalized their decision on the matter of Dred Scott. The Missouri Ruffians celebrated in the streets when word of the decision made it to Leavenworth City. So let it be written one time that I do assist in the liberation of fugitive slaves out of the town of Leavenworth City with the assistance of many friends of whom I will not mention.

To end this entry, I have learned that Governor Geary has fled the territory in the dark of the night a few nights ago. It was said he had to escape members of his own party, who had ambition to assassinate the governor.

    May 30, 1857   Esplanade
    Saturday Night   Leavenworth City, Kansas Territory

Leavenworth City continues to grow at a remarkable rate since its first thoughts three years past. Another 320 acres of land south of Threemile Creek was purchased from the Delaware Indians and has rapidly become the residential area for the Leavenworth City as downtown has expanded west to the Military Road. The newest section pays tribute to the trees in our region: Oak, Pine, Spruce, and so forth and so on. They run in the east west directions and the numbered streets try to line up on the other side of the creek. Peter

Abele bought the land and built a farm south of the new city edition. The firms of Russell, Majors, and Waddell have built fine wooden bridges crossing the creeks along the trails that benefit the freighting company and the citizens of Leavenworth City.

Jeremiah Clark, who built the first actual house in Leavenworth City at Fourth and Walnut, donated a parcel of his land to build a court house, for all our city business, and court was still being conducted on the second floor of J. B. Rowdy's Furniture Store at the corner of Shawnee and Fifth. Our newest and fourth governor, Robert J. Walker, has arrived in the territory finally. He is a man that has lived in both the north and the south, so we shall see how he governs the territory. When Governor Walker arrived in Lecompton, he gave a speech that seemed fair and just, but as said before we shall see if he can back his words up with action. Although the new governor is pushing for the Lecompton Constitution and the Free-State Party is in an uproar about his politics. Governor Walker was a former slave owner who released his slaves about ten years past.

    July 4, 1857   Esplanade
    Saturday Night   Leavenworth City, Kansas Territory

As I sit here at my desk scribing by the candlelight around the room, I can see the night sky light up with the brilliant colors of Independence Day, and even though gunfire is not permitted in the city limits, we can hear the blasts from every direction around us. It was almost the normal Saturday night but with the magic of fireworks.

We had a family portrait taken downtown at the studio of E. E. Henry, who we met while walking along the Esplanade overlooking the river. We try to get a family picture every year but with me on assignment, the last two years were missed.

In the last week of last month, the territory of Kansas sold surplus Indian land off to new settlers. The Peoria, Kaskaskia, Wieh, and Pinkashan tribes were moved again further west into Kansas Territory. With the gold rush in the west and finding of other minerals, cities are being built all over the new frontier.

In Governor Geary's reign in office, he did stop an abundance of violence and mayhem in the area, dispersing the right military to handle the situation but the killings and ransacking still continues because of the two governments in the territory. On June 29th, there was another altercation at a polling station. It appears that citizen voter W. M. Haller was voicing his opinion of some matters corresponding to the City Recorder James T. Lyle, who is a very pro-slavery man. Mister Haller was a witness to what happened to Captain Reese P. Brown and swears on his Holy Bible that James T. Lyle was a Kickapoo Ranger that day Mister Brown was murdered.

The words became more belligerent and threatening between the two gentlemen and Mister W. M. Haller drew his revolver and shot James T. Lyle in the chest, mortally wounding him there outside the polling station.

| August 1, 1857 | Esplanade |
| Saturday Night | Leavenworth City, Kansas Territory |

Governor Walker took another position with the Pro-Slavery Party when he declared that the men that were in the Lawrence and Topeka Free-State Legislature are in rebellion of the territory of Kansas and cannot establish a government of their own. Many abolitionists want the Topeka Constitution to replace the Lecompton Constitution for possible statehood.

As of July 24th, Brigham Young, the Mormon leader in the Utah Territory, has declared war upon the United States of America. Orders from the President James Buchannan have the troops from Fort Leavenworth going to Utah Territory to extinguish this uprising. Russell, Majors, and Waddell have the freighting contract for the army to Utah Territory. Back in Kansas Territory, the army at Fort Leavenworth is constantly on alert trying to repress the uprisings of attacking Indians on the wagon trains while the pioneers travel on the trails in Western Kansas Territory. Colonel Edwin Sumner was following a renegade band of Cheyenne Indians when the two forces met on the 29th of July at a location called Solomon's Fork. Colonel Sumner received word that there was an Indian encampment nearby with approximately three hundred warriors. The army of Colonel Sumner was around five hundred men.

The initial confrontation near Solomon's Fork ended with nine Cheyenne dead and many others wounded; the army lost two soldiers, and less than a dozen soldiers were wounded by the Cherokee. In the pursuit after the Cheyenne retreated, the Army came around to a recently departed Indian Village with around a dozen or more structures intact. The village was ordered to be destroyed and was burnt to the ground, so no piece of the village could be used again. His pursuit of the renegades continued until Colonel Sumner received his new orders to report to the Utah Territory. One of the wounded soldiers is being recommended for a medal of valor during this expedition and his name is Jeb Stuart.

Closer to home, on the same day that Colonel Sumner was fighting the Cheyenne on July 31st, another abolitionist was murdered. James Stevens, a free-state member from Leavenworth City, who was brutally killed by

Missouri Ruffians' John C. Quarles and W. M. Bays. This morning, a mob of free-state friends of James Stevens liberated the two murderers from jail and escorted them down to the river where a big old oak tree has stood for over one hundred years on Cherokee Street and the Levee.

Ropes were tossed over the thick strong branches of the oak tree and then the two men on horseback were placed under the branch with the noose of the rope placed around their necks. The ropes were tightened around the base of the thick oak tree and John C. Quarles with W. M. Bays were both asked if they had any last words to deliver to their loved ones. Both ruffians cursed the mob and as they were screaming their profanities, an unknown participant of the lynching fired his weapon and the horses darted out from under the men and their bodies quivered until there was no more movement from either man.

The bodies of the men were left hanging from the oak tree to show the Missouri Ruffians that there will be an eye for an eye in the battle on Kansas Territory soil. When the town became dark that night, the bodies were taken down and buried over in Weston Missouri.

Stewart Iron Works

Chapter Fourteen
Laws of the Land

September 2, 1857 Esplanade
Wednesday Night Leavenworth City, Kansas Territory

In my eyes, Leavenworth City is the greatest city west of the Mississippi River. The town's growth and port usage have surpassed Weston and any other town on the Missouri River. In the main section of town, the streets have expanded to past Tenth Street now. The freighting company of Russell, Majors, and Waddell are employing over one thousand men in Leavenworth City with various businesses that help make this a town for any needs. Outside of town, fields of lumber, oxen, cattle, horses, crops of hay, wheat, corn, barley, and beans are worked in between the fields of sunflowers that are everywhere in the prairie. Rope still comes from the hemp houses in Weston, but every other device one would need to live and travel can be found in Leavenworth City.

In political news, Charles Robinson was finally acquitted for his shenanigans in the treasonous acts of the Free-State Party in Topeka. The Territorial District Court on the 20th of August 1857, set Mister Charles Robinson free after almost a month of being on trial.

September 10, 1857 Esplanade
Thursday Night Leavenworth City, Kansas Territory

A few days past, I had the privilege of meeting our ex-governor but now standing as Territorial Governor, Daniel Woodson, when he made an appearance for the governor who was in our nation's capital on business. A Leavenworth County Territorial Legislation Meeting was being held in the Rees's Warehouse down on Delaware Street.

Just a note from last week that there was a lunar eclipse that made all the animals uneasy as well as the people who believed that the world was coming to an end.

September 20, 1857   Esplanade
Sunday Night   Leavenworth City, Kansas Territory

Marisol and I had the honor to attend the wedding of my friend Hugh Miles Moore at the Shawnee Hotel between Main and Second Streets on the 15th last week, and that is the only good news I am scribing tonight, because my latest trip to Fort Leavenworth has brought me news of a tragedy that has occurred in the Utah Territory.

My sources in Fort Leavenworth say that there was an incident in an area called Mountain Meadows. The Wagon Train Expedition of Baker-Fancher from Arkansas was looking for a new home in California when they were surrounded by a group of two hundred Paiute Indians. After a few days of occasional attacks by the Paiute Indians, a group of fifty Mormon men came into the wagon circle and persuaded the Baker-Fancher group to lay down their arms and they would be escorted out safely past the Indians by the Mormons, who said they were friendly with the Paiute Indians.

With the assurance of the Mormons who knew the area, the wagon train disarmed and in a single file marched out of the protection of the wagons. After about two hundred yards, the pioneers entered a small ravine where the fifty Mormon men and two hundred Paiute Indians had conspired together to ambush and massacre the one hundred and twenty men and women, sparing only the lives of seventeen children under the age of seven years old. Fort Leavenworth dispatched more troops to Utah Territory to suppress the uprising.

There was also news from the west coast about a steamer ship sinking named The Central America, killing four hundred people and losing a large portion of America's treasury gold shipment that was being transported from San Francisco. With that news, the east coast at New York City began to panic about the financial crisis that is occurring with a major banking system failing and gold being lost in the ocean.

I must write about another eclipse but this time it was a solar event, meaning in the daytime on September 17th of 1857. The middle of the day became as dark as night in just a matter of minutes and then the sky began to fill with light again as the moon passed in front of the sun. The confusion of the animals again with the reaction of the people who have never experienced a phenomenon like the one that just occurred was comical.

October 10, 1857   Esplanade
Saturday Night   Leavenworth City, Kansas Territory

The territorial election a few days past has put more Abolitionists or Free-State Representatives, into office who now have control over both houses in the Kansas Government. The laws of the land will be changing and the Pro-Slavery Party is in turmoil with the loss of political power. Some riots have occurred, started by the Missouri Ruffians, but their efforts will not change the fact that the Free-State Party will change the direction the territory was heading.

A vote was also taken to move the county seat from Delaware City and the new county seat of Leavenworth County is Kickapoo City. The buildings intended for the government use in Delaware City will still be used by the city but no ideas or names have been mentioned. The town of Quindaro is rapidly growing, and will be a very important riverport soon.

November 20, 1857   Esplanade
Friday Night   Leavenworth City, Kansas Territory

Winter seems to have arrived early this year with fierce winds and freezing temperatures. River traffic has ceased for the season and everyone is bearing down for a winter worse than last year. More land was acquired by the Kansas Government by the acquisition of surplus Shawnee Indian land south of the Kansas River and Leavenworth County. A new town of Monticello was established and its constable is a young man I met in the streets of Leavenworth City by the name of William Hickok.

December 27, 1857   Esplanade
Sunday Night   Leavenworth City, Kansas Territory

Political unrest has taken over our governor's office again in Kansas Territory. A group of political men forced the resignation of Robert Walker our fourth territorial governor as the previous office holder John White Geary. In between unelected officials during the times, the position was vacant or the governor had responsibilities in Washington. Daniel Woodson and Frederick P. Stanton became acting governors during the vacancies. Our newest and fifth territorial governor is James W. Denver, who was sworn into office on December 21, 1857.

The Lecompton Constitution that was passed by Kansas Legislature will be put to the vote of the Kansas citizens in our next election. More conflicts are occurring in Bourbon County in an area called Fort Bain, where James Montgomery and John Brown are using the free-state militia to transport slaves along the underground as it's called from southern Kansas to the Northern States. In the Northern states, the former slaves will be free and live safe lives.

January 2, 1858   Esplanade
Saturday Night   Leavenworth City, Kansas Territory

I did not mention Christmas in my last entry. The holiday was festive with the family here in our house this year. The children were spoiled by Swiety Mikolaj (Santa), and the children's mother with lots of presents and confectionaries. The New year was brought in by a bang as fireworks filled the skies of Leavenworth City again. A feeling of change is in the air for the year, but we shall see what the political parties decide to play the game. It is still hard to determine where popular sovereignty is taking Kansas, but it looks to be going the free-state way. The little battles over the last three years have taken a toll on all the residents of the territory. Families have lost loved ones and all sorts of property damaged by the war in Kansas Territory.

January 20, 1858   Esplanade
Wednesday Night   Leavenworth City, Kansas Territory

Another bitter winter has been dealt to us in the cards of Mother Nature, so news is as slow river water. The debate over the Lecompton Constitution was put to rest again as it was rejected by the voters in Kansas Territory in an earlier election this month.

The only other news I have to offer today is the news that a new mail route has been started out of the warehouse of Lewis Rees's to carry parcel to Hyatt in Anderson County. Then to the city of Humbolt in Allen County.

February 4, 1858   Esplanade
Thursday Night   Leavenworth City, Kansas Territory

The temperature outside has not risen above freezing for over the last three weeks. Again, the news is slow due to little outside activity but the latest from Lecompton is good news for Kansas Territory. A newly formed Kansas Educational Association was chartered by the territorial legislation to begin a school of higher education in the town of Palmyra southeast of Lawrence. The first school will be run by the Methodist Episcopal Church.

The delegates in Lecompton are also speaking of granting charters to sixteen businesses to build roads and also railroads across Kansas Territory. The Missouri River and Rocky Mountain Company here in Leavenworth City has a charter to build a road from Leavenworth City to Delaware City. John C. Calhoun and D. A. Grover are proprietors of that company.

    March 31, 1858   Esplanade
    Wednesday Night   Leavenworth City, Kansas Territory

The river has begun to thaw out in some places but travel still will not be able to go up or down the river for at least a week or so. Still the news is nothing to even mention, so I will scribe to you an event.

A new market hall was constructed on the corner of Third and Delaware. In the basement there is a billiard's room along with a bowling saloon. The ground floor consists of the city market and part of the theater that extends to the second floor. The second floor also consists of more theater and the offices of the City Recorder and Marshall's Office. It is said that the theater has the capability to hold over five hundred people. H. T. Clarke and company have made this building into a very beautiful updated theater.

Levi North's Circus Newspaper Ad

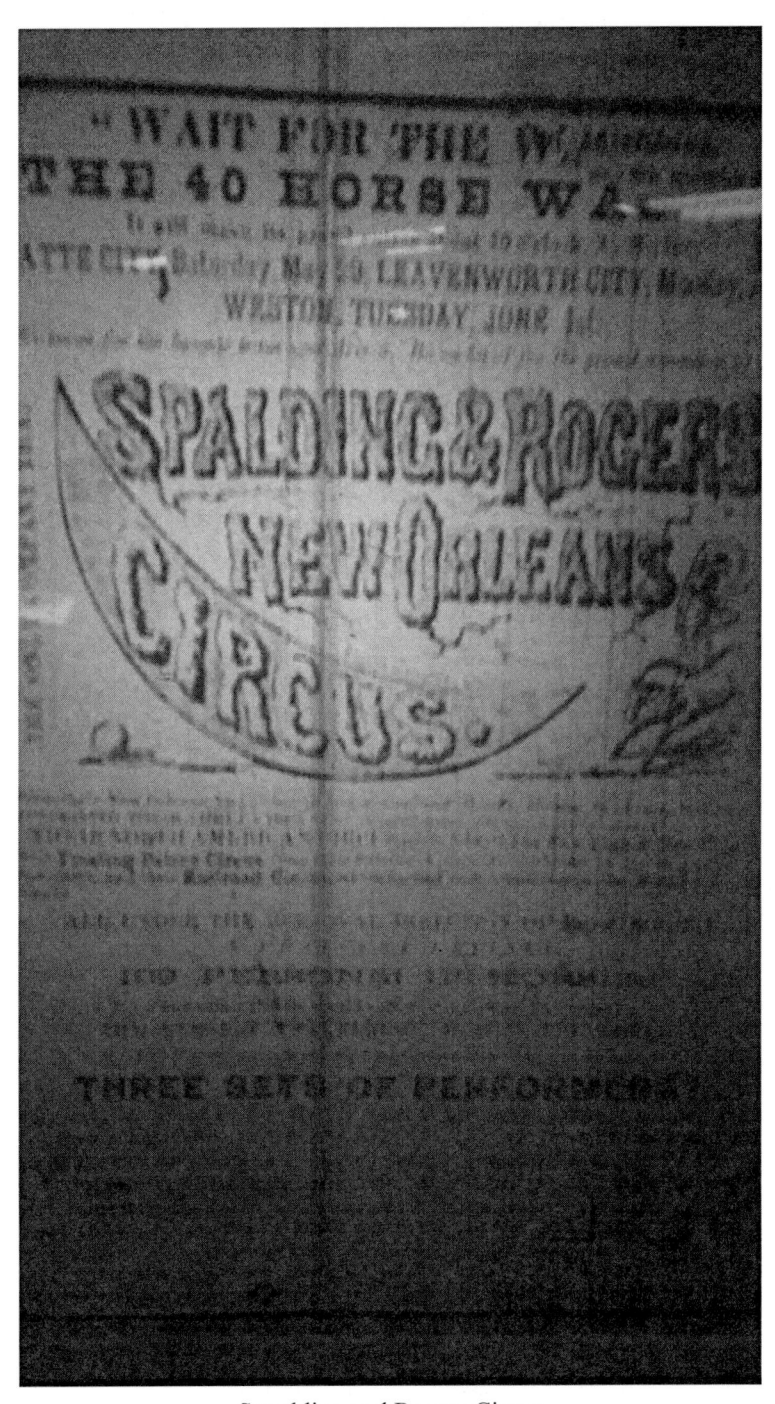

Spaulding and Rogers Circus

Chapter Fifteen
Underground Railroad

We continued to read the journal until almost two o'clock in the morning of Wednesday and everyone was still full of the excitement of the stories. As the saying goes, "I wish these walls could talk." Well, the walls in this house were telling us its story tonight. The kids and my brothers wanted to go down into the tunnel right then but due to the recommendations of the mothers and wives in the room, the exploration of the tunnel was to be in the morning after breakfast.

After a restless night of no sleep, Natalie and I rolled out of bed and helped the family make a nutritious and delicious breakfast. My brothers and all the kids also did not get any sleep last night as well. We cleaned up the kitchen and then grabbed our flashlights and phones to record the event.

Ric and Ken went down first and then the children, with me following. There were a dozen flashlights moving around, making the tunnel brighter than I had before. We walked past the bottles that we left and I showed them where Natalie and I found the saddlebag. As we approached the end, we could see that it was just a little cave-in, and the children immediately started moving the boulders by pushing them, but we stopped them and proceeded slowly to avoid any accident or another cave-in. As all of us removed the rocks, my brothers went back up and returned with wood to support the ceiling of the tunnel. Securing our advancement, we proceeded further southeast, finding more bottles and a newspaper remnant but we couldn't make out the writing.

About one hundred yards further at a slight downgrade the entire length, we saw a black rod iron gate that was off its hinges with what appeared to be a stairway going up but was covered up again by another cave-in. The gate had a name on it from Cincinnati, Ohio; 'The Stewart Iron Works' was casted into the scrollwork. This gate seemed to be the end of the line. Ken and I decided to use our phones and track the tunnel from above by walking above each other. He stayed in the tunnel and I went outside to the bay window and by what we decided, I was standing on top of him. So he told me how far and what direction the tunnel went and I walked across the front yard and across the street. Ken said the first cave-in was almost in the middle of the Esplanade. We continued southeast and where the gate was located appeared to be where the backside of the Planter's Hotel was.

After our latest discoveries in the tunnel that we brought up were placed in the library, we cleaned ourselves up, fed the kids, and did some chores around the house for Mom and Dad. Dinner was served early, so we could continue our reading of the book and after we put everything away, the entire family grabbed their pillows and blankets and made them little nests in the library for more stories.

    April 13, 1858   Esplanade
    Tuesday Night   Leavenworth City, Kansas Territory

Today we celebrated Thanksgiving and tonight we feasted on roast turkey with all the fixings of a New England Holiday. Our neighbors and friends started arriving midday and we had the honor of hosting Bishop Miege, who told us they are planning to build a cathedral in town to replace the smaller Immaculate Conception.

The Catholic Church now has three services on the Sabbath. Sunrise services start at six in the morning, the next mass is at seven in the morning, and the last at ten and a half in the morning. Bishop Miege has three assistants that assist in the masses.

There was a third Constitution Convention held here in Leavenworth City to determine a new constitution for Kansas Territory on the 3rd of April. A new constitution was written and approved by the people to be voted on in the upcoming elections on May 18th. The new document was the boldest piece of legislation that I have ever encountered to this day. It not only banned slavery from the territory but stated all men were equal no matter what color their skin was. Another never-heard-of-before attachment was that women were given certain rights that had never been allowed to women in history.

    April 29, 1858   Esplanade
    Thursday Night   Leavenworth City, Kansas Territory

The river has completely thawed and the traffic on the river is back to its chaos. Ships of every size appear at the levee at all times of the day. The hustle and bustle noises of a busy city fill the streets of Leavenworth City with the sounds of many languages, wagons, and work in progress. Pioneers fill their carts with supplies to travel across the country to the west that takes around three months to complete.

As the population in Kansas Territory grows, there is still the debate over popular sovereignty, which still causes mischief and mayhem throughout the territory. The Leavenworth Constitution is the abolitionists' or free-state response to the Lecompton Constitution that is all pro-slavery, and now the Lecompton Constitution is being endorsed by Congress with an add-on of what they are calling the English Bill. This is a bribe to the people of Kansas Territory by William Hayden to pass the Lecompton Constitution by giving Kansas Territory more land but only if the Lecompton passes into statehood.

A good piece of news is that Kansas Territory has also put in a continued education system in the territory. The Methodists have founded a college that they are naming after their Bishop Osmon Cleander Baker, and the college will be built in the town of Palmyra. My old acquaintance George Park added his influence on a new college named Bluemont Central College. A site was claimed by Mister Park on a site he called Polistra on the north side of the Blue River near Fort Riley. While George Park was back in Parkville, a group of educated men from the northern states arrived at the same site Mister Park landed, but these men set up their claim on the west side of the Blue River.

Later, Mister Park was conducting business in Texas when his claim was jumped by Professor I. T. Goodnow. When George Park returned to Kansas Territory to check his claim, Professor Goodnow and Mister Park were able to resolve the conflict after a number of meetings. The idea of an agricultural college was adopted and approved by both men. They also will call the new town Manhattan.

The Honorable Reverend Bishop Miege had two Benedictine monks visit him in Leavenworth City a few months ago and they toured the town of Atchison in which they picked a location on the cliffs overlooking the Missouri River, just a short distance north of Atchison. A boarding school was built on the site and six men are enrolled into the school to become future priests.

I have news from the southeastern part of Kansas Territory of more disputes between the Ruffians and the Jayhawkers. Jim Lane's Kansas Free-State Militia in the Fort Scott area, under the supervision of James Montgomery, was camped out at a place called Yellow Paint Creek, resting their horses, when the pro-slavery group called the Dark Lantern Society, based out of Fort Scott's Western Hotel, a former army barracks of the old fort, started a firefight.

Seventeen regulators for the Free-State Army were ambushed by Captain Anderson and twenty men in his troop ordered by the Marshall John Little to make the abolitionists leave the county or face death. Montgomery's men decided to stay in the county and started to fire upon the Ruffians while taking cover in the brush and trees nearby. During the bullet exchange, one free-state man was mortally wounded and many men on both sides were wounded. A truce was called while both sides can collect their wounded and patch them up, and during that time Montgomery and his men snuck out of their place of safety and escaped the larger force of Ruffians.

      May 12, 1858   Esplanade
      Wednesday Night   Leavenworth City, Kansas Territory

With all the rain we have received in April, the foliage, flowers, and landscapes are full of vibrant colors that make Leavenworth City I do declare one of the most beautiful cities I have been in. The covered bridges across the creeks out in the country are picturesque as you approach them.

Making this spring day even better is the news I received that Minnesota has been declared a state by Congress and President Buchannan as a non-slavery state. Being in a great spirit, I will now scribe my involvement in the free-state movement. The Planter's Hotel down the Esplanade from this location is run by two gentlemen. Len T. Smith, a pro-slavery supporter, along with Jep Rice, an abolitionist. Compromise has made this hotel a place both parties can be accommodated at. At the bar there are always two bartenders behind the bar that represent both parties, so no fighting over who serves. As long as the guests remain civilized and gentlemen-like, they are more than welcome to stay at the Planter's Hotel.

I have my new horse, Running Water, still boarded at the stables behind the Planter's and along with Colonel Rice have made a secret tunnel that runs from my storage box in my pen, my storage box has a false bottom in it down some stairs, into the tunnel that goes to the back of my house to my gentleman's room. I then escort the train passengers through town to William Mathews at his boarding house.

      May 26, 1858   Esplanade
      Wednesday   Leavenworth City, Kansas Territory

Levi J. North's National Circus came to Leavenworth City on Monday May 21st and set up their tent in the north of town near Fort Leavenworth and put on a good horse and pony show with lots of clowns. Acrobatics and ropewalking along with the trick horse riding made it a very enjoyable event. Their next stop was in Weston the next day, so after the afternoon show here, they broke down their tents, loaded the wagons, and disappeared in the night, leaving only a small trace that they were there.

I did not mention this, but a major accomplishment occurred over a week ago for the citizens of Kansas Territory in the Free-State Movement. There was scribed into the Leavenworth Constitution that African Americans can claim citizenship in the state and that slavery will be forbidden.

The conflict that occurred with Marshall John Little last month and James Montgomery has brought more retaliation. James Montgomery and his forces attacked a town called West Point on the border in Missouri. It was said that this was the headquarters for the Missouri Ruffians and that Charles Hamilton was there after Montgomery attacked Hamilton's home and chased him out of the territory into Missouri.

Of course Charles Hamilton wanted revenge for his attack, so he enlisted around twenty-five men and went into Kansas Territory to a town called Trading Post, located in the Marais des Cygnes River Valley. Hamilton and his men rode from businesses and farms in the area, kidnapping a total of eleven anti-slavery activists that Hamilton was aware of. The total would have been twelve prisoners, but one man escaped his kidnappers by firing back on them and fortifying himself in his blacksmith shop, and in the end, the blacksmith was only wounded by the Ruffians.

The eleven prisoners were taken into a ravine and lined up along the bank making a single line. Hamilton ordered his men to fire at the abolitionists. Five souls were taken that day, five were injured, while one man remained alive with no wounds falling under the bodies of his comrades who were murdered by Hamilton. The bodies were found by the wife of one of the men taken. She was able to follow their trail and locate the massacre after the bushwhackers departed the area.

Changing the subject, gold has been found in the Rocky Mountains in the far west of Kansas Territory. D. R. Anthony in his newspaper, *The Leavenworth Conservative*, mentioned that twenty men from our city have departed to the area called Pike's Peak to strike it rich. Well, good luck to them I say.

    June 8, 1858   Esplanade
    Tuesday Night   Leavenworth City, Kansas Territory

Another traveling circus came to town on May 31st called Spaulding and Rogers Railroad Circus. This group of entertainers traveled across Missouri on the Hannibal Saint Joseph line and set up their tent in Platte City on the 30th and will be performing in Weston on June 1st. After arriving in Saint Joseph, all the gear was loaded into wagons and they are traveling to where they have never performed. I recall seeing Spaulding and Rogers before in Hannibal, but then they were called Spaulding and Rogers Floating Circus Palace.

In Hannibal, Missouri, during the year 1853, one of the largest ships I have ever seen docked at the pier in Hannibal. Two hundred feet in length and thirty feet across with a height of a two-story building, with seating capacity of over two thousand people on board the vessel inside a grand auditorium. A forty-two feet wide circus ring is the center of the ship where they put on a variety of acts that entertains the guests for two to three hours, all for fifty cents. A towboat provided heat and held a menagerie for the Floating Palace and a steamboat was the means of moving the large vessel up and down the rivers. On board as you walk toward the theater, there is the opportunity to witness over one hundred thousand curiosities displayed on the main floor under the seating. Some are stuffed exotic animals from around the world or you can see wax figures of important people. There are also sideshows where you will see an 'Invisible Lady Act,' or won't you?

The circus wagons chose to cross the Missouri River at the Leavenworth Ferry and make a grand entrance into town. When all the wagons had crossed the river, they formed a single line and a parade started from the levee to the northland where Levi North's circus set up last week. A twelve-piece brass band walked in front of the wagons but the music was being played out of a calliope that I am sure you could hear from miles away.

Spaulding and Rogers are claiming to be the largest traveling show in the world with an equestrian act of over forty horses, tightrope act, acrobatics, clowns, comedians, singers, actors, dogs, and monkeys. The circus was amazing and should be shared by all ages.

Back to the reality of life in Kansas Territory, I must sadly convey this tale I have heard of evilness on the Missouri and Kansas borders. This tale begins on Friday night, June 4th, when a group of free-state men took the Rialto Ferry to Weston for a night of debauchery and mayhem. After hours of women and drinking, the men, who shall be nameless, became angry with some of the locals about their words in an establishment downtown and were kicked out to the street by the owner of the bar.

Now angrier and drunker, the Leavenworthians set fire to some still existing wooden buildings on Main Street. The fire was slow spreading, so only did minor damage to a few buildings and the town was better prepared for fires this time than the last. I am not much of a conspiracy person but the following night in Leavenworth City, disaster struck.

On Saturday night June 4th, 1858, a fire of unknown origins was started in the area of the dressing rooms of the new theater in the Market House on the southeast corner of Third and Delaware. Some say that it was started in the Marshall's Office and ex-Marshall Sam Jones was reported seen leaving the building shortly before the fire. Unfortunately, the witnesses were drunker than skunks and their testimony was not considered. The fire overtook the entire structure, consuming the bowling alley and billiard's room in the basement and then continued eastward on Delaware Street to Second Street.

Like the night Weston burned, the sky was a brilliant reddish orange in the early hours of the morning, and after recollecting visions of that night fire. Being awakened up to the commotion and havoc, I raced down to Delaware Street to try to help the fire brigade as they continued to battle the devastation of downtown Leavenworth City. We fought the fire with whatever water we could retrieve as quick as we could if it was not for the stone and mortar buildings that slowed the fire down to a controllable flame and the sudden rain storm that put the fires out by sunrise.

A total of thirty-five buildings were lost to the fire that night with what they are saying will cost over two hundred and fifty thousand dollars to replace the loss of the city. Doctor Park's Drugstore, J. B. Davis Furniture Store, Conway's Boarding House, Beecher's Shoe Store, Weaver and Seaman's Store of Dry Goods, the grand opening of The Grazier Brother's Ice Cream Parlor and Confectionary was held that night, and of course all the business in the city market building plus many more that were here since that first day in October of 1854.

There is a benefit for the fire victims to be held at the Public Hall at an upcoming date that I do not recall at this time, but I will remember and scribe the date. Over two square blocks of downtown Leavenworth City have been destroyed by fire.

In other fiery news, James Montgomery tried to retaliate for the Marais Des Cygnes Massacre by riding into Fort Scott with his troops and attempt to burn down the Western Hotel.

This hotel is noted for being the headquarters for the pro-slavery supporters in southeast Kansas Territory. Montgomery's forces who were fortified made it within a few hundred feet of the hotel but were driven back by the pro-slavery forces fortified in the two-story hotel.

Word has traveled down the road from Lawrence that Jim Lane was involved with the shooting of Gaius Jenkins. Apparently, Mister Lane was at his home when Mister Jenkins, armed with a revolver drawn, approached the front door of the Lane family home with a few other men because the two men have been having a land dispute over the property line between their farms. Mister Lane came onto his porch with a shotgun and then heated words were exchanged by Gaius Jenkins and Jim Lane. With anger in his eyes, Gaius

Jenkins shot his revolver, hitting Jim Lane in the knee, falling down onto the porch, and at the same time Jim Lane lifted the barrel of the gun and shot Gaius Jenkins right off his horse. The men picked up Gaius and put him on his horse, riding away as fast as they could.

A mob was formed to lynch Jim Lane, but the vigilantes were stopped by and talked out the hanging by the new Sherriff, Samuel Walker, when Sherriff Walker noticed the ex-Sherriff Sam Jones in the crowd.

June 6, 1858   Esplanade
Saturday Night   Leavenworth City, Kansas Territory

The heart of Leavenworth City's business district downtown is still in chaos trying to repair the fire-damaged buildings through times of rains, lightning, and thunderstorms that make you want to go underground. Money was raised at a benefit to assist with the rebuilding and the choice was made to rebuild with brick and mortar using only the wood for floors, interior walls, and covered sidewalks.

The main news I have tonight is that the after the Rebellion of Brigham Young, the Governor of the Utah Territory was replaced by a non-Mormon, Alfred Cumming. For over one year, Brigham Young fought the United States Government about religious freedom and then tried to secede from the United States and start his own country. Even after all the blood spilled by the war in Utah, a pardon was offered to Brigham Young and his followers, stating that if they played nice, they could go free.

Locally, our Governor Denver went down to Fort Scott to see what all the troubles were going on down there with and if a resolution could be penned. A meeting was held at the Western Hotel where both parties only agreed to try to be less aggressive and there was no official handshake to end the meeting between James Montgomery and Marshall John Little.

Bringing the news even closer back to town, Mark Delahay is on top of the world with his cousin-in-law Abraham Lincoln was selected as a candidate against Stephen Douglas in the race for a senator's seat in the State of Illinois. Mark and a few others from Leavenworth went to Illinois to hear a debate between the two men in Springfield at a Republican Convention.

Mark Delahay reported back to his paper saying basically that although Mister Lincoln spoke about our nation as a whole, his words were felt in the hearts of the Kansan's that were present in the crowd. Slavery was not a needed institution in society today and will not be tolerated anymore. If the citizens of the United States do not come to the realization of that fact, then there will be more unnecessary violence that will occur though the United States Government was the basic platform Lincoln was standing on.

Sad news from the parents in Hannibal is that our family friend Henry Clemens was injured in an explosion on the steamboat Pennsylvania floating on the Mississippi River just south of Memphis, Tennessee. The boiler exploded, killing over two hundred and fifty souls on board. The survivors were picked up by other steamships that were passing by soon after, The Imperial, The Diana, and the A. T. Lucy.

Henry was transported back down to New Orleans where his brother Samuel was taking his leave off the ship that he started at the last docking of the Pennsylvania a few days before the explosion. The boy's parents told my parents that Samuel met Harry at the dock and was taking care of him the best he could.

    July 4, 1858   Esplanade
    Sunday Night   Leavenworth City, Kansas Territory

We had a lovely day today celebrating the Independence of our nation. It started with the sunrise service at Immaculate Conception with Bishop Miege and with the day being fresh and young, I took the family on a tour of the ever-growing Leavenworth City. After breakfast, we sat out on our adventure. I harnessed Running Water with another horse I borrowed from the stables to a wagon and loaded up the family. Being near the Gardens at Broadway and Olive, we enjoyed the yard games provided by the owners, Mister and Misses Stahl. We played for a few hours and enjoyed the brass band that was set up in a gazebo. Lawn bowling was the children's favorite while I enjoyed throwing horseshoes and drinking the Green River. A large barbeque was set up and two beeves were turned over a large fiery pit similar to the first Independence Day celebration I encountered in Kansas Territory at the home of my departed friend Isaac Cody in Salt Creek Valley.

After the Gardens, we went south on the Military Road looking at all the houses and farms in the county and then took a trail east that led us to another trail that took us up north to Leavenworth City where the family had a nice dinner and a fireworks display that we watched from the top of the tower of the house. The fireworks can be seen in the skies above Weston, Platte City, Farley, and even Delaware City along with the displays being set off all over Leavenworth City.

A mention of an event that occurred earlier this week in Leavenworth City is that our Governor James Denver departed Kansas Territory for business in Washington, our nation's capital. A small party was given for the governor and then he boarded the New Lucy and went down the Missouri River toward Saint Louis, Missouri. Our city has organized a Board of Education and have nominated a man called George Wetherell to be the first public school teacher, even though we all know that the Reverend J. B. McAfee was the first teacher with the first school in Leavenworth County.

        July 22, 1858   Esplanade
        Thursday Night   Leavenworth City, Kansas Territory

The summer here has been very wet, muddy, and humid; in easier words, very agonizing. The nightly rains and the high temperatures are not a good combination, but the scenery here is quite remarkable all the seasons.

Sherriff Roberts of Fort Scott reports that he had retrieved all of the horses that were stolen by the Reverend John E. Stewart, who is also known as Captain Plum in the area because of the purple partridge feather that flies high on the top of his hat. This is interesting because the Reverend stole the horses because he believed that the horses were in favor of pro-slavery and did not want to be owned by southern supporters anymore. It was the horses' choice to follow him. The Reverend Stewart was not in custody long because a congregation member James Montgomery liberated him out of confinement with no shots fired during the encounter.

With all the rains, the river and creeks are swelling over the banks in some areas. Stranger Creek in west Leavenworth County is already flooded over into the fields.

        July 25, 1858   Esplanade
        Sunday Night   Leavenworth City, Kansas Territory

Leavenworth City was devastated by nature's fury in the flooding of the town from the river and all the creeks that are running through town last night and the flood waters are still rising tonight. A heavy rainstorm came down from the heavens on Saturday night with the lightning and thunder to accompany the nightmare. Threemile Creek was already at the height staying in the brim off the banks but, with this new rain the lower sections of downtown and areas in low lying creek land are now under water.

With the rising water at the Government Crossing and Threemile Creek at the cross streets of Cherokee and Shawnee, there is an area called Cincinnati Town because the houses in that area are prefab houses sent up in packages from Cincinnati, Ohio. Well, the water was so swift Saturday night that it took four houses off of their foundations.

Only the lightning strikes were the rescuers only way to see the family floating down Threemile Creek in their Cincinnati house. The cries of panic were heard from the bedridden woman and children who were looking after their mother. A great effort was made by some very brave men to save the family. I wish I knew their names for my writings.

This morning I arose in the sunrise to gaze across what once were fields of tobacco, corn, and to where the little village of East Leavenworth, Missouri was now under water on the eastern side of the Missouri River to the hills that are about a mile distant to the east. People's cellars, basements, and low-lying houses are now submerged in water. The last of the store that was destroyed by the fire downtown are not quite replaced at this point and will be further delayed with this new city catastrophe.

View of Leavenworth City, Kansas Territory 1858

Chapter Sixteen
Saloons, Breweries, and Brothels

August 8, 1858   Esplanade
Sunday Night   Leavenworth City, Kansas Territory

On Monday earlier this week, the voters of Kansas Territory put an end to the Lecompton Constitution, and the rider added on to the constitution called, the English Bill. Rejecting the Lecompton Constitution for the third time, a new constitution will be drawn and approved by the Kansas Legislature, and then it will have to be passed by both houses in Washington, and then receive the president's signature.

    When the bill passes through all those hoops, Kansas Territory will be granted statehood. With the reality of two stubborn parties who each believe in their way of life, there is still a long road ahead for all in Kansas Territory. The polls were under tight security provided by Governor James Denver. No conflicts were reported on voting day with a turnout to the polls of over ten thousand Kansas citizens.

August 25, 1858   Esplanade
Monday Night   Leavenworth City, Kansas Territory

For years, a man named Cyrus Westfield had the idea to take a cable for telegraphic communications and make a connection between the United States and England, laying it on the bottom of the Atlantic Ocean. Sometimes the depth of the ocean was over two miles with a span of over two thousand miles. In the beginning of this month, Mister Westfield's idea became reality when on August 16th, President James Buchanan had a brief conversation with Queen Victoria from across the ocean.

    This was the fifth attempt to give communication between the countries and a fleet of four ships was necessary to complete the task. The Niagara and The Gorgon from the United States, and from England the ships were The

Valorous and The Agamemnon, who worked together and completed the connection.

As I noted previously, the rains in Kansas Territory have been quite heavy and torrential downpours have caused more flooding in other areas of the region. Flooding on the Kansas River has taken out major crossings and bridges going over streams and creeks have been washed away in the high waters. In Weston, the Missouri River has risen and flooded its ports, but the worst news is that when the water receded from the town, it actually moved further west by one hundred yards creating a new channel in the river.

The flooding in Kansas Territory has even went as far inland as Fort Riley where the crossing at Smokey hills was washed out and other bridges along the Military Trails were washed away from the fast high waters. Saint Louis even experienced high waters in their levee, going in as far as the business district, but in Beardstown, Illinois, the entire town went under waters of the Mississippi River on an early Sunday morning. There was an island made at the highest point of the town where a few buildings were saved. In Leavenworth, the lower section of downtown along Threemile Creek was under water for a spell and our city officials are putting their heads together to come up with a solution.

Senator Steven Douglas from Illinois is running against the cousin-in-law of Mark Delahay for the Republican seat of senator. Abraham Lincoln and the current senator have set up seven debates across Illinois in the next three months. In the first debate, Mister Lincoln was not mentally prepared for the lifelong politician, Senator Douglas's tactics.

Abraham Lincoln won some votes on his views on slavery and spoke of all men being created equally, but the southern sympathizers backed Senator Douglas, and Mister Lincoln lost the first debate according to the people.

    September 7, 1858   Esplanade
    Tuesday Night   Leavenworth City, Kansas Territory

It was with great enthusiasm that the Levi North Circus came back into town on their tour of Kansas Territory. On Monday, August 30th, they brought their wagons back to town and had another fantastic show even though the field was a mud pit by the end of the show.

The ignorance of my fellow men has baffled me to laughter at times but in reality, what the actions of these men in this territory do make my heart break. Man's inhumanity to each other because of what makes a person different to someone else is exactly what the other person sees as well. Respect the opinions of your fellow man, no matter what color, creed, or any genetic difference, and let's learn from each other to make this country a better place in peace.

Why I am ranting is the treatment of the American Indians with the treaty breakage and now a conflict in the Washington Territory at Spokane Plains.

By order of the United States, Colonel George Wright took six hundred troops into the Washington Territory area for the sole purpose of Colonel Wright to cause extreme harm to the natives. Hostile Indians were causing havoc in the area and Colonel Wright was ordered to settle matters at any extreme. On the campaign of Colonel Wright, he destroyed every Indian village that was in their view. This action of the army rallied up the tribes in the Spokane Plains area, and at Four Lakes the Indians went up against Colonel Wright and his forces. Twenty Indians were reported as causalities as the Indians fought the modern-day armed soldiers who were armed with new long rifles and the cannons of the United States against the bows and arrows of the Indians. Some Indians did also battle with musket loaders and knives against the army if they could get that close. It was reported that there were close to six hundred Indians who battled that day in Spokane Plains from all the tribes joining forces.

At a meeting of surrender between the two armies, the two Indian chiefs, Polatkin and Palouse, arrived with their escorts of nine warriors. Colonel Wright recognized one of the escorts as a suspect of being participant in the murder of a miner. At that moment, the young Indian warrior was seized and bounded. He was then taken to the gallows without any trial and swung from the noose as soon as it was tied around his neck.

My other news of bewilderment is of an event that took place out east in the Richmond, Virginia area. If you recall, I mentioned Reverend Frederick Star in Weston for teaching his slaves to read and write, but the news from Virginia is that there was the arrests of ninety Negros for learning. No word on who was teaching or where that person could be found.

Back to Kansas Territory, news is that another governor has resigned from running this hostile state. James Denver will take over the position until October. Mark Delahay keeps us informed of his wife's cousin, Abraham Lincoln, and his debates against Senator Douglas. A second debate was held on August 27th in Freeport, Illinois. The town of five thousand tripled that day when the men clashed words and shared their ideas and beliefs. The main topic of this debate was Popular Sovereignty in Kansas Territory and across the nation.

September 24, 1858   Esplanade
Friday Night   Leavenworth City, Kansas Territory

The city has announced that they have a plan for the flooding issues in downtown. The streets will be leveled and macadamized along with a quarter mile of the levee receiving the same process, starting at Threemile Creek and heading north. Mark Delahay reports that he is traveling to Illinois to hear the debates himself and report back to his paper. Since last entry, two more debates have taken place, the first to mention on September 15th at the Union County Fairgrounds in the town of Jonesboro, Illinois. Being a border state, the southern half of the state lean more to sympathize with the south and likewise with the northern part of Illinois. In Jonesboro, Mark Delahay reports that there were actual fisticuffs amongst family members. Brothers, who defend each other from harm, are fighting their other brothers about national issues.

The fourth debate between Abraham Lincoln and Senator Steven Douglas took place in Charleston, Illinois, at the Cole County Fairgrounds on September 18th. In this debate, Mister Lincoln had seemed to have found his tongue and was swaying the crowd to his beliefs. Using his boyish charm and jokes, his support grew not only in Illinois but all over the nation. Mister Delahay also stated that he was able to spend time with the wife's relatives on this visit to his wife's hometown. Mister Lincoln also ran a law office from Charleston.

      October 17, 1858   Esplanade
      Sunday Night   Leavenworth City, Kansas Territory

Not much in the news to offer except for a few mentions. First thing is that the city has started leveling the streets of downtown. The stores that were on the first floor are now the basement of the establishment in some areas. Walkways will be provided under the sidewalks to the stores, and tunnels will be made to extend the shopping in the lower areas. Over twenty foot of bluff was removed from the end of Delaware at the levee, removing the public well from that bluff.

The shenanigans of Abraham Lincoln and Senator Douglas are keeping the nation entertained. At the debate at Knox College on October 7th in Galesburg, Illinois, there was an estimated crowd of over twenty-five thousand people there to hear the men discuss the issues of Illinois.

The weather was uncooperative and the stage had to be moved because of tornado advisory weather. To get to the new stage, the men had to climb out a second-story window and down a ladder to the stage. On the 13th, they met again with better weather in Quincy, Illinois, in an area called Washington Square. Quincy is across the Mississippi River from Hannibal. so my wife's family was able to attend and report the speech to me.

Marisol's sister expressed how aggressive Mister Lincoln was toward Senator Douglas, who, even though the weather was fine, seemed to be under it for some unknown reason. Abraham Lincoln was better prepared and to my family's accord, they believe Mister Lincoln won this round.

On October 15, 1858, the last debate occurred between the two delegates. Morals, slavery, equality, and certain freedoms that should be granted by the government were the topics of this debate. Mister Lincoln looked road-worn by the end of the debate, and Senator Douglas was drunk as a skunk and did not make any sense through most of the talks.

October 31, 1858　　　　Esplanade
Sunday Night　　　　　Leavenworth City, Kansas Territory

The citizens of Platte County have decided to bring some of the east traditions to our neck of the woods and have planned the first county fair in Platte County. After years of all work and no play, an announcement was made earlier this month. Land was allocated for the event about a mile west of Platte City on the route to Weston. The land was cleared from any brush and a show ring was laid out with a rope barricade around the perimeter. Bleachers were built to hold the crowd they hoped would attend.

The event took place on October 23rd through the 25th, and folks from all over the region came to see the finest foods and critters that Platte City had to offer. The highlight of the show did not occur in the ring or stables but in the bleachers when the bleachers collapsed with Professor Todd's Female Academy that consisted of one hundred and fifty girls as they were sitting in the bleachers at the time of collapse. The entire crowd rushed to the rescue of the young women and not a single young lady was injured in the horrific accident.

November 20, 1858　　　Esplanade
Saturday Night　　　　　Leavenworth City, Kansas Territory

The news is flowing as fast as the frozen Missouri River and the thermometer has been below freezing for a few days now. The downtown renovation has shut down for the winter and the fire victims who decided to rebuild have done so, while the others sold out and new owners have improved the lot.

Mark Delahay is disappointed as his cousin-in-law did not win the senate seat in Illinois, but Abraham Lincoln has gained national attention and is being considered for a presidential nominee.

December 20, 1858   Esplanade
Monday Night   Leavenworth City, Kansas Territory

I am very proud to announce our newest governor appointed by President James Buchanan as Samuel Medary. This will be our sixth territorial governor in the four years and a half of being a territory. Hopefully, Governor Medary will last more than a year in office, but this office has brought down the strongest of wills.

Colonel James Montgomery, on the sixteenth of this month, took his troops into Fort Scott to retrieve one of the members of the Montgomery Militia named Benjamin Rice, who was being held for a murder charge at the Western Hotel. The releasing of the prisoner went off with no altercation but as the Jayhawkers were leaving, the departing troop fired their weapons into the Western Hotel and took the life of Sherriff John Little. No pursuit followed that encounter from Fort Scott being outnumbered and without leadership from the pro-slavery supporters.

January 4, 1859   Esplanade
Tuesday Evening   Leavenworth City, Kansas Territory

The Abolitionist John Brown two weeks ago liberated eleven slaves in Vernon County, Missouri, from Harvey Hicklan. Brown went to this location to assist a freed slave given the name of Daniel. Before getting the assistance of John Brown, Daniel attempted to plead with Master Hicklan to let Daniel's family free to save them from the impending sales at the auction block that they were headed too.

With twenty heavily armed Jayhawkers, John Brown led his army to the place of the auction and liberated the family of Daniel. David Cruise, a Missouri slave owner that was at the auction, was killed by one of the men freeing the slaves. Aaron D. Stephens claimed that it was self-defense, as Cruise was about to shoot Stephens. Along with the family of Daniel, the Brown Party liberated wagons, horses, food, oxen, cash, and jewelry from the audience members at the auction house.

From the last report of John Brown's whereabouts, he was headed for Jim Lane's Trail, making back into Kansas Territory successfully after the raid. It is also reported that a baby was born on the trail shortly after the liberation was completed in Kansas Territory. A Christmas miracle happened when a boy was born, and in honor of their savior who saved the family, the child was christened John Brown.

January 30, 1859   Esplanade
Sunday Night   Leavenworth City, Kansas Territory

    This entry I will start from what I witnessed off my front porch at the Planter's Hotel. In employment at the Planter's Hotel, there is a barber who goes by the name Charlie Fisher. It was claimed that Charlie was an escaped slave from Kentucky from a man staying at the hotel who recognized the fugitive. This man notified the supposed owner of Mister Fisher in Kentucky who made the trip from there to Leavenworth City to reclaim his property.

    Charlie was arrested under the Fugitive Slave Act with the allegations brought on by the Kentuckian, but being part of the Leavenworth City community for so long, the residents valued his work and personality, and his arrest did not sit well with the citizens. The protection of Charlie was in question by both free-state men and southern sympathizers. With the Planter's Hotel being a neutral ground, it was decided that Charlie would be kept in a room on the fourth floor. Guards from both parties were stationed outside and inside Charlie's room.

    In the early morning hours of either the thirteenth or fourteenth, it doesn't really matter, a group of twelve abolitionists stormed the Planter's Hotel and seized the room of Charlie Fisher. Claiming him not to be the man from Kentucky that they say he is, Charlie refused to leave with the Jayhawkers so the men fortified the hotel room as the Missouri Ruffians started to organize and try to recapture Charlie Fisher. The southern supporters gathered in front of the hotel and with torches in hand threatened to burn down the building. The free-state men pulled Old Kickapoo out of hiding and confronted the Ruffians on the Esplanade and Shawnee Streets to defend the hotel and the city from another fire.

    It was decided for the safety of Charlie Fisher that he would leave the building and show up at his trial the next day. A diversion was created and Charlie left his room, and secretly taken down to the stables. Some reports say that he escaped Leavenworth City to Lawrence dressed as a woman. Marisol did have the dress returned to her later that week and Charlie did show up for his trial on time.

    The trial of Charlie Fisher was one-sided due to the southern sympathizers who control the city commissioners, and the outcome of the trial did not look good for Charlie Fisher. The Marshall Jas. McDowell was guarding Charlie in the front of the courtroom when a ruckus broke out in the back of the room. The Marshall ran to the back to stop the fight and Charlie was rushed out a side door and down the outside steps of the furniture store to a horse waiting for him to ride out of town and never return.

John Brown is still on the run with the fugitive slaves from Vernon County. Last report of his whereabouts was northeast of Grasshopper Falls at a stage stop called Fuller's Station. Aaron Stephens, who was on patrol, came across a Federal Army troop of about eight men and attacked the patrol. Mister Stephens captured one of the soldiers while the other seven men retreated.

Another group that liberated some slaves from Missouri met a different fate when they were captured by Missouri Ruffians outside of Lawrence. Doctor John Doy and his son Charles freed thirteen slaves from Missouri and them themselves were tied up, captured, and taken back to Platte City, Missouri, where the trial will be held along with the liberated slaves.

    February 4, 1859   Esplanade
    Friday Night   Leavenworth City, Kansas Territory

John Brown has escaped capture once again on his quest to deliver the fugitive slaves to the promise land of freedom in the north. A short while ago in the early morning sunrise with fog rolling across the lowlands of Spring Creek, the twenty-one-man army of John Brown decided to cross the creek at that time. There were Federal Troops over a hill who heard the men crossing the creek with so much noise, the federal troops believed they were being sieged by a larger army. The army of forty-five federal troops mounted their horses and, in the fog, the only noise the army of John Brown heard was the pounding of spurs on the horses of the retreating Federal Army. A witness who was there called the incident the Battle of the Spurs, with no sound of a shot being fired, only the sound of spurs from the retreating army.

    February 25, 1859   Esplanade
    Friday Night   Leavenworth City, Kansas Territory

Oregon Territory has officially become a state on February 14, 1859. There are now thirty-three states in the United States of America, with more territories hoping to enter the union. It was entered as a free state, and the southern states want the next state entered to be a slave state. Last week, news from Saint Joseph is that a railroad from Hannibal, Missouri, to Saint Joseph was completed in Cream Ridge just north of Chillicothe. The final spike was hammered in after eight years of development and planning.

    March 5, 1859   Esplanade
    Saturday Night   Leavenworth City, Kansas Territory

The first official public school in Leavenworth City was inaugurated on March 1st on the southeast corner of Shawnee and Fifth Streets. It was a former tin shop owned by George Russell. A. D. McCarthy is the appointed headmaster for the school.

The trial of Doctor Doy took place in Weston Missouri on March 4th but was called a mistrial and another date has been set for the trial. Charles Doy, the son of Doctor Doy, was released after a few days in jail.

March 28, 1859	Esplanade
Monday Night	Leavenworth City, Kansas Territory

News has trickled down from the north that John Brown has successfully arrived in Northern Iowa on the 9th of March with all the fugitives of Daniel's family now free and surviving through a cold and bitter winter in Nebraska and Kansas Territories. Almost three months on the trail hiding out from bounty hunters with a price tag on John Brown's head from the governor of Missouri, Mister Brown decided to visit relatives in Virginia and let the hostilities settle in Kansas Territory.

The trial of John Doy has another obstacle in its path and is being moved from Weston to Saint Joseph where it is believed that there will be a fairer trial in Saint Joseph rather than in Weston. The new trial is set for latter part of July.

Chapter Seventeen
The People of Kansas

April 14, 1859　　　　Esplanade
Thursday Night　　　Leavenworth City, Kansas Territory

We celebrated another Thanksgiving in our lovely new house last night. Marisol fixed a turkey dinner with all the fixings of a seven-course meal that will last us more than likely a week to finish the leftovers. A few neighbors came by to celebrate with us and we reminisced about the years in Leavenworth City.

The population is now well over ten thousand souls living in the city limits. A business directory was created for Leavenworth City this year with every store and person from A to Z. Leavenworth City is now the largest city from Saint Louis to San Francisco.

More cities have been established all over the Kansas Territory, but the majority of the folks are staying in the hills rather than go to the wide-open plains where the buffalo roam. Here in Leavenworth, Shawnee, Douglas and Atchison Counties is a list from the top of my head, of towns that are established in these counties. Alexandria, Fairmont, High Prairie Township, Eastin, Eudora, Lawrence, Millwood, Monrovia, Mormon Groove, Mount Pleasant, Delaware City, Weimar, Arrington, Kennekuk, Port Williams, Sumner, Oak Mills, and Kickapoo City are just some of the towns that I have traveled through in my time here in Kansas Territory, not including the counties to the west of the three counties I have mentioned. From Quindaro to Fort Riley, along the Kaw River, are some cities I did not mention but are on the list as there will be many more to come and some were gone before I could ever visit them.

The business directory I mentioned earlier is called the Barclay's Business Directory, Leavenworth, and I am amazed at the amount of diversity this city provides in all commodities and with the address of the store, makes it very convenient. My lawyer and friend H. Miles Moore has his office on Delaware between Second and Third Streets, and he is also a neighbor of mine on the Esplanade near Miami. Another neighbor and my insurance Agent is D. R. Anthony and his office is on Main Street between Delaware and Shawnee Streets. I liked what Davis had to offer as far as variety in furniture, but Abernathy has a quality that with children can last a while. Mister Davis switched over to the funeral business when he came upon the notion that while making the coffins, he found out he could bury them as well a few years back. There is a soda factory, drug stores, carriage makers, confectionaries, bakeries, stove makers, broom makers, and many more items are made here in Leavenworth City. Barclay's Business Directory even was printed in different languages.

There are six different newspapers being printed now in town. *The Leavenworth Journal* is edited by Hutchison and Campbell, George W. McLane prints *The Ledger*, and Champion Vaughn and J.K. Barlett publish *The Times*. The other papers are a German edition is printed by Fritz Braunhold and in the same office on Cherokee Street, Mister Frank Barclay prints the news in the French language. All the offices for the newspapers can be found on Delaware between Main and Third Streets. I sell my stories to all the papers in town and still work for the Hannibal newspaper.

Last year, the Jewish population of Leavenworth with Jonas Wolman, Simon Abeles, and Joseph Ringolsky as the main contributors created the organization called the Society of the Sons of Truth. There was a benefit for the clearing for a cemetery and a mausoleum for the Jewish members in our community. Jonas Wolman donated thirty-six acres of land about a mile out of town at the northwest end. Mount Zion will be the name of the Jewish Cemetery.

April 28, 1859   Esplanade
Thursday Night   Leavenworth City, Kansas Territory

Easter Sunday was on the last Sabbath, and Bishop Miege said a lovely service to a full room and with the new addition of the Sisters of Charity, who arrived in Leavenworth City last November 11th, starting their mission from Tennessee. Sister Xavier Ross and her fellow sisters now provide what they can for the sick and the poor while trying to educate young women of Leavenworth City.

This is such a diverse town that I believe every religion has a place of worship. If a congregation does not have a place to meet, the city can provide one with the Public Hall. The Episcopal Church started construction last year on the southeast corner of Fifth and Chestnut, but due to the land not being donated and costs more than they expected, so a new location was picked at Seventh and Seneca to be called Saint Paul's. The German Lutherans have their mass held at the Seventh and Miami, while the English Lutherans conduct their services on the northeast corner of Seventh and Spruce.

Planter's Hotel

The First Congregational Church built their church on the northwest corner of Fifth and Delaware, while the Jewish Synagogue is on the corner of Sixth and Osage Streets. The Baptists have their place of worship on the southwest corner of Sixth and Seneca. If I have failed to mention a particular religion, I am sorry, but that is all I know that have about the different churches, and as mentioned before if a congregation does not have a place to worship, the Public Hall is at their means.

After our Easter service, this time I took the family on a carriage ride to the Gardens of the Joseph Kuntz Brewery, spending most of the morning and afternoon there. Mister Kuntz' brewery is located on the south side of Threemile Creek with access to that side of the creek at the Fifth Street Bridge. The big stone house on top of the hill is the family home, but it is also used as malt house storage, and the beer is stored in the caves between Threemile Creek and his house through a series of tunnels. His tunnels are used for the same purpose as my tunnel at times from what I hear through the wind. The natural springs that run underground provide fresh water for brewing and keeps the caves very cool to keep the beverages.

A beautiful groove of trees line the side of the hill with benches placed under some of them to enjoy the grounds. Flowers and bushes are blooming in the spring and the flowering cotton and dogwoods are quite amazing in the spring. In the middle of a meadow, a bandstand was built to house the musicians that play daily to entertain the guests as they relax in town. Stahl's Beer Gardens located around Second and Cheyenne is a much more promiscuous place that is not suited for children at any time of day. Always a party, twenty-four hours a day. It is the soldiers', trail workers', and travelers' last stop before heading west and the first place they want to come to when they arrive in town as well.

Another brewery is called Fritzlen and Mundee, who built their shop on the South Esplanade into the side of the hill to the river. They built a two-story stone structure and dug a vault to store their product further into the bluff. A boiler house was built in another building for cooking their product at all times of the day.

| May 10, 1859 | Esplanade |
| Thursday Night | Leavenworth City, Kansas Territory |

The spring rains have come with a vengeance this year, raining every day for the past week.

Newspaper The Daily Times July 4, 1859 Leavenworth, Kansas

The newly leveled off downtown with its new streets are easy to travel on with no holes or wagon wheel tracks embedded in the streets at this time.

Sidewalks that are now street level are covered walkways along the storefronts, and easy access has been provided to the lower levels of the city by stairwells at each corner. They have minimal water flowing into the tunnel entrances.

A mentor of mine, Horace Greeley, the editor of the *New York Tribune* and a founder of the Republican Party, has expressed interest in seeing what the west is really like firsthand other than just reading stories about how untamed it really is. Although he is not a young man at this present date, he is going west to California through Kansas Territory.

    May 26, 1859   Esplanade
    Thursday Night   Leavenworth City, Kansas Territory

The last two weeks have been an adventure for me, or should I say my misadventures with Horace Greeley. My paper assigned me to follow Mister Greeley around northeastern Kansas Territory. The travels west of Horace Greeley started on a train ride across the Northern United States. On Monday morning, May 9th, he departed from New York City to the fair city of Quincy, Illinois. From Quincy, he boarded a steamship and disembarked at Hannibal where he was able to ride the newest railroad, The Hannibal, to Saint Joseph. At the end of the line in Saint Joseph, Mister Greeley boarded a ferry steamship named Platte Valley and floated down the Missouri River into Atchison, Kansas Territory, where I met up with the gentleman at the Massasoit House on May 15th.

At Horace Greeley's arrival in Atchison, he was met by the Mayor General S. C. Pomeroy. Atchison, like Leavenworth City, is becoming more free-state thinking, although it is still strongly a pro-slavery town. The small parade of happy citizens walked down the streets of Atchison to the Massasoit House where Mister Greeley was able to rest the remainder of the evening and hear stories of Kansas Territory from the citizens of Atchison.

The rains continued again Sunday night into Monday Morning. The sounds of the storm with the lightning made it quite a noisy night. Before sunrise the storm had ended and Mister Greeley wanted to get a start on our eighty-mile adventure, so Mayor Pomeroy, the carriage driver, and an unidentified man rode with Mister Greeley to be at a convention in Osawatomie. I and another reporter rode our horses behind the two-team carriage.

The trail with all the rain was a muddy road, slowing down the speed of the journey, and at the fords for crossing streams or creeks, it was near impossible or even impossible at most crossings with the strong currents of the water. At one point along the trail we were traveling on, we came to a crossing of the California Trail and there was a wagon train heading west with their wagons, so fully loaded even an eight-oxen team pulling the wagons were moving at a snail's pace. With the weight of the wagon, the wheels dug deeper into the earth making the struggling oxen struggle harder to pull the wagons.

By eleven o'clock in the morning, Horace Greeley was becoming aggravated with the roads and the weather as the carriage reached Leavenworth City. Hearing that Stranger Creek was out of its banks and stage coaches were not able to cross the trails going south, we were able to board passage on the steamship D. A. January at three o'clock that afternoon with the hopes of still making it to Osawatomie by nightfall. As luck would have it, our voyage ended in Wyndot where the vessel had to stop for the evening.

With our destination still sixty miles away, we started our morning at six o'clock. We found the Santa Fe Trail and headed south crossing the Kansas River on a wooden toll bridge that was still under construction. The bridge spans over twelve hundred feet across the river from bank to bank. The carriage had a better day of travel passing through Shawnee, making a stop at McAffrie's Stage Stop in Olathe, Spring Hill, and to Stanton where we had to bed for the night not being able to cross the Marais des Cygnes River along with about thirty other men, who were also going to Osawatomie for the convention.

The next morning on the day of the convention, the wagon train that we joined to Osawatomie was stopped in our tracks for a spell when the rope of the ferry boat broke and was lost in the current of the Marais des Cygnes River. With true determination, the men on the mission found another rope and strung it across the river saving the day. A few hours later in the morning around nine o'clock, we reached the convention.

Over one thousand men were present for that convention in Osawatomie that day when Horace Greeley gave his speech that would change a political party in Kansas Territory. The mud-stained faces looked and listened to Mister Greeley speak for over an hour that day to the free-state men and at the end of the convention, there was the birth of the Republican Party in Kansas Territory.

On May 19th, we departed Osawatomie for Lawrence, still having to cross the Marais des Cygnes River at a place named Bundy's Ferry and then travel through Prairie City near Palmyra, and then staying in Baldwin for the night. With fifteen miles to Lawrence, we had a short journey that morning and were greeted with honors by the townspeople, who gave us a tour of Mount Oread where Jim Lane and Charles Robinson lived and defended the city. That afternoon, Horace Greeley spoke to a large crowd at the Eldridge House.

The next day, Mister Greeley departed Lawrence to Leavenworth on a stage coach where at a ford crossing on Stranger Creek, the passengers had to leave the stage they were riding on and walk across a fallen log to finish the journey on another stage coach waiting for them on the other side of the flooded creek. Mister Greeley stayed in Leavenworth a few days to recoup and talk to our townspeople. On May 24th, Horace Greeley departed Leavenworth City for Topeka by stagecoach and made it safely with no flooded trails.

    July 5, 1859   Esplanade
    Tuesday Night   Leavenworth City, Kansas Territory

We had a lovely Independence Day Celebration yesterday with the family playing outside games in the beautiful summer day. We went to the Gardens today where there was a picnic for the whole town. A baseball game was played by the boys and men, while the ladies sat under the shade trees and were entertained by the sports around them. There were also horseshoes, racing games for the boys, and the girls played house.

Rains came in the afternoon so the games were moved inside and to our house. The boys played a game board game called Traveler Tour through the United States. It is an older game that is not current on the additions that the United Sates have made along the west coast with California and the other western territories. It is a great geography game for the Eastern United States. The girls played a game called The Mansion of Happiness that teaches Christian virtues, morals, and good personal values.

In political news, a fourth attempt to find a constitution to make this territory into a state was held at Wyandotte. This convention was represented by fifty-two delegates who will hopefully write the proper words to end the war in Kansas.

    July 30, 1859   Esplanade
    Saturday Night   Leavenworth City, Kansas Territory

There has been lots of excitement in the region during the last two weeks. The first bit of information involves Doctor John Doy, who has been imprisoned for the stealing and transportation of slaves since January of this year. His second trial was held on July 20th and at the time was found guilty and sentenced to five years in prison.

At the trial. the health of the doctor was noticeably deteriorating with disease and malnutrition that left the good doctor weak and unable to walk without any assistance. This was noticed by a friend, Major James Abbott, who quickly put together a misfit group of men loyal to Doctor Doy to liberate the doctor from the conditions that he is currently under.

On the 23rd of July in Saint Joseph Missouri, the mission took place. Three men of Major Abbott's crew went into the jail with two of the men posed as bounty hunters and the third was a fugitive they were bringing in for the bounty. The three inside overtook the unsuspecting guards and the rest of the team enters the jail. They carried Doctor Doy out and threw him on the back of a waiting horse. The other men mounted their horses and rode off out of town without firing a shot or any wounded. Major Abbott and his nine other men made it safely back to Lawrence. Last word from Lawrence is that Doctor Doy is slowly recovering and will be leaving Kansas for his protection when able to travel.

My other bit of information pertains to the Wyandotte Convention. The convention went on with the Democrats refusing to sign the new written constitution, so they left the gathering but with the Republicans, now as they are called, had a majority vote to pass the new legislation on to the territorial voters, Congress of the United States, and then the President. Charles Robinson was absent, as he had prior commitment in the city of Quindaro, and Jim Lane was in court proceedings over his killing of Gaius Jenkins. The new legislation will be presented in October to the people for voting.

The new constitution is a very radical paper that hopefully will change the way America treats each other. This document gives women the right to vote in school district elections and that women can own their own property without children. The western boundary of Kansas Territory is becoming further east, creating the Colorado Territory. It also clearly states that only white men over the age of twenty-one can vote in elections. The efforts of Clarina Nichols is what gave women these new rights in Kansas Territory.

August 16, 1859   Esplanade
Saturday Night   Leavenworth City, Kansas Territory

Tonight, I am happy to announce two modernizations for Leavenworth City. We now have telegraphic communications running through our great city heading north to Saint Joseph; it is said it will be complete by the end of the year. Yesterday, Mayor S. C. Pomeroy of Atchison sent the first telegraph communication from the furthest western union station ever in the west to the mayor of Saint Louis, Missouri, who answered with a successful response received in Atchison.

My other news in this entry is we now have in Leavenworth City the Leavenworth Gas and Light Company. The gas company has built a pump and started to lay pipes in downtown and to some residential areas.

October 8, 1859   Esplanade
Saturday Night   Leavenworth City, Kansas Territory

There has been a little activity other than the continuously growing city of Leavenworth. Wagons of every color leave the downtown area after filling their wagons with supplies to last a few months for the voyage west. Looking onto the valley sometimes in Salt Creek with all the trails, it looks like a colony of ants traveling across the land. The population has to be close to ten thousand souls in the city limits of Leavenworth. Factories of many products are now operating. satisfying the needs of all in town. This is now the largest town in between Saint Louis., Missouri, and Salt Lake City, Utah. The weather is now unusually dry for this time of year with no rain since springtime. This has been the worst year for the crops of the farmers in the territory since farming was started in the area.

In political news, the United States Senate refused a bill that was presented to them admitting Kansas as a state, but the Wyandotte Constitution was passed by the territory voters by a margin of two to one in favor of this new legislation. This new bill will now go to Washington and be presented for statehood.

October 19, 1859   Esplanade
Wednesday Night   Leavenworth City, Kansas Territory

With our new telegraph in town, we receive news quicker than ever before from the eastern states. It has been communicated that our own John Brown has started his shenanigans again in Harpers Ferry, Virginia. Apparently, Mister Brown decided to start a revolution and overrun an ammunitions depot in that town. His attempt was going well with his small army of slaves and followers, but the adventure came to an end yesterday when the United States Marines led by Robert E. Lee and Jeb Stewart surrounded the arsenal. After a standoff, John Brown surrendered to the army and is being held for a trial.

October 31, 1859   Esplanade
Monday Night   Leavenworth City, Kansas Territory

The children had a festive Halloween Party with bobbing for apples, pin the tail on the donkey, and more games inside and out all day, and we adults enjoyed the antics of the children on the Eve of all Saints as well.

The troops of Fort Leavenworth were sent out to build forts along the Santa Fe Trail to protect the pioneers from Indian attacks along their journey west.

Their first encampment was on the Pawnee Fork where the Kiowa and Comanche Indians have been raiding the wagon trains.

Bad news again happened for downtown when another fire was reported at Main and the Esplanade and around Shawnee Street a few blocks from our present location. The billiard saloon of S. A. Bassford is said to be where the fire was initiated. Luckily with the response of the volunteer fire department and our water wagon, the fire was contained to fourteen buildings this time. Some of the businesses were just rebuilt from the last fire downtown.

Chapter Eighteen
Abe Lincoln Visits Leavenworth City

December 7, 1859　　　Esplanade
Wednesday Night　　　Leavenworth City, Kansas Territory

This last week I received an assignment to follow another figure around Kansas Territory. This man I have written about before as an up–and-comer in the Republican Party. With the efforts of his cousin-in-law Mark Delahay and friend Daniel Webster Wilder, they persuaded Abraham Lincoln to visit the territory of Kansas and to spend some time in Leavenworth City.

I, with a small party from Leavenworth City, traveled up to Saint Joseph on a riverboat to meet the honored guest at the Hannibal and Saint Joseph Railroad Train Station on the 30th of November. It was a bitterly cold day that day as the train arrived in Saint Joseph. Pleasantries were exchanged between the men on the platform of the station, then they loaded onto an omnibus to take Mister Lincoln to a barber shop for a shave and a haircut. I brought my horse with me to ride behind the carriage when on tour.

No big bands or mayoral greeting for Abe Lincoln in Saint Joseph that day, and a quiet ride across the Missouri River on the ferryboat is when I was able to chat with the fine gentleman from Illinois. After a short chat with Mister Lincoln, we docked our ferryboat in Elwood, Kansas Territory. Our arrival in Elwood again was met with no bells or whistles, but a nice crowd did escort us to the Great Western Hotel where Mister Lincoln made a small speech to the crowd that assembled, then he turned in for the night.

The next morning, Thursday, December 1st, our little party departed Elwood for Troy about fifteen miles to the west on the trail. A few miles before reaching the city of Troy, after passing through the towns of Blair and Wathena, a carriage approached from the west toward our carriage and horses. The rider started hailing Abraham, and to Mister Lincoln's astonishment, it was an old acquaintance of his, Mister Henry Villard. It was another cold morning and Mister Villard noticed that Abe was in only a short coat, not dressed warm enough to ride in the prairie, so he reached into the back of his buggy and pulled out a buffalo coat for Abe to wear while traveling the territory. Mister Lincoln thanked him and promised to return the coat to Mister Villard one day.

We reached Troy in the early morning hours so Mister Lincoln visited with another acquaintance that just happened to live nearby the city hall, where Mister Lincoln was going to give a speech to the citizens. Mister Sidney Tennet and his wife, Chloe, entertained their guest and even offered a prayer up for a mutual friend who passed away six weeks prior. He was a former land surveyor for Kansas Territories, our own John C. Calhoun, who passed away from unknown causes.

After a speech at the city hall, we departed for the town of Doniphan ten miles to the southwest of Troy. In Doniphan, Mister Lincoln spoke a lengthy time for the crowd that assembled to hear him speak and then we all settled in for the night at the hotel.

On Friday December 2nd, we said goodbye to Doniphan and started our day going to Atchison, arriving in the afternoon hours. We all purchased rooms for the night at the Massasoit House on Second and Main Streets. Tom Murphy is still the proprietor of the establishment and welcomed us all into his house. About the time we reached Atchison, the telegraph lines were buzzing from the news of the execution of John Brown by hanging in Charleston, Virginia. I did not go into detail what occurred at Harpers Ferry, so I will now clarify any questions one might have.

Going back to October 16, 1859, John Brown and eighteen men, five colored men and thirteen white men, overtook the federal government building and an arsenal in Harpers Ferry, Virginia. John Brown and his small army killed four people and wounded nine others in their siege of the buildings. A thirty-six-hour standoff followed with the United States Marines under the command of Robert E. Lee. Brown held off the Marines until following the orders of Lee, Jeb Stewart went to knock down the doors of the arsenal; Brown was barricaded in with his men.

Eight of Brown's men were killed or captured that day in the exchange of gunfire when the Marines breached the doors on October 18th.

The trial of John Brown continued till November 2nd when the jury came back with a guilty verdict of treason, and death by hanging is the penalty for such offence. The day of the hanging, Lee put over one thousand troops in the courtyard recruited from the Virginia Military Institute to prevent any abolitionist from freeing John Brown from his sentence. Mister Brown was escorted to the gallows by Major Thomas Jackson, a teacher at the institution and the superintendent of the school, and its founding father, John T. L. Preston.

John Brown was escorted to the gallows and as he walked up, he was able to say some last words to his wife who was present in the crowd. Just after eleven in the morning, the executioner under the white hood put the noose around the neck of John Brown and adjusted the slack to keep the drop short. John Brown was then asked to step forward tree steps to be in the center of the trap door. For ten minutes, the crowd bellowed out their praises and ridicules to Brown, who was also under a hood himself not being able to see the boisterous crowd.

The order was yelled and the trap door opened, dropping John Brown a few feet making his body spasm for a few minutes then hanging there lifeless. His body was cut down and given to his wife who placed him in a walnut coffin to be taken back to his land in the north.

The news of John Brown's execution did not deter Mister Lincoln from showing up to speak at the Methodist Church that evening in Atchison. Abraham Lincoln spoke for over two hours for the very large crowd that filled the church. The Atchison newspaper, *The Freedom's Champion*, was written by a Seward supporter, so no support was written in the papers for Lincoln in Atchison. After the speech that night, like the other nights, Mister Lincoln returned to the Massasoit House to turn in for the evening after a short speech for the crowd at the house saloon.

In the morning of Saturday, December 3, 1859, the Lincoln party of five headed toward Leavenworth City. It was another bitterly cold, wintery, windy day riding the trail in an open carriage. D. R. Anthony joined in the carriage ride with Mister Lincoln wearing a new silk topper that Abraham liked very much. The military trail to Fort Leavenworth was the trail chosen by Abe.

We traveled through Sumner, Port Charles, Oak Mills, and then passed through Kickapoo City arriving in Leavenworth City around noon time. At Leavenworth City, a parade was led by a brass band, the firing of the cannon Old Kickapoo, down Shawnee Street to the Mansion House. He spoke for a short time in his carriage to the crowd then settled into his room at the boarding house to warm up before spending the rest of the afternoon at his cousin's house until his next speech.

That night, Mister Lincoln spoke to a large group at Stockton Hall and before the speech, a friend of the late Isaac Cody was there with his daughter. Joseph L. Stein and his daughter, Mary, who was in the crowd of people in Stockton Hall. They were walking around when Abe Lincoln approached them and had a small conversation, shaking the little girl's hand before taking the stage for his speech. Stockton Hall was standing room only that night as

Lincoln spoke to the excited crowd that was even outside the building looking in through the windows.

On Sunday, there was a day of rest for Abraham as he went to church and then spent the day at the Delahay House playing billiards and drinking the beer of Leavenworth. The beer was delivered to the Delahay House located on Kiowa Street from the John Grund Brewery at Sixth and Delaware.

On Monday December 5th, Mister Lincoln spent the day walking up and down the streets of Leavenworth, meeting the people and gazing around in amazement of what a busy town this was. That afternoon a large crowd gathered outside the Planter's Hotel to hear Mister Lincoln speak again. He climbed the few stairs in front of the building so the folks could see him and he spoke to the crowd, giving us a speech that had promise and hope for the United States.

On Tuesday December 6th was an election day and Mister Lincoln wanted to stay and watch the event in Leavenworth City. He was seen walking the streets and talking to the voters at the polling station to get a feel of the movement that is happening in Kansas Territory. The Wyandotte Constitution was accepted by the majority of the voters so the bill will be sent to Washington and with the majority vote himself, Charles Robinson will be the next Governor of Kansas Territory.

On Wednesday December 7, 1859, Mister Lincoln left Leavenworth City for Weston crossing over a frozen Missouri River to Weston, where Mister Lincoln caught a stage for Saint Joseph to ride the rails back to Illinois that afternoon.

    December 31, 1859   Esplanade
    Saturday Night   Leavenworth City, Kansas Territory

Another year is at its last day and what a year it has been. This has indeed been an adventure of a lifetime, covering the turmoil of the politics and how far people will go to make you believe what they do. With all the mayhem and madness, Marisol and the children have taken to Leavenworth City like ducks to water, enjoying the city that has become bigger than Hannibal, their hometown. Although now they are not innocent to the world and the problems that it faces, I hope they make the right choices through Marisol's and my teachings of life. Tonight, the babes were playing cards and waiting for the midnight hour, while Marisol and I sat by the fireplace to keep warm on this bitterly cold night.

January 29, 1860   Esplanade
Saturday Night   Leavenworth City, Kansas Territory

The freighting firm of Russell, Majors and Waddell has announced another company that they will be forming in Saint Joseph, Missouri. Now beside the freighting, stagecoach, banking, wagon making, farming, and iron works, the firm is going into the mail delivery business from the starting point of Saint Joseph, Missouri, to San Francisco, California. An advertisement was placed in the paper that they are looking for orphans, preferably small boys, to ride ponies across the country. Also laborers to build post stations along the route.

February 17, 1860   Esplanade
Saturday Night   Leavenworth, Kansas Territory

The Wyandotte Constitution was placed before the House of Representatives one week ago and after five days of no mention, on the 15th Galusha A. Grow of Pennsylvania introduced the bill to admit Kansas Territory into the Union of the United States. The bill was read a second and third time and was then passed on to the next stage the passing of the bill by the Committee on Territories.

February 30, 1860   Esplanade
Wednesday Night   Leavenworth, Kansas Territory

The Kansas Legislation is at odds with Governor Medary and passed a bill that the Governor vetoed abolishing slavery in the territory on February 23, 1860. In Washington, news has said that William Seward introduced a different bill for Kansas to become a state and was hissed and booed by the southern state representatives at his proposal.

March 23, 1860   Esplanade
Friday Night   Leavenworth, Kansas Territory

Great news for Kansas Territory as the first iron rails have crossed over the Missouri River onto Kansas Territory soil. On March 20th in Elwood Kansas, the Elwood Marysville Railroad drove the first spikes into the ground. This should be a day to be celebrated every year from this day forward.

April 3, 1860   Patee House 12th and Penn.
Tuesday Night   Saint Joseph, Missouri

This morning, I rode Running Water to Weston, taking the Leavenworth Ferry to East Leavenworth and then rode north to Rialto into Weston, where I boarded Running Water in the stables that I used to keep Wildfire while I stayed at the Saint George. I bought a ticket for a stage and headed for Saint Joseph to report about the new business venture of Russell, Majors and Waddell. When I reached Saint Joseph, I was able to retain a room at the Patee House Hotel.

The Patee hotel is a beautiful four-story brick hotel with one hundred and forty rooms and a grand ballroom that exceeds all the hotels that I have ever ventured into. The new offices of Russell, Majors and Waddell are located on the first floor called The Central Overland California and Pikes Peak Express Company.

This new company is referred to as The Pony Express, because the mail carriers will be riding ponies across the country. The horses cannot exceed over nine hundred pounds and be over fourteen hands high. Thoroughbreds, Mustangs, Pintos, and various breeds of Morgans will be ridden by the young boys over a two-thousand-mile route in ten days' time. A stagecoach could take from three to six weeks to cover the same trail. The firm had to build relay stations along the route every ten to fifteen miles apart, so the horses can be switched out as well as the riders for a total of around one hundred and ninety relay stations. These stations had to be stocked with fresh horses for the riders and manned to protect the station from Indian attacks and thievery.

The number of horses purchased is close to five hundred head distributed along the route. The stations have two or three men working them, so over four hundred men were hired to work the stations to keep them functioning. The riders number around two hundred boys who cannot weigh more than one hundred and twenty-five pounds and be under the age of eighteen. Even at that age, being expert horsemen was required to be a rider for the express making twenty-five dollars a week, while the station hands only will make a dollar a day.

The riders are only to carry on them a bag called a *mochila*, a Spanish word for backpack. These bags were made of leather and shaped to hold four reinforced leather boxes, or *caja de cueros*, another Spanish name for leather box. Each *caja de cuero* is secured with a small padlock and can hold up to five pounds of mail. The *mochila* is secured around the horn of the saddle and held down by the rider's weight. The riders are also carrying on them a canteen, a Bible, a revolver, choice of second revolver or rifle, and a small horn to announce their arrival at the relay stations, so the next horse or rider is ready for the relay.

The events I am about to describe almost did not take place today. The courier from the east missed his train connection in Detroit, Michigan. That put his arrival in Hannibal, Missouri, two hours late, missing the train for Saint Joseph. The Station Manager in Hannibal knew the importance of the parcels, so he cleared the track and took a locomotive named The Missouri to make a record-breaking trip across the state of Missouri in four hours and fifty-one minutes arriving at the Saint Joseph train station at Olive and Eight Streets in Saint Joseph in the early afternoon today.

Just after seven o'clock tonight, William Russell, Alexander Majors, And the Mayor of Saint Joseph gave short speeches to the crowd assembled for this event outside the Patee House Hotel. There were two riders present at the ceremony that were hired to ride from Saint Joseph to the first relay station in Kansas Territory named Johnson William Richardson and Johnny Fry.

Johnson William Richardson was selected to be the first rider in this historic moment of what will be The Pony Express. At that time, the young rider was handed the *mochila* that consisted of forty-nine letters, five private telegrams, and papers for San Francisco and various points on the route. I believe I witnessed a *Saint Joseph Gazette* being placed in the *mochila*, making it the only newspaper to be delivered across the country.

John Richardson, after he was handed the *mochila*, ran and secured the *mochila*, jumping on the pony. A cannon was fired to announce the departure and the rider galloped off to the ferryboat that was waiting for him at the Missouri River. The steam ferryboat called The Denver was at full steam when Richardson arrived at the foot of Jules Street and as soon as he was on board the vessel, it also made a record trip across the river, letting the rider off in Elwood. He started for the city of Seneca where he switched horses and then rode to Marysville, Kansas Territory, in which the *mochila* was to be handed off to another Pony Express rider from Richardson.

I was also informed by Mister Russell that they had a ceremony occurred in San Francisco today as well sending off a rider from there. The mail was carried on the steamboat Antelope from San Francisco by James Randall who transferred his *mochila* to William Hamilton in Sacramento, California, the starting point of where Hamilton began to ride his pony from.

    April 24, 1860   Esplanade
    Tuesday Night   Leavenworth City, Kansas Territory

Spring has arrived again in Kansas Territory finally this year after a long cold winter. The weather is warming up and the rivers again are open for businesses traveling to the northwest. The latest news from Washington is that the Wyandotte Constitution was passed by the territorial committee in the House of Representatives on April 11th and is now waiting for senate approval. To follow up on the Pony Express, the mail was delivered successfully in both directions. The route from the east made it to Sacramento on the morning of April 14th, and the western route arrived in Saint Joseph on Thanksgiving morning, April 13th.

There is an incident that occurred in Topeka that I must scribe in this entry. There is a gentleman by the name of John Ritchie who resides in that town, who, like me, has helped in the liberation of slaves from their confinement. Mister Ritchie was a member of John Brown's militia and was involved in the attack at Hickory Point back in 1856. At that time, John Ritchie was arrested and incarcerated until he escaped his confinement in November of that year, leaving Kansas Territory. He ventured to Indiana returning to the territory after Governor Geary's pardon for all the so-called crimes committed against Kansas Territory in March of 1857.

Upon his return to the territory, he rode again with John Brown at the Battle of the Spurs, north of Holton, assisting in the transportation of fugitive slaves. On April 20th of this year, the Deputy Marshall Leonard Arms went to the Ritchie home with a warrant from 1856 to arrest John Ritchie. An argument started and the temperatures of both men rose to the point in the confrontation that Mister Ritchie defended his freedom and shot the deputy, ending his life on the spot. A quick trial was held and John Ritchie was found innocent for the killing of Deputy Leonard Arms.

April 30, 1860   Esplanade
Monday Night   Leavenworth City, Kansas Territory

I kept my ears to the rails so to speak and was able to be assigned to cover the excitement of the first locomotive crossing over the Missouri River into entering Kansas Territory. The crossing was not over a bridge but it was transported across the river on a steamboat ferry. The Great Pacific Railroad completed lying of five miles of iron rails from the riverbank on the Missouri River to Elwood, Kansas Territory. The locomotive Albany was loaded onto a ferry and was set on the rails, followed by the fire car and five flat train cars. The train was prepared for the five-mile journey with dignitaries from the railroad, and both Kansas Territory and the State of Missouri. The five flat cars that were brought over were equipped with chairs for the special guests to ride on as they entered Elwood.

The Albany was received in Elwood with a jubilant celebration with speeches made by the Railroads President, Willard P. Hall, and also the

Governor of Missouri, Robert M. Stewart. The speakers spoke of hope and prosperity for the territory and the railroads, and what an important day it was in the history of the Kansas Territory.

Chapter Nineteen
On the Road to Statehood

May 9, 1860   Esplanade
Wednesday Night   Leavenworth City, Kansas Territory

Leavenworth now has a population of over ten thousand residents living within its city limits.

A new census of the territory tells us that the territory now has over one hundred thousand people in Kansas Territory. With that amount of folks and a good state constitution, there is a good possibility of becoming a state in the union.

As I converse with the immigrant pioneers who chose to visit our city before they venture further west, I asked them about their experience seeing America and how they felt when they set foot on solid ground. As of August 1, 1855, all the immigrants coming to America have to be documented for census as by the Passenger Protection Act of 1855. This was a bill passed to ensure safe entrance into New York City, where many immigrants were killed and robbed of their earthly possessions. This place of documentation was established at the southern tip of Manhattan Island in the New York Harbor.

What once was a fort built to defend our new country from the British in the war of 1812 called Fort Clinton, and also known as Castle Clinton, is now called Castle Garden. Castle Garden is the nation's first Immigration Arrival Station.

May 25, 1860   Esplanade
Friday Night   Leavenworth City, Kansas Territory

No big news in Leavenworth other than the political talk of the presidential campaigns. There are four candidates running for this position. The Northern Democrats elected Stephan Douglas for their candidate, the Southern Democrats chose the current Vice-President John C. Breckinridge.

The Republicans have chosen for their choice Abraham Lincoln over Seward as candidate, and the Old Guard of the Constitutional Party have nominated a slaveholder from Tennessee, John Bell.

    June 4, 1860   Esplanade
    Monday Night   Leavenworth City, Kansas Territory

In a Leavenworth town meeting last month, it was decided by the city that a Poor Farm was to be established to house the people that cannot take care of themselves in society. A quick reaction by the citizens resulted in a land donation outside the city limits in High Prairie. The term poor is a broad expression or what today's society feels about the sick, incapacitated, aged, or just unable to support themselves in anyway. On the land of the Poor Farm, they built what are called Pest Houses for the members of society that are not breaking any laws but are disturbing the general flow of the town's streets and businesses.

Another act the government of the country initiated last month was the passing of the Indian Removal Act of 1860 that removes the remaining tribes that live east of the Mississippi River to lands west. This bill did just narrowly pass in both houses in Washington. One other bill was passed as well three days later called the Preemption Act giving squatters the first dibs to the land, they improved on illegally prior to being put up for sale by the government.

    June 21, 1860   Esplanade
    Thursday Night   Leavenworth City, Kansas Territory

Earlier this month in the House of the Senate, a Senator Wade made a motion to pick up the Wyandotte Constitution for consideration for the admittance of Kansas Territory as a state. The motion was defeated thirty-two to twenty-six votes. One Democrat voted for the passage of the Wyandotte Constitution and that man was Mister George Ellis Pugh of Ohio. Now the fate of Kansas Territory will have to wait until the next session of Congress in the winter when the newly elected members take their seats and a new President of the United States is in office.

    July 5, 1860   Esplanade
    Thursday Night   Leavenworth City, Kansas Territory

Platte County has advanced their educational system to fit the needs of the growing population in our region of the country. When Platte County was formed in the 1846, twenty-seven school districts were formed and set up with schools for the public in each district. And now by the end of this year, they will have built a number of continuing education facilities for both men and women.

There are two of the schools that are being called high schools built in Weston for the purpose of further educating men and women, of course the women in one and the men the other. A few male academies were established at Camden Point, Platte City, and Pleasant Ridge built an academy that taught both sexes. Camden Point also built an academy for women as well as the men. Weston has also built Union College and a Young Ladies' Select School.

September 5, 1860   Esplanade
Wednesday Night   Leavenworth City, Kansas Territory

The hemp and tobacco industries in Weston have reached an all-time high for the city. Their product is now shipped around the world. The Missouri River has boats going up and down its currents from the first ice melts to the first freeze over.

Since the devastation of Leavenworth City with fire and flood, our city and territory now are in a drought. Rain has not fallen since last winter and grasshoppers have eaten many of the crops grown in the region. As the grasshoppers fly from crop to crop, it appears to look like a black cloud moving up and down the horizon line of the plains.

September 28, 1860   Esplanade
Friday Night   Leavenworth City, Kansas Territory

Governor William Seward paid a visit to Kansas Territory on his presidential campaign even though the citizens of the territory cannot vote for that position. Governor Seward spoke to a crowd of over six thousand people in Lawrence two days ago and this morning he gave a rousing speech here in Leavenworth that may have persuaded a few Lincoln followers to Seward's ideals.

Stockton Hall was once again filled to capacity when the governor spoke about how proud he was of the citizens of Kansas Territory put the issue of slavery on the nation's minds. After his speech, Governor Seward bought passage to Atchison on a stage line and was going to speak there tonight.

November 7, 1860   Esplanade
Wednesday Night   Leavenworth City, Kansas Territory

Yesterday, the United States of America held its election for the President of our country and Abraham Lincoln came out victorious in the election with the majority of votes. The Popular Vote was split by the candidates, but again forty percent went to Mister Lincoln with the other sixty percent going to the other candidates.

The Pony Express carried the news to Fort Churchill, Nevada Territory, and then telegraphed the remainder to San Francisco, setting a record time of delivery across the United States in seven days and seventeen hours.

November 30, 1860   Esplanade
Friday Night   Leavenworth City, Kansas Territory

The Territorial Governor Samuel Medary has requested troops from Fort Leavenworth to assist in the conflicts that are still occurring in Lynn and Bourbon Counties. Skirmishes are being fought in the honor of John Brown and are increasing the number of wounded and property destroyed by both sides. A heavy rainfall finally occurred in our region before winter after almost a year without. The dried-up streams and creeks now have water trickling across the rocks once again. The river water level has also increased, so ships may now carry heavier loads without the worry of bottoming out their vessels before the river freezes in winter.

December 29, 1860   Esplanade
Saturday Night   Leavenworth City, Kansas Territory

Earlier this month on December 6, 1860, the thirty-sixth Congress of the United States began their session. The newly elected Republican delegates of Kansas Territory took their seats with Kansan pride, holding the majority of the seats in both territorial houses and in Washington. With a Republican president, the southern democratic states are now not liking the direction the country is heading and changing their way of life with slavery.

Coming back to local news, I must now scribe the events of a snake in the grass that became a traitor to the free-state men of Kansas Territory and let it be known that if this traitor ever shows up in Kansas Territory, that varmint will be hung on the spot. This is about a young schoolteacher that lived outside of Lawrence named Charley Hart.

I had met this young man a few years back in August of '57 when Jim Lane was recruiting men for his regiment in Lawrence. Jim Lane had come to Leavenworth City looking for respectable individuals to help defend Kansas Territory from slavery. He not only outwitted me that day but Jim Lane as well, who not only recruited him but also gave him a job as a schoolteacher in the Lawrence area.

Mister Hart, and I am using that term loosely, had joined a group of Quaker Abolitionists who wanted to free some slaves over the border in Missouri. The six young men rode into Jackson County, Missouri, to a large farm that was owned by a man named Morgan Walker.

Arriving in the early afternoon, the men hid in the woods about a mile from the farmhouses. Now as the story went, Charley went to do some spying to see where the slaves were kept on the farm but on his way, he rode up upon Andrew Walker, the son of Morgan, at Andrew's house.

Charley at this time told the plans of the Jayhawkers to Andrew Walker, who then took Mister Hart to the house of Morgan Walker. There, Charley repeated his story of the robbery tonight of their slaves by the Jayhawkers from Lawrence inside the house, where when he entered the house was asked to remove his pistol and did so, leaving the revolver on a table by the front door as they went to the parlor. Morgan Walker sent Charley back to his group and told him to go ahead with the plans but hold back, there was going to be an ambush.

A few hours after dark around seven, a rainstorm started as the Jayhawkers arrived with a wagon to free the Walker slaves. Charley stayed in the woods watching the trail so no one came up to the farm. Another man stayed at the wagon while the other four men crept quietly in the shadows toward the slave quarters. When the men were crossing an opening between some buildings, a bolt of lightning lit up the dark sky and then Morgan Walker and four neighbors opened fire upon the men. Ed Morrison was killed instantly, a man named Lipsey was shot in the hip. And a man named Dean was shot in the foot escaping down the trail into the woods. The man in the wagon rode off as soon as he heard the shots escaping back to Lawrence. Another man named Ball made a safe escape and also returned to Lawrence. Lipsey and Dean were tracked down by the Walker's mob and Lipsey was shot on sight by Morgan Walker himself with Lipsey's own gun.

The townsfolk around Independence, Missouri, believed all the Jayhawkers should be hung for the act they tried to commit. A mob gathered at the Walker Farm and demanded to hang Charley Hart for his part in the ruckus. Later still that night, Sherriff John Burns of Jackson County, Missouri, took Charley Hart into town for his protection. Unbeknownst to the citizens,

Charley was let out the back door as soon as he entered the jail, and himself and Andrew Walker stayed at the hotel until morning when Charley was told to leave town until things settled down and then return to the Walker Farm. The next morning, the crowd assembled outside the Jackson County Jail to hang Charley Hart. Who was a Missourian that changed his name from William Charley Quantrill.

On December 17, 1860, the Territorial Governor Samuel Medary resigned from his office stating that he felt he was not challenged in this position and wanted something else. He returned to his home state of Ohio and George M. Bebee, the Territorial Secretary, will be temporary governor.

December 20, 1860, the State of South Carolina voted without any opposition in the South Carolina Legislature by a vote of 164-0 that the state of South Carolina will no longer be called a part of the United States of America. Their Union is dissolved with the election of the Republican President, Abraham Lincoln. With that announcement, the sixty-eight federal troops stationed in Charleston withdrew from the city to Fort Sumter, a federal fort in Charleston Harbor.

Chapter Twenty
The Battle in Kansas Territory Becomes the Nation's Civil War

January 22, 1861 Esplanade
Thursday Night Leavenworth City, Kansas Territory

Our new territorial legislation has met in Lecompton at the Constitution Hall for their last meeting on January 7, 1861. The new legislation has voted to move the legislative offices to Lawrence until Kansas becomes a state and its capital is voted upon.

The news from Washington brings us hope of statehood but at the cost of the nation. More southern states have left their Senate positions to protest against the election of Abraham Lincoln. Six more states have left Washington and returned to their homes. William Seward took the opportunity to readmit the Kansas Territory under the Wyandotte Constitution and with little opposition to deny the motion, the bill has been delivered back to the House of Representatives to pass the amendments added on to the bill.

January 29, 1861 Esplanade
Tuesday Night Leavenworth City, State of KANSAS

Kansas is now the thirty-fourth United State of America. Earlier today, President James Buchanan signed the Wyandotte Constitution, proclaiming Kansas as a free state. The House of Representatives passed the amendments made by the Senate and the president had the papers on his desk yesterday afternoon at the White House.

When the news was deciphered from the telegraph machine, the news spread quicker than wildfire. In fact, Daniel Anthony printed a special edition of his newspaper and made a Paul Revere ride to Lawrence to tell the territorial legislature that Kansas is now a state. The streets were full of cheering and celebration. Even though illegal in the city limits, guns were fired into the air to bring awareness to the citizens along the firing of the Old Kickapoo cannon.

Patriotic songs were sung in the streets and dancing in some spots occurred in the streets. Thousands of people filled the streets downtown of Leavenworth Kansas. The celebration continued into the night with a spectacular firework display over the river on the levee. We watched from our front porch as the merriment went into the morning hours.

In other news in our nation, President Buchanan was taking care of our troops at Fort Sumner by sending in an unarmed merchant ship, The Star of the West, with supplies for the troops to live. As the ship entered Charleston Harbor, it was fired upon by the South Carolina Militia.

Having no defense, the Star of the West had to retreat and return to its port of departure, unable to deliver the supplies for the men on the island fort.

February 24, 1861   Esplanade
Sunday Night   Leavenworth City, Kansas

The states in the south that have left the Union with the United States held a convention in Montgomery, Alabama, on February 4th and formed the Confederate States of America. There are seven states in the Confederacy at this time that has nominated Jefferson Davis as their President of the Confederate States. In our own governor's seat, Charles Robinson is the first Kansas State Governor on February 9, 1861.

I have been following the reports of Abraham Lincoln and his train ride to Washington from Springfield, Illinois. His adventure started on February 11th, traveling with his son, Robert Todd Lincoln. The next day on his birthday, his wife, Mary, and his two other sons, Willie and Tad, joined the train in Indianapolis, Indiana. Along the way, they would see the historical sites in the cities they travel through and giving speeches to the crowd from the back of the train when they were departing the city.

As the train entered Philadelphia, Pennsylvania, a detective named Alan Pinkerton discovered a plot to assassinate the elected president. Under careful protection, Abraham Lincoln delivered his speech to the people of Philadelphia at Independence Hall. He then traveled to Harrisburg and delivered a speech to the legislature at Pennsylvania's State Capital. As the group was heading back to Philadelphia, Mister Pinkerton disguised the president-elect and secretly traveled by carriage to Washington, arriving there unnoticed by anyone on the early morning hours on February 23, 1861.

March 29, 1861   Esplanade
Friday Night   Leavenworth City, Kansas

The inauguration of President Abraham Lincoln took place on the 6th earlier this month along with his Vice-President Hannibal Hamlin. President Lincoln in his speech tried to heal some wounds by saying that he was not wanting or to interfere with the established slavery institution for he has no right by law to do so. There is hope in the country and the differences should not be settled on a battlefield.

When the Wyandotte Constitution was approved, there were amendments, making Kansas smaller in size. In doing that, a space of unnamed land opened from Kansas to Utah. On February 28, 1861, the Colorado Territory was created. That is all the news I have. Spring is arriving with high winds and rain again. The levee reopened its port a few weeks back when they were clear of all the ice. With Kansas now a state, the tension level has decreased and Leavenworth is on the road for a great future. The first state legislative convened in Topeka on March 26, 1861, with Governor Charles Robinson presiding over the houses.

There is a story now I must scribe to remember for later. It is about a Pony Express rider named Robert 'Pony Bob' Haslam. As the story goes, Pony Bob was riding his eastern-bound leg of the route from Lake Tahoe Friday's Station to Fort Churchill's Buckland Station seventy-five miles to the east. When Pony Bob reached Buckland Station, his relief rider grew a yellow belly and hid himself under his bed at the station bunk house. Seeing that the rider was not leaving for the fear of the local Indian attacks, Pony Bob mounted his new horse and rode another hundred and fifteen miles to Smith's Creek Station.

Being able to rest for nine hours, Pony Bob mounted up again taking the westbound mail carrying President Lincoln's inaugural address speech in print to San Francisco, California. At a horse relay station called Cold Springs that he had been to the day before, as he rode upon the station, he noticed it was attacked by Indians. Arrows were surrounding the windows and door openings, but when Pony Bob was close enough, he saw the station keeper's body in front of the station full of arrows. The Indians also stole the horses so there was not another horse to exchange for the one he had just ridden. Again, he mounted his horse and headed westward and before he could reach the next station, Pony Bob had ridden up on an Indian hunting party. Pony Bob escaped the Indians but not without injury. He had taken an arrow into his jaw and knocking out all his teeth on the side the arrow entered. He returned to Fort Churchill's Buckland Station making a three hundred and sixty mile trip as a Pony Express rider, the longest ride a rider had made and setting a record time of the distance traveled of one hundred and twenty-eight miles in a time of eight hours and twenty minutes.

    April 13, 1861   Esplanade
    Saturday Night   Leavenworth City, Kansas

The predecessor of President Abraham Lincoln, President James Buchanan left quite a dilemma with the situation at Fort Sumter, South Carolina. With the troops on the island fortress still needing supplies of basic human needs, President Lincoln sent word to the Governor of South Carolina that a ship with no weapons or ammunition will be transporting supplies to the men at Fort Sumter.

The South Carolina's Governor Francis Wilkinson Pickens sent word to President Jefferson Davis of Lincoln's intent. Jefferson Davis in response to the governor's notice tried to persuade the fort's commander to surrender the fortress over to the south and leave peacefully. Major Robert Anderson refused to surrender the fort so in the response to Major Anderson's response, President Jefferson Davis ordered General Pierre Beauregard to attack Fort Sumter on April 12, 1861, before the supply vessel could reach the island in the harbor.

Today, this Thanksgiving was not a very thankful day in our nation. With a heavy heart, I do believe this will be the last Thanksgiving to be celebrated for a spell. The fighting over slavery has the entire nation wondering what direction Lincoln will put us in.

    April 21, 1861   Esplanade
    Sunday Night   Leavenworth City, Kansas

The battle over Fort Sumter lasted until the 14th of April 1861, when the Union Major Anderson raised the white flag of surrender after a three-day siege of the island fortress by the Confederate General Beauregard. Then the next day after the news spread about the confederate attack on the United States, four more southern states seceded from the United States and joined the Confederate States.

President Lincoln then called to action seventy-five thousand volunteers from every corner of America. The men of this country need to defend the United States of America from the treasonous southern states who call themselves The Confederate States of America. The nation is divided in two and a civil war has begun in America. So now our men, who have been fighting in our own front yards for seven years to make Kansas a free state, now have to go off and fight the same war in someone else's yard a thousand miles away to. Our Kansas hearts will show the southerners that slavery is wrong and that all men are created equal.

If I failed to mention this before, Jim Lane was elected senator for the state of Kansas in our last elections. He was in Washington when he had heard the news about Fort Sumter and mustered a group of men together to defend the White House from Confederate forces.

Senator Jim Lane took control of the east room of the White House and secured the President and his family. Back in Leavenworth, tensions mounted when a southern-owned riverboat, named the Sam Gaty from Saint Louis, arrived at the Leavenworth Levee, flying the Confederate flag stars and bars. Members of the Turner Society noticed the peculiar flag flying from the jack staff of Sam Gaty and with high determination, the society was going to remove the flag from its height.

As the men of the Turner Society were bringing out Old Kickapoo and pointing it in the direction of the Sam Gaty, the captain of the vessel removed the flag from the jack staff. The society was not content with just the removal of the flag, they wanted it destroyed, so the men of the society forced their way onto the riverboat and forced the captain to hand over the rebellious flag. The captain was also asked to fly the United States flag for his duration in Leavenworth.

Yesterday, rumor was spread around that Missouri Ruffians were going to attack the Fort Leavenworth Military Base from the cities of Parkville and Independence. Mayor McDonald mustered up over one hundred men to help defend the fort from the bushwhackers of Missouri.

May 10, 1861   Esplanade
Friday Night   Leavenworth City, Kansas

The Pony Express has run into troubles both financially and physically. The freighting firm of Russell, Majors, and Waddell went bankrupt, and had to sell of most of their assets to various businesses like Bella M. Hughes of Saint Joseph, Missouri, who is a relative of Ben Holladay from Weston. The Pony Express is also suffering from Indian attacks on their stations. The Paiute Indians attacked a station in the Nevada Territory. The station was set fire to and burned to the ground while three of the men who worked there were tortured and killed. It is said that the owner of the station, J. O. Williams, abducted two of the Paiute Indian women and soiled them to the world. The Pony Express has halted service until the conflict with the Indians, that is being called The Pyramid Lake War, can be resolved.

Ruins of Rialto, Missouri

June 5, 1861　　　　　Esplanade
Wednesday Night　　　Leavenworth City, Kansas

At some time last week, Daniel R. Anthony was taking passage on a riverboat from Fort Leavenworth to Saint Joseph on a day business trip. As the riverboat was moving up the Missouri River passing the city of Iatan, Mister Anthony, along with the other passengers on board the riverboat, noticed a Confederate State of America flag flying from the city pole downtown.

On the return voyage back to Leavenworth that day, Daniel Anthony asked the captain of the riverboat to let him and his associate off at the Iatan Landing. As the men disembarked, the gentlemen noticed that the flag was not flying on the pole it was first noticed on that morning. The men continued into the town and found the gathering place of the townsfolk at a grocery store. As the two men entered the establishment with about a dozen men already in the store, Daniel Anthony noticed the folded Confederate flag on the store's counter by the register.

Mustering up the strength of a troop, Daniel from what the story goes, in a very deep voice said, "I will take that!" Every man that was in the store quickly drew their revolvers pointing them at the two men standing in the doorway. Mister Anthony and his associate mumbled something about a misunderstanding and stepped backward till they were outside the grocery store then ran as fast as they could back to the landing where they paid a fisherman to get them out of town quickly.

The news of the encounter at the grocery store was spread all over Leavenworth by the Missourians who disliked Daniel Anthony and believed that would be the last they heard from the Kansas activist. The story continues by what brought to my attention as a newspaper writer that a spy was used by a group that wanted the Iatan flag captured to locate its position and see what resistance the operation would receive in the town. The location of the flagpole by the railroad tracks, and the flag at night was determined, and as the fact that there was over one hundred and forty men camped within the town's earshot.

On a night with no moonlight, seventeen members of Company A First Kansas Infantry took the initiative to secure the flag for Colonel Anthony. In the early morning hours before the sun was even ready to raise, the men procured a small flatboat to cross over the Missouri River. Five men took that craft while another craft was found and four more men crossed the river on that boat. The first boat returned to pick up the remaining men but five had changed their minds and went back to camp before the boat arrived on the shore.

Twelve men marched into Iatan to face over one hundred and forty armed men that morning to capture their flag. Arriving at Iatan as the sun was raising and the men expected the flag to still be in the grocery store not seeing it up in the air on the pole. As the men from Company A entered Iatan thinking that they had to cross about one hundred and fifty feet to the grocery store, but as they rounded the corner of a building, the flag was being raised by five Missourians. As the flag was tied off, the Kansans charged the Missourians and surrounded the flagpole. A demand to lower and hand over the flag was made by Company A and choice words were exchanged by both sides until Mellen Lewis of Company A pulled out his knife and cut the flag's rope, dropping the flag into the dirt.

As Company A was retrieving the flag off the ground, shots were heard coming from the grocery store's door. The Kansans quickly made it back to the river and across with no causalities. The flag was handed over to Colonel Anthony and the men returned to their camp by dusk. Frank H. Drenning, Thomas Merrick, Frank M. Tracy, G. Mellen Lewis, Fred Amberine, William Smart, and James Little are all original members of the Elwood Guards and Emil Umfried, Theodore Kroll, Richard Lander, and Henry Laurenzier are from the Stuben Guards making up part of Company A First Kansas Infantry.

| June 22, 1861 | Esplanade |
| Saturday Night | Leavenworth City, Kansas |

The Iatan Confederate Flag's story was not over when it came into the hands of Colonel Anthony. On June 13, 1861, R. C. Saterlee made some ungentlemanly remarks about the Colonel. Insults were thrown by both men and a duel was emplaced. The two gentlemen squared off outside the office of

Colonel Anthony and the life of R. C. Saterlee ended that day in the streets of Leavenworth. A quick trial followed and Daniel R. Anthony was acquitted by a judge from Kansas City.

      July 22, 1861   Esplanade
      Monday Night   Leavenworth City, Kansas

    I, James Michael Urbaniak, have been assigned to cover the war now brewing in the east.
    Marisol and the children will stay in Leavenworth City and I will visit back to Kansas when I will be permitted. Theses journals I will place in a safe location until my return hopefully in a few months, and those were the last words in this journal.
    You could hear a pin drop in the room as I finished reading the last page in the journal. The eyes of everyone in the room were wide open and their jaws hung low. The looks of bewilderment and awe had the children wanting more of the story and I had to tell them the next time we meet that we will read the next journal. Everyone picked up their pillows and blankets, and we headed off to bed.
    With Dad feeling better the next day, we packed up our things and said our goodbyes to all who came to see all of us off to the airport. My brother Ric had his family drove up from Gulfport, Mississippi, so they took off after six o'clock. Ken and his family had an early flight to West Palm Beach, Florida, with a layover in Atlanta, so they left for the airport after breakfast around eight o'clock. Tammy and her family drove home to Melvern and our kids Michael and Cera drove home to Wichita; Laura and Hope went back to Kansas City along with Christina.
    Natalie and I were the last to leave Mom and Dad's, and as we headed to the airport, we drove around the downtown area with a bit more pride of what our city had accomplished and all the famous people that had walked on the streets and sidewalks of Leavenworth City. Wishing there was still a ferryboat crossing, we departed Kansas into Missouri, picturing all the events we just read about in the journals I had in my luggage to read the further adventures.

THE END FOR NOW

Bibliography

A / B

Andreas, A. T.	History of the State of Kansas (Reproduction 1976) Andreas 1883 Chicago. A Bicentennial Project of the Atchison County Historical Society Atchison, Kansas in cooperation with The Kansas State historical Society Topeka, Kansas.
Arnold, Anna	A History of Kansas Published by The State of *Kansas W. R. Smith State Printer Topeka, Kansas 1915*
Atkeson, W. O.	From The Marais Des Cygnes. Kansas City, Missouri Burton Publishing Co. 1920
Bird, Roy – Kansas, Day By Day	1996 Particle Press Tucson, Arizona 85754
Bless, Mrs. B. I. – Weston: Queen of The Platte Purchase	The Weston Cronicle January 1, 1969
Braden, Lester	The History of Leavenworth County. Leavenworth County Genealogical Society, May 1990 Kansas Printing and Advertising Salina, Kansas 67402
Bright Ph.D., John D. (editor)	Kansas The First Century, Volumes 1-4 Louis Historical Publishing Company 1956
Brown, Ann Bromell	Fact and Folklore of Bell School Community Of Leavenworth County, Kansas 1986-1987
XXX	
Brown, Mary Ann Sachse	The Cody Family in

	Leavenworth County. Leavenworth County Historical Society 2011
Brown, Mary Ann Sachse	Remembering Lowemont Copyright Oct 29, 2010 Mary Ann Sachse Brown

C

Connelley, William	A Standard History of Kansas and Kansas's. Lewis Publishing Company. Chicago/New York 1918
Cord, Julius	Lickskillet Revisited Julius Cord Publishing 2008
Cutler, William G.	History of the State of Kansas. A.T. Andreas Publishing Company. Chicago, Illinois 1883

D

Duncan, Dayton/ Burn, Ken Lewis and Clark	The Journey of The Corps of Discovery. Alfeda Knope Publishing, New York 1997

E/F

Fitzgerald, Danial – Mad Money	The Steamboat Era on The Kansas and Missouri Border. The Dan Fitzgerald Company 2011
Foster, E. G.	History of The United States. State of Kansas. Published by The state of Kansas. Topeka, Kansas. B. F. Walker State Printer. 1925
Frederick Ph. D., J.V.	Ben Holladay The Stagecoach King. The Authur Clark Company. Glendale, California. 1940

G

Goodpasture, Lorene — Historical Legends of Iatan.1996

Grant, Bruce — American Indians Yesterday and Today. E. D. Dutton and Company Inc. 196

H

Hall and Hand — History of Leavenworth County Kansas. Historical Publishing Company, Topeka, Kansas. James A. Hall/ Leroy T. Hand

Holbrok, Stewart H. — Wild Bill Hickok Tames The West. Random House. New York. 1952

Holland, Hjalmar R. — Norse Discoveries and Explorations in America 932-1362. Lief Erickson to the Kensington Stone. Dover Publications. New York. 1969.

Hoole, William Stanley — A Southerner's Viewpoint of the Kansas Situation 1856-1857. Kansas Collection May 1934 Vol. 3, No. 2

Howes, Charles C. — This Place Called Kansas. University of Oklahoma Press.1952. Third Printing January 1961.

Hughes, J. Patrick — Fort Leavenworth Gateway to the West Kansas State Historical Society Mennonite Press Newton Kansas 2000.

I

Isley and Richards — The Story of Kansas Published by the State of Kansas under the authorization of the State Board of Education. Printed by Ferd Voiland Jr. State Printer Topeka, Kansas 1953

J

Johnson III, J. H.	Early Leavenworth and Fort Leavenworth Copyright 1977 J. H. Johnson III
Johnson III, J. H.	Hundred Year Hurrah Copyright 1994 J. H. Johnson III
Johnson III, J.H.,	Leavenworth: Beginning to Bicentennial Published by J. H. Johnson III Printed by Benedictine College Press, Atchison, Kansas 1976
Johnson III, J. H.	A. Looking Back in Postcards. Copyright 1991 J. H. Johnson III
Johnson III, J. H.	Tales of Old Leavenworth. Copyright 2003 J. H. Johnson III
Johnson III, J. H.	The Leavenworth Register. Copyright 2001 J. H. Johnson III
Johnson III, J. H.	They came This Way. Copyright 1988 J. H. Johnson III

K

Kansas Publishing Company	KANSAS AS SHE IS. Second Edition: 1870 Kansas Publishing Company Lawrence, Kansas.
Kramer, Julia Wood	The House on the Hill. The Story of the Abel's Family of Leavenworth Kansas. Chicago, Illinois.

L

LaBorge, Joseph	Early Steamboat Navigation on the Missouri River Volume 1/ Volume 2 – Life and Adventures of Joseph LaBorge H. M. Chittenden. New York. Francis P. Harper 1903
LaMaster, Kenneth M.	Fort Leavenworth Arcadia Publishing Leavenworth Branch of the American

	Association of University Women. Other Days… Other Ways. One Hundred Years of Freedom and Progress in Leavenworth Kansas.
	1861-1961. Booklet in reproduction size.
Lowe, Percival G.	Five Years a Dragoon and other Adventures of the Great Plains.
	The Franklin Hudson Plains Publishing Company Kansas City, Missouri. 1906.

M

Majors, Alexander	Seven Years on the Frontier. Lifetime on the Border.
	Rand McNally and Company Publishers Edited by Colonel Prentiss Ingram 1893.
McKale, Young	Fort Riley: Citadel of the Frontier West.
	Kansas State Historical Society 2000. William D. Young/ William McKale.
McNamara, John	Three Years on the Kansas Border by a Clergyman.
	Miller, Orton, And Mulligan
	Edward O. Jenkins Printer 1856
McNeal, T. A.	When Kansas was Young.
	The McMillian Company New York
	Published September 1922
McNulty, Elizabeth	Saint Louis: Then and Now
	Thunder Bay Press Advantage Publishing Group
	2000
Meerse, David E.	"No Property in the Late course of the Governor." The Geary Sherrard
	Affair. Kansas Collection Kansas Historical Quarterly. Autumn 1926
	Volume 42 Number 3.
Mildfelt, Todd	The Secret Danities Kansas, The First Jayhawkers
	Todd Mildfelt Publishing 2003

Miller, Nyle	Kansas: A Students Guide to Localized History.
	Teachers College Columbia University Editor; Clifford L. Lord 1965
Miller, Sandra	Memories of Weston, Missouri. 1837-1992.
XXX	
Minor, Craig	Kansas: The History of the Sunflower State. 1854-2000. University of Kansas Press 2002. Lawrence, Kansas.
Moore, H. Miles	History of Leavenworth County Kansas. Sam'l Dodsworth Book Co. Leavenworth, Kansas 1906

N

Nichols, Alice	Bleeding Kansas
	Oxford University Press New York 1954

O/P

Partin, Dr. John W.	A Brief History of Fort Leavenworth
	Edited by Dr. John W. Partin: combined Arms Center Command Historian
	Combat Studies Institute U. S. Army Command and General Staff College
	Fort Leavenworth, Kansas 1983
Paxton, W. M.	Annals of Platte County
	Hudson Kimberly Publishing Company 1897
Phillips, David R.	The West: An American Experience
	Henry Regnery Company 1973 Chicago, Illinois
Phillippi, Laura/Sunderman Nolan, Lansing	Arcadia Publishing 2008
Ponce, Pearl T.	Kansas's War
	Ohio University Press. Athens Ohio 2011
Prentis, Noble L.	History of Kansas

Published by E. P. Greer Winfield, Kansas 1899

Q/R

Rich, Everett	The Heritage of Kansas University of Kansas Press Lawrence, Kansas 1960 4th Edition 1966
Richmond, Robert W.	Kansas; A Political History University of Kansas Press Revised Edition 1992
Riegel, Robert E.	America Moves West Taird Edition. Holt Rinehart and Winston I. X. Copyright 1930, 1947, 1956. February 1963
Russel, Don	The Life and Legend of Buffalo Bill University of Oklahoma Press. Second Printing 1961

S/T

Saint Louis National Historical Company	History Of Clay and Platte Counties Published 1885
Settle, Raymond and Marylund	War Drums And Wagon Wheels: The Story of Russel, Majors, and Wadell. University of Nebraska Press 1966
Shortridge, James R.	Kansas City and How it Grew. 1822-2011 University Press of Kansas
Spear, Bob	Leavenworth: First City of Kansas Spears Mint Editions 2005
Spring, Leverett	American Commonwealths of Kansas Riverside Press Cambridge, Mass. 1885
Socolofsky and Self	Historical Atlas of Kansas Second Edition Norman Publishing division of The University of Oklahoma Press. 1972-1988

Throne, Guenther, Klingele.	Reflections of Leavenworth County The Leavenworth Times Copyright 2000 Compiled By: Tom Throne, Judy Guenther, Kirk Klingele.

U/V

Vaughn, Joe H.	Kansas City Kansas. Arcadia Publishing 2012

W/X

Walter, George	History of Kanzas: Also Information Regarding Routes, Laws. Kanzas League No. 110 N.Y. N. Y. 1855
Whittemore, Margaret	Historic Kansas: A Century Sketchbook University of Kansas Press 1954
Wilder, Danial W.	The Annals of Kansas 1541-1885 Topeka Kansas and Dwight Thatcher Kansas Publishing House 1886

Y/Z

Zeinert, Karen	Tragic Prelude: Bleeding Kansas First Published as a Linnet Book in 2001. An imprint Of the Shoestring Co.
Zornow, William Frank	Kansas: A History of the Jayhawk State. University of Oklahoma Press 1957

Special Thank You To

Clara Vanderstay
Kansas City Kansas Community College Leavenworth Campus.
Ken LaMaster
Leavenworth County Historical Society
Leavenworth City Museum
Leavenworth Public Library Kansas Room. Zac Baker
Mary Ann Sachse Brown
Natalie Marie Urban
The Pony Express Museum
The City of Leavenworth for the Inspiration
The Weston Museum
Jeff and Holly Pitman
Danial Schiffbauer
Mike and Mary Stephenson
Keith Long
Lynn Zielinski
The Lexington Historical Association and Museum
Kansas State Historical Society
…and to all the people I have spoken to over the six years of research writing this book.

Hope you enjoyed the journey as much as I.

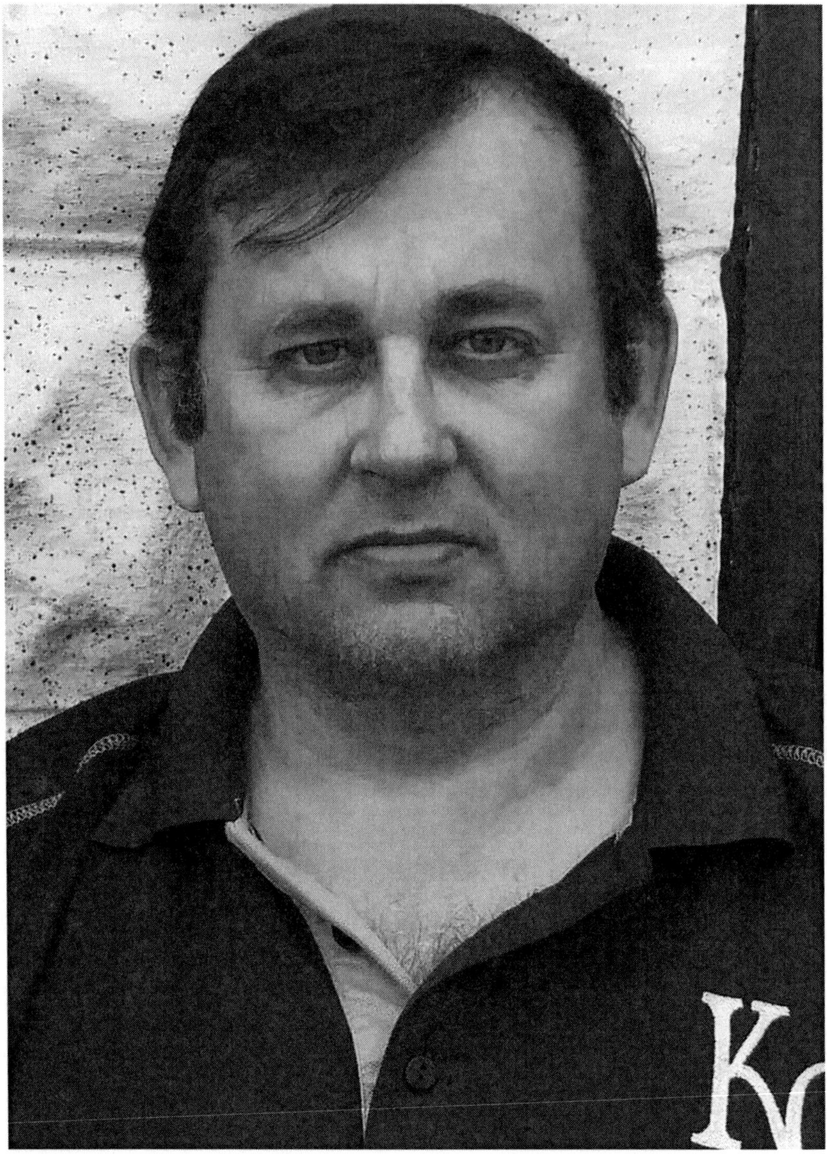
Ko

Pictures Provided By

1) Cover Picture: Centennial Bridge Leavenworth, Kansas- Missouri Border
   Picture provided by: Austin Macauley Publishers (color photo)

2) Picture p.34/35: Polar Star Newspaper Ad. (B&W pic)
   Picture provided by: The Weston Museum, Main St. Weston, Mo.

3) Picture p. 38/39: Plat of Weston, Missouri (B&W pic.)
   Picture provided by: Weston Museum, Main St. Weston, Mo.

4) Picture p. 42/43: Entrance to Trinity Catholic Church, Weston, Mo. (B&W pic)
   Picture provided by: Author's personal photo collection.

5) Picture p. 55/56: Kickapoo Mission 1854 (B&W pic)
   Picture provided by: Leavenworth Public Library, Leavenworth Ks.

6) Picture p. 74/75: View looking west from Weston Bend Bluff overlooking Missouri River and Western Kansas. (B&W pic)
   Picture provided by: Author's personal photo collection.

7) Picture p 89/90 Stephan Naeher's Only chance Saloon. (B&W pic)
   Picture provided by: Leavenworth Public Library, Leavenworth, Ks.

8) Picture p 97/98: 5th and Shawnee Streets looking north (B&W pic)
   Picture provided by: Leavenworth Public Library, Leavenworth, Ks.

9) Picture p 102/103: View looking south from Rialto Landing at Missouri River (B&W pic)
   Picture provided by: Author's personal photo collection.

10) Picture p 123/124: Stewart Iron Works Gate (B&W pic)
    Picture provided by: Author's personal photo collection.

11) Picture p 126/127: Levi North's National Circus (B&W pic)
    Picture provided by: Leavenworth Public Library, Leavenworth, Ks

12) Picture p 128/129: Spaulding and Rogers New Orleans Circus. (B&W pic)
    Picture provided by: Leavenworth Public Library, Leavenworth, Ks.

13) Picture p 137/138: View of Leavenworth City, Kansas Territory 1858 (B&W pic)
    Picture provided by: Leavenworth Public Library, Leavenworth, Ks.

14) Picture p 148/149 Newspaper The Daily Times July 4, 1859 Leavenworth, Ks. (B&W pic)
    Picture provided by: Leavenworth Public Library, Leavenworth Ks.

15) Picture p 154/155 Planters Hotel, Leavenworth City, Kansas (B&W pic)
    Picture provided by: Leavenworth Public Library, Leavenworth, Ks.

16) Picture p 174/175 Ruins of Rialto, Missouri (B&W pic)
    Picture provided by: Author's personal photo collection

17) Picture of Author: Michael J. Urban (color photo}
    Provided by: Author's personal photo collection